WHEN THE
DEAD
RISE

The Outbreak

D.K. FRASER

WHEN THE DEAD RISE

D.K. FRASER

Willowtree Press

When the Dead Rise

Copyright Willowtree Press.

CONTENTS

WHEN THE DEAD RISE

CHAPTER ONE
Dr. Ferguson

Lance Ferguson slumped himself down on a bench at the light rail station in downtown, the same station he'd been using to catch the train car home every day since he'd arrived here in Portland. He was exhausted from a grueling day at OHSU where he taught medical students and where he also gave medical diagnoses from local hospitals a second opinion. Lance sat there relaxed in the uncomfortably hard chair that right now, after being on his feet all day, made him feel like he was on a cloud. As with the last couple of days, he rubbed his temples, contemplating why he chose this new career path. This wasn't the reason he'd left his job as a lead Supervisor at the CDC in Atlanta. In fact, it was the opposite, he'd come here to get away from the seemingly endless workload. A "cushy number in the Northwest" his good friend and former colleague Malcolm had said.

He was distracted by some girls laughing loudly and he looked over to see a group of girls with signs. Another group of people were walking onto the platform being rowdy and also holding signs. For a moment he was puzzled then remembered there was a protest going on in downtown Portland. There had been a lot of absences due to people being sick, both teachers and students. He couldn't help but think maybe a few of the students not being in class or even professors he'd covered for had played hooky to attend these protests. He looked up and down the platform and saw there were dozens of people all waiting to head further downtown on the light rail.

"Dr Ferguson!" a girl's voice said loudly. He looked round to see Cheryl, a student nurse from one of his classes, walking towards him smiling. "Are you headed downtown to the protest?" the young girl asked.

Lance smiled and shook his head. "Afraid not. Headed home, it's been a long day, in fact it's been a long week already," he said with a small chuckle.

"I bet it's flu season," Cheryl said, smiling.

He nodded in agreement with a forced smile, he wanted to correct her that the flu isn't a season, it's a virus.

"You stay safe, Cheryl, and I'll see you tomorrow, right?" he asked, raising his eyebrows and smiling.

The young girl nodded smiling then waved goodbye before turning and walking towards a group of girls who were just arriving at the platform.

All day at school then protests and partying, oh what it must like to be young and have all that energy again, Lance thought to himself smiling. When a girl like Cheryl called him by his title it always made him feel old and reminded him of his age.Lance felt the phone in his pocket vibrate just like it had been doing all day. Being so busy with lectures and covering for other doctors who had come down sick, he'd barely had time to even look at his phone. His wife was probably upset that he'd not texted her or called her all day. Pulling his phone out, he was surprised to see it was Malcolm on the caller ID. He hadn't spoken to Malcolm in months, not since he left the CDC in Atlanta. The two had exchanged some texts and funny emails and he kept meaning to call but was just too busy.

"Hi, buddy!" he answered the phone.

"Lance! Thank god you answered!" Malcolm said sounding flustered.

"You okay? What's up? Sorry I haven't called but it's been so busy settling in-" Lance began but was cut off.

2

"Look, Lance I've been trying to get a hold of you all day, so have a few other guys and we've sent you some emails" Malcolm said.

"Sorry, I've been so busy today I haven't checked them yet and was going to check them when I got home... is everything alright?" he asked.

Lance knew if Malcolm and some of his other former peers were trying to get in touch with him must have been important.

"We need you to take a look at some test results and samples we have. There's been a few major outbreaks of an unidentified virus in countries all over the world. The world health organization is in a panic and have been blanketing as much of it out from the media as they could for the last three weeks" Malcolm said taking a breath before continuing.

"We got some samples from a couple of the countries and now we've gotten a few dozen samples back from here in the US too that are matching." Malcolm said sounding scared.

"What kind of virus are we talking about?" he asked.

" It's mimicking symptoms. of Ebola and Rabies but with rapid incubation times, we've had conflicting reports of how it's transmitted and that it mutates" Malcolm told him.

"Jesus..." Lance muttered to himself.

"Lance, the virus is spreading rapidly... A few of the guys are talking that it's following the path of the model you did a couple of years ago" Malcolm said.

Lance knew exactly what his friend was talking about; he had done a projection based on a bioweapon attack on the US utilizing the hand wipe stations at various large supermarkets like Costco and Walmart. The ones used for wiping the carts which not only infected the people using the carts but spreading to everything else they touched.

3

Lance felt his gut twist as he knew he had taken a very aggressive approach when designing the model and calculating the infection rate of the biochemical weapon. If someone had in fact released a virus spreading like this then an epidemic would be inevitable.

The fact that Malcolm was stating the symptoms. were like rabies, Ebola and then mutated reeked of a man-made bio engineered virus. "Have you guys been working on anything like that? Do you think someone got a hold of the model and used it to let this virus loose?" Lance asked.

"We're not sure, The World Health Organization is putting pressure on us to release all the information we have on viruses and strains we've been working on, the model simulation you designed as well as containment and quarantine measures" Malcolm said.

"You're wanting my help?" he asked knowing Malcolm and his former peers needed him onboard ASAP.

"You are the best person we know who has experience the Ebola virus, projecting infection dynamics and you're one of the few people still alive who were there for the initial incident in Somalia" Malcolm said.

The light rail train arrived, and everybody started to board but Lance sat there on the bench still on the phone looking at all these young people boarding to head to the protest. He couldn't help but feel sick to his stomach that all these people gathered together with a virus like this was a recipe for disaster. As the train pulled away, he saw Cheryl on the train laughing happily and he knew he had to do what he could.

" I can be on a flight tonight!" he said knowing if there was some kind of mutating virus that was sounding bio engineered, he would have to be there in person to get the best results and experiment hands on with live specimens.

"What else can you tell me about this virus?" he asked, needing as much information as possible to come up with a plan and timetable for infection, incubation, and contamination.

He could do this while on route to the CDC in Atlanta as time was of the essence and every second right now counted.

"Lance. There's more...a lot more" Malcolm said.

Lance could tell his friend was hesitating now. He wondered what his friend was holding back.

"While we're not exactly sure how the virus is transmitted, whether it's a blood borne pathogen or spread via bodily fluids or it could be airborne. The end result has reportedly been the same, though. That it starts with a high fever, some highly aggressive behavior in some reports, bleeding orifices and then leading to death..." Malcolm said but Lance knew there was still more by the way his friend was talking.

"Go on Malcolm... I can tell there's more" he said, wondering what his friend was keeping for last or just hesitant to tell him.

"Once they flatline, they reportedly...come back alive- but not as themselves...like cannibals, more aggressive, limited awareness, high pain tolerance." Malcolm said.

"You mean like zombies?" Lance asked.

"I wish there was a better word, Lance, I do but we've not been able to hold a live specimen so I'm just going by the footage and reports we've read," Malcolm told him.

LANCE DIDN'T KNOW what to say, he'd seen zombie movies growing up and always thought to himself that these stories must have originated somewhere. After all, his grandfather always told him all made up stories come from some truth. Could this new virus or pandemic, as it was seeming to be turning into, be the cause of zombies? The genre that so many movies and video games had been based on?

"Lance they've been rushing orders and containment plans through for the last couple of weeks, involving FEMA, the National Guard, and all branches of the emergency services. We've asked for several doctors that we need to be evacuated from their current locations and brought here" Malcolm said.

"My God! Malcolm, I need to see these samples ASAP, I can talk to the wife and be on a plane in a few hours!" he said, knowing something like this, no matter how far fetched it seemed, needed to be addressed. If it was true, then this was the type of virus that would be a nightmare for not just the CDC but the whole world.

This was the reason his friend had been trying to get a hold of him, he thought, they needed his expertise on virus mutations and spread patterns. Better to analyze and thoroughly investigate the virus before announcing to the world that there is in fact a real Zombie virus.

The pounding of his heart was echoing in his ears as it thumped dully inside his chest.

"There's no need to fly here, Lance...." Malcolm said and Lance could hear the tone drop in his friend's voice. Sirens from emergency vehicles were filling the air making it hard for him to hear his friend.

"Sorry, Malcolm could you speak up, it is crazy here because of these protests," he said covering his other ear with his hand to try and hear his friend better.

"That's another reason why I'm calling." Malcolm began, "A few of the test results we've been sent from inside the US are from hospitals in Portland. Yours."

CHAPTER TWO
Jake

The yellow Nissan Frontier truck rocked back and forth as it bumbled along the pothole riddled back roads surrounded by huge open fields that led from the sleepy little town of Battleground to Vancouver. Jake sat in the passenger seat as the truck jerked at every bump of the road which hadn't been taken care of since it had been built, he had always thought. This wasn't the main route from Battleground to Vancouver but right now it was definitely the safest. Jake sat expressionless, sunk into the passenger seat staring at his hands hanging down between his lap. Blood covered them with some dripping on the floor mat of Benny's truck with every bounce.

Benny was driving and without looking asked "Jake you okay, bro?"

Benny put his hand on Jake's arm and gave him a shake, Jake squirmed and sat up more "Yeah," he mumbled "I'm fine... I guess," he said as he looked at the mini dream catcher hanging on the rear-view mirror.

"We're almost there, bro, you're just in shock" Benny meekly reassured him. He sounded more like he was trying to reassure himself.

Jake zoned out again, wondering if this whole day had been a dream, but if it was, it was a nightmare. His eyelids fluttered and he rested his head back against the headrest, trying to remain calm. He thought about how the day had started off and how he had no idea it would have ended up like this or that he would have blood on his hands from taking a life.

Jake lay in bed blinking away the fogginess of just waking up, he glanced over at the alarm clock beside his bed, he wasn't due to get up for another fifteen minutes but the noise of the boys getting ready for school and arguing over something had woken him up. He thought about laying there trying to get back to sleep before his alarm went off or he could even hit snooze a couple of times and just lay there but he realized that was pointless and climbed out of the sheets.

He pulled on his underwear and blue scrubs for work then headed out into the living room, still a little groggy from being woken up by the chaos in the small single wide trailer, he walked into his son Paul and his stepson Greg arguing over something. "Whoa, whoa, whoa! What is going on?" He asked "You guys didn't know how loud you were being or what? I had to work late last night!" he shouted.

Both boys stopped and looked at him, Paul opened his mouth to talk but was cut off by Greg.

"It was his fault!" Greg shouted, pointing to his brother, Paul.

"He wanted to watch the news, but we said last night we should finish building our castle in Minecraft before school," his face was bright red and his cheeks puffing.

Emily came from the kitchen, the sun glowing behind her from the kitchen window, her dark skin and big brown eyes, bleached blonde hair, even first thing in the morning she looked super hot, Jake thought instantly, making him smile and taking the edge off his irritation.

"I told you boys not to wake Jake up! Go get your bags ready for school and maybe you can play some video games or TV before school, but I don't want to hear another peep." she didn't shout but had an authoritative tone.

He just smiled as both boys wandered past him with their heads lowered. He was always quick to get angry, but his wife was always the cool tempered, level headed one. She walked towards him with two cups of coffee as if reading his mind.

"I love you," he said chuckling as she handed him a cup and flashed him a smile, " I don't know how you do it." he complimented her.

She took a sip of her coffee and replied back "It still amazes me how after three years you've not gotten used to it or learned to drown them out," she said and they both laughed.

"Why did you have to work late last night? That's the latest you've had to stay," she asked.

He turned and walked back into the living room taking a seat on the couch.

"This fucking flu or whatever it is, we're short staffed with all the call outs and a lot of our patients are getting it bad," he said, and he knew today would probably be the same if not worse.

Emily took a seat beside him and put her legs across his and cuddled into him. Emily always told him he cared too much for the people at the home he worked at.

Emily had been a caregiver before becoming a hairdresser, she knew how tough it was and how hard it was dealing with the elderly and not getting too attached.

She snuggled into him and kissed his neck "Aww, poor daddy, anything I can do to take your mind off it?" she asked in a sexy tone and he looked down at her but before he could answer they both laughed as the two boys walked back into the room, backpacks in hand.

Both boys stood there looking at them as if waiting for a verdict "So?" Greg asked, "What are we allowed to do?"

Paul spoke up "I just wanted to watch the news to see about the riots, my teacher said the protests today would turn into a riot so people could get free stuff."

Emily started to laugh but Jake took a breath "Protests? Riots? Aren't you guys a little young to be watching stuff like that?" he asked the boys as he didn't understand why a teacher would be talking about protests and riots. Jake was curious, too, though as people at work were talking about the protests the last few days. "Okay we'll put the news on for a minute to see what's going on but just so you know, even if there are riots, you won't be getting a free PlayStation." He knew his son all too well and knew that would be what his Paul was going to ask for next.

"But Daaaad, if people are getting free TVs why can't Greg and me get PlayStation?" Paul was so serious and Greg, smiling, piped in, "Yeah! Let's watch the news! I love free stuff!" Greg cheered.

Jake smiled and he could tell Emily was trying hard to hold in her laugh, "It doesn't work like that, buddy, if you want stuff you have to work for it." he told them.

Greg just grinned from ear to ear and took a seat in front of the TV, throwing his backpack down beside Paul. Emily shook her head still trying not to laugh as they turned on the TV.

The bottom of the screen had a red banner scrolling across the bottom saying, "continued coverage..." Lately there had been protests over literally everything.

He read the info scrolling along the bottom of the screen detailing several incidents involving police that had escalated all over the US. Bullet points and info on different events were all popping up in boxes on the screen along with facts and figures as a live feed was being shown of downtown Portland.

Jake wasn't a TV person, but he had picked up most of what was happening with the protests from news clips he had seen at work. The protests and the super flu going around were the main topics of discussion in the break room and among the residents.

From what he was able to gather, there had been a number of people in various states getting shot or brutally killed by police officers and the families of the people had said that they were sick and had begun being delusional and aggressive.

"What a joke!" Emily commented as they all watched the people on TV waving signs and walking on the road blocking traffic.

"It's like they use any excuse to protest these days," she said, shaking her head.

Jake nodded "Yeah, I would just run them over," he said out loud and both boys laughed.

"LOOK!" Greg squealed.

The screen switched to a shaky video taken from a cell phone and a warning stating "WARNING: footage is graphic and may be disturbing to some viewers." Jake was about to change the channel when Emily put her hand on top of his. The clip showed a man well dressed with blood around his mouth fighting with a police officer up against a wall.

"That looks like Portland!" Emily said, "Oh my God, it is in Portland…." she gasped.

This made him a little uneasy, he knew they were protesting downtown Portland because of the shootings but he didn't realize there had been one so close to home.

The man on the screen was struggling with the police officer when more cops came into view and the officer being attacked fell. The man covered in blood was standing over him but before he could get any further two shots rang out.

"YEAH!" both boys cheered together.

The man on the screen was staggered back by each shot then looked at the officers firing and began moving towards them. The man wasn't running but moving fast like he wasn't bothered by the bullets then another shot rang out causing his forehead to erupt in a spurt of crimson red and he dropped to the ground. The officers closed in on him and the video ended then it switched to the two

11

reporters in the news studio and the protest still live in view behind them in the top corner.

"Did you see that headshot?" Paul said to Greg,

Laughing, Greg replied "Yeah! That was awesome! Epic fail with the first few, though!"

Emily cleared her throat, "Okay, how about you guys just play video games now?"

Both boys were still laughing as they headed off towards their room to play Xbox.

"Fuckin' idiot protesters! The guy was attacking a cop, of course he got shot." Jake said to his wife as he finished off his coffee and got up "I'm going to finish getting ready," he told her then headed towards the bathroom. He was still pretty tired but knew it would probably be another long day with a lot of sick people, so he liked to get some time to himself before leaving.

Jake stepped into his bedroom and opened up the drawer of the bedside table and looked at the lockbox that was inside. He opened it to make sure his gun was still in there; it had become a habit lately and he wasn't sure why. The 9mm was still there with a fully loaded clip beside it and their passports. Emily had made him lock the gun away as she was always worrying and safety conscious of everything. He thought that was a good thing though, as that was also why she'd let him get the gun.

When he came out of the room, the boys were getting ready by the door to head out to school.

"You driving them today?" he asked a bit confused as he saw Emily grabbing the minivan keys. The boys usually rode the school bus every morning since it stopped right at the entrance of their trailer park.

"Yeah the school sent out an automated voicemail last night saying buses could be up to thirty minutes late and if you could get your kids to school another way." Emily said, grabbing her coffee mug from the kitchen. He nodded to himself as neither of them could afford to be late and they didn't trust both boys on their own at the bus stop for more than ten minutes.

"Your ride's here," Emily said looking out the kitchen window and then he heard the sound of Benny's truck horn as it honked to signal   he   was   here.

CHAPTER THREE
Nick

Nick stretched his legs as the train pulled to a stop at the Seattle Amtrak station and he got out the seat he'd been stuck in since Portland. He grabbed his luggage from the compartment above his seat. There was a duffle bag with his clothes and his EDC one strap messenger backpack that went with him everywhere. He slowly made his way off the busy train along with everyone else. As he walked into the terminal building it seemed chaotic. People were rushing past each other and some were even pushing through the crowd that had just gotten off the train so they could get to the platform faster to board the train.

Nick had only been to Seattle one other time; it had been with his wife, but he definitely didn't remember them being this rude as they bumped into him going in the opposite direction. As he walked into the terminal there was a police dog and its handler sniffing around the benches that people were sitting at. The dog approached Nick as he walked in and took a big sniff before moving onto more benches. Judging by how packed the station was. Nick knew he had to get to the taxi line pretty fast.

As he left the station. there was another sniffer dog at the entrance and then another by the taxi cabs. Nick got into the first cab he saw, the man looked at him in the rear-view mirror.

"Where to, boss?" the man asked in a thick African accent,

"The Motif hotel, please," he told the driver with a smile.

"You got it, boss" the driver replied with a huge pearly white grin of his own. The cabby peeled out and the taxi roared up the hill.

Nick clutched his bag close as the taxi flew up the hill almost taking off. He wasn't sure if the driver was practicing for the Grand Prix or was maybe a street racer in his off time. You can't judge a book by its cover or a person by their first impression or appearance and Nick knew this all too well, but he always liked a good laugh to himself.

He maybe looked like a geeky pencil pusher to the average Joe, but Nick was a "prepper" and a Survivalist, he liked to think of himself as being prepared for anything and everything. Which is why he always kept his EDC bag with him at all times because "you just never know" he always told his family and friends. He'd given his wife an EDC bag for her car too, she always laughed at him, but he didn't care, he was her dorky husband but better safe than sorry.

She would always get the acronym wrong for EDC, too. "Every Day Carry" he always told her laughing when she got it wrong. He was thinking of her with her short dark hair and big brown eyes, and their daughter, Amber. He was shaken out of it when the cabby slammed on his breaks.

"Fook sake mudda fuck ass bitch" the cabby blurted out.

They were stopped at the top of a hill with a line of cars in front of them going all the way down the hill for about four blocks, Nick just looked at the cabby in the mirror and thought of something quick to say, "Traffic, huh?" he said trying to ease the man's tension.

The cabby smiled and nodded "So what brings you here, sir?" the driver asked.

Nick looked him and cleared his throat, it was hot. "I'm here to meet with a company that leases out food carts." he began telling the driver "I'm going to sell gourmet grilled cheese sandwiches." he said, trying to sound as serious as he could about his idea. Nearly every time he had told someone his idea, they had laughed but he had made his girls over twenty-two different types of grilled cheese and they loved every one of them.

The cabby let out a big deep laugh.

15

"I like that idea, friend!" the cabby said giving his approval with a thumbs up then went on.

"I came here from Africa three years ago," the cabby said, "Always a cab driver and hear a lot of crazy things but this idea I like," the driver said with his eyes widening.

Nick didn't know whether to take this as a good sign of approval or to be worried. He had known the driver for barely five minutes and he clearly drove like a maniac so hopefully his taste in ideas was better than his driving.

The cabby started to go on about all the crazy ideas he had heard from people, like inflatable full size unicorns for floating on, to a monthly subscription box full of rocks. It was hot so Nick started to roll down his window. As he did, he could hear shouting coming from outside, he looked at where it was coming from. There was a homeless man growling and screaming at the cars that were stalled in the line behind them which now stretched back quite a bit.

The man started to walk towards a car behind them waving his arms. when two police officers appeared on bicycles. They hopped off as they got close to the man, the sending the bikes clattering to the ground. As the taxi started to move again, Nick twisted his neck so he could keep watching to see what was happening, but the line moved at a decent pace and he lost sight of them.

"Look! Look!" the cabby exclaimed, "This is the fuckin' hold up, man!" the cabby was waving his hand at the passenger window in frustration. Nick looked out to see four officers in the middle of the road in the other lane with caution tape up connected to cones. It was hard to see what was going on, but he could see a black body bag lying beside them on the ground. Nick looked at the cabby with a puzzled look.

"Is it always like this up here?" he asked but the cabby shook his head

"No, it's hot and lately people are going crazy, it will only get worse, I've seen this happen before. Back home when the government was destroying our land," the cabby stopped smiling as he stared off into the rear-view mirror at Nick. Nick was starting to get a little creeped out then saw the Motif logo lit up on the corner.

The cabby started banging on his horn as they got to the corner, pedestrians scurried across the road as the cabby continued laying on his horn and waving his arms. about, not caring that he was in a motor vehicle and they were on the road.

As they pulled up outside the hotel, Nick glanced at the meter, the fare was at eight sixty,

Nick gave him a ten and told him to keep the change, he smiled and nodded a thank you. As Nick got out the cabby rolled down the passenger window and shouted "Stay safe, Mr. Grilled Cheese! Here my card if you need a ride back!" he said in his broken English, handing Nick a business card. Taking it, Nick nodded back with a smile and a wave.

As the Cabby drove off, Nick walked into the hotel lobby, he tried to call his wife, but the line was busy, so he walked up to the checkout desk. The lobby was pretty full, and he could only see two of the check in desks staffed. When it was his turn in line the receptionist apologized for them being short staffed today. Nick thought she maybe should have called in too, as she was sweating quite a bit and wiping it with her sleeve and looked very pale.

Once he was all checked in, he headed to his room, He got into the elevator and as it hummed, he was starting to get nervous so he figured he would go over his presentation notes on his laptop before the big day tomorrow soon after he had called home.

Once he got to his room, he swiped the key card and opened the door, the luxury of the room amazed him; a white bathrobe hanging outside the frosted glass bathroom door, a huge flat screen TV, big white turned down bed. He put his EDC bag down beside the door and threw his duffle bag on the bed, he had been sitting on that sweaty train for three hours and needed a shower. He turned on the shower so it would be nice and steamy then started unpacking, throwing his clothes on the bed and put his laptop and cellphone on the desk. He could hear sirens outside and looked out the huge glass windows, he was on the twenty ninth floor and the ground looked so far down, the people moving like ants, he could see them all scurrying around, he could see flashes from red and blue lights bouncing off of windows. He was surprised by the amount of police he had seen on the streets and sirens he was hearing in the short time he had been here, made him glad he hadn't brought Amber, as she would have been terrified.

He decided he would take his shower then give his girls a call, he had only been gone a few hours but missed them a lot and with all the craziness in Portland right now and apparently everywhere he knew talking to his girls would calm his nerves a bit.

CHAPTER FOUR
Jake

Emily walked out of the house waving to Benny, who was Jake's daily ride to work and was parked at the end of the driveway. Jake locked the door behind them all as he was the last one out. The kids rushed up to Benny's truck "Hey, Uncle Benny!" they both cheered,

"Hey guys! What's up?" Benny said, leaning out the window giving high fives, flashing his trademark gleaming white smile, standing out against his deep dark Native American skin. The boys began asking him if he had seen the news and the guy getting shot, Benny shook his head "Nah. I was playing video games all morning," Benny said, laughing.

Emily walked up behind them "Okay boys, let's go, mommy has to get to work, too" and both boys got into the minivan. Jake walked up behind her.

"Love you," he said as she turned and give him a kiss and a hug.

"Love you more, have a nice day and don't work too hard" she said, and he squeezed her butt. The boys were already buckled in and playing around in the back. Emily got in smiling and him and waved as she reversed out the driveway.

A door slammed, it was their neighbor Pete, he was coming out of his trailer fast carrying some suitcases with his wife Susie right behind him with bags of groceries and both began loading them into Pete's Subaru. Pete's two girls came out behind Susie carrying backpacks and more bags of food. Pete ran back into the house without even acknowledging him or Benny, Susie was always quiet and really only spoke to Emily and the boys, but she looked up and gave a sad look. Jake could tell she was upset and trying to fight back tears.

"Hey, Susie! Everything okay?" he asked. Pete seemed to be in a frenzy shouting from inside the house with banging and the sound of things being thrown around. Then Pete appeared out the doorway carrying more bags.

"You guys going camping?" Benny asked Peter.

Pete looked at them. "You guys better get your shit together and get the fuck out of here. This place is going to go to shit! And Jake you have kids! Trust me! You need to leave!" Pete said as he got in slamming his car door. Susie and the kids were still buckling themselves in when Pete peeled out and sped towards the entrance of their trailer park.

Benny looked at Jake confused then shrugged his shoulders as they both got into the truck.

"Weird," Jake muttered.

"This fuckin' trailer park," Benny chuckled trying to change the subject. Benny and he had worked together for about four years, He had no family so Benny was like a brother and they carpooled every day.

"Your kids really see that on the news?" Benny asked. Jake nodded as they headed the same direction Peter had just driven, it was a small park shaped in a circle with only one entrance/exit.

"You know I think I might move in over here, it's so cute and friendly" Benny said waving to an old lady on her bike, but she didn't wave back.

"That's Marge, she's a bitch…always stoned" he told Benny

Benny rolled his shoulders honking his horn as they passed Emily, who had stopped at the mailboxes, she waved from inside the mail room that had no door and looked more like a bus shelter.

Benny glanced at the huge white wooden map beside the mail room, it was a map of the trailer park. A circle of units all numbered with sixty around the outside and fourteen in the middle and beside it was a huge piece of what looked like driftwood with the trailer park's name on it

"The Great Western Trailer Park," Benny said, smiling. Benny had always told him it had reminded him of some shanty old cowboy town.

"See how cute this is? The map, the weird old sign and..." Benny began then hesitated "but all these old people, don't you get enough of them at work?" Benny asked. Jake just smiled and nodded; he knew Benny was just trying to lighten the mood before they got to work. They joked and laughed all the time but today he wasn't in the mood to joke, something about the news and what was going on bothered him, but he couldn't figure out what it was. Pete's behavior didn't feel right, and he knew today was going to be longer than usual with more people probably out with this flu, but he also knew that if he didn't start laughing at Benny's jokes Benny wouldn't give up.

"That's why we moved here in the first place," he started to explain "All we could afford was an apartment but Emily hated apartments and this was just as cheap but a lot safer." he started to tell Benny the reasoning behind the decision, "There's only one way in or out, small community mostly of older people or people who've lived here since it was built and it's far enough out of the way from town that it's quiet."

They turned out onto the main road from the park and an apartment complex came into view further down the road.

"Then there's that" he groaned, and Benny chuckled,

The 'low income housing' as it had been labeled went up less than a year ago and was full of large families over crowded into the three five-floor high buildings, the people who lived there probably

21

couldn't afford or find housing elsewhere which was fine but the worst part was all the criminal activity that had increased since they went up. As they drove past, they could see several groups of people outside smoking out on the sidewalk, glaring at them as they drove past, Benny nodded over to the other side of the road from the apartments to another trailer park which was closed off with large iron gates.

Jake raised his eyebrows, "Oh they were pissed! Still are," he told Benny and they both laughed. It was a trailer park for the elderly, no kids were allowed and all the trailers that could be seen looked very well taken care off.

This had been another reason why they had moved here. The only neighbors at that time were the people in their park and this other park that was adjacent to theirs and full of rich old people who kept to themselves with a big empty field that separated them.

Benny looked at him and laughed "Emily had a list of pros and cons to moving here?" Benny asked trying to hold in his laughter.

Jake looked at him and sighed, "Yeah," he said in a dull tone and they both laughed as they headed towards I-205 which would take them to Battle Ground, Washington where they worked.

It was close to nine o'clock when they pulled into Vitality Health and Rehab where they worked. It was a posh name for what it was, a glorified old people's home. A lot of the residents checked in after having an injury and not many of them checked back out either due to families not being able to properly care for them or just not wanting to anymore.

He always thought it sad that life had gotten so busy for people that caring for the elderly, the people who cared for them as they grew from a baby had become an inconvenience.

They hopped out the truck and noticed an ambulance parked at the side fire exit, this usually meant a resident had passed, neither of them wanted to think who it could be as there was a lot of residents

22

who were very sick right now. As they entered the lobby, they both looked at each other and Benny muttered, "Uh oh," as he noticed the piano in the corner of the room was vacant and the air silent. Ms. Munroe would be playing that thing every morning from around 8:00 am right up until lunch at 11.

They both swiped their time cards and headed for the morning meeting which was held every day at the main nurse's station in the center of the complex beside the main dining hall.

They passed several rooms. with residents inside watching TV or reading, some still asleep. The complex was divided into three halls. 1 and 2 for regular patients with injuries and the third was locked and secured as it was full of what Benny liked to call "the crazies", he didn't really like Benny's term as he knew most of them suffered from dementia, Alzheimer's, schizophrenia, and other age related mental illnesses. He knew they couldn't help but come across as "crazy", but he didn't like them being labeled as that, even jokingly.

The main dining hall and nurse's station was located right beside the entrance to hall 3. The hall 3 entrance was two wide heavy fire doors with only a small glass pane on each about half a foot wide to let you see inside and there was an illuminated keypad on the side.

They could see some paramedic equipment on the floor beside the doors, this let both men know that whoever had passed during the night had been from hall 3.

They walked into the meeting room and everyone was already there who hadn't called in sick, he walked away from Benny towards Sandra the day shift supervisor "It's going to be another long day?" he asked as he collected his charts from the table then looked around the room trying to eyeball who wasn't there. Sandra nodded, "We've had six call ins, another two possible no call no shows and three residents passed last night." Her eyes were cloudy with sadness. He was stunned by being told three, he wanted to ask who, but he knew once the meeting started in a few minutes he would find out. He took his and Benny's charts and gave Sandra a somber nod.

Benny was busy chatting to a young girl whose name he couldn't remember when he walked over, she had only been at the facility for a week or so, she was on some kind of training placement from her college. He handed Benny his charts, "Three gone," he told him quietly so he would be ready for it getting announced in the meeting. The girl's giggling stopped, and he looked down at her name tag. "Michelle."

Benny's flirty behavior changed, "Oh shit, three in 24 hours means the state will be getting involved and investigating, man our day – no, our week just got a whole lot fucking worse," Benny sighed.

Michelle looked at Benny and asked, "Why what does the state do?" Benny started to explain that once more than two residents passed in a 48 hour period then the state would send a team in to audit and investigate the facility to make sure it was operating correctly and 100% to state safety codes, essentially they would be under a microscope until the team the state sent out had reported back that everything was 100% by the book. This would not be fun for anyone, not the nurses, residents, or even visiting families.

Michelle just nodded as Benny explained all of this and Jake looked out the window on the other side of the dining room. He could see the parking lot of the high school that was next to them and there were trucks pulling in with long white trailers.

CHAPTER FIVE
Caleb

Caleb's farmhouse sat on a hill on the huge plot of land he owned in Amboy, Washington. He loved being a little bit away from the hustle and bustle of the people in town and not having to deal with much drama. He stood in the kitchen of his custom-built three-story home sipping a beer while his wife Janice and two girls, Madison and Haley, were in the living room adjacent laying on the huge luxurious couch big enough for ten people watching a movie. Nate, his son came in rushing into the kitchen grabbing his attention

"Dad, there's two cars coming!" Nate blurted out. They lived out of the way in the country and didn't get many visitors unless invited and certainly weren't expecting any. Caleb finished off his beer and tossed the bottle into the recycling bag hanging from a cupboard door. He dragged his sleeve across his face wiping his lips then walked into the huge living room which took up one whole corner of the second floor of the house. Windows ran along both walls, he looked outside at the panoramic view of the hills and trees that surrounded them. Far off in the distance he could see some smoke, it was south and pretty far for him to be worried about. He knew his crops or family were in no danger, but he had heard on the news about the craziness going on across the country. He walked towards the spiral staircase smiling at his girls as he passed through. They were both in their twenties, but he still sheltered them as best he could, his little girls were his world. He went down the stairs that led to the front door and opened it. He stepped outside onto the gravel driveway that snaked from the house all the way to the road about three hundred yards to the edge of the property. Then the gravel drive turned into a road that ran all the way into town. The bottom floor of his house was a large three car garage and behind the garage was his wife's interior greenhouse. Above the garages was a large balcony that spanned the width of the house, it had two doors leading onto it. One from the living room, the another from his master bedroom. Linda, his wife, walked out from the living room door looking at the cars coming down the driveway then at Caleb, "You expecting anyone, honey?" His wife asked.

He could see two cars flying up the driveway, a Camaro and an Escalade he knew right away who it was, he had thought the last time he had a visit like this the man was just ranting and raving being high on whatever but he knew now most of what he had been told before was starting to come true from what he was seeing on the news.

Victor Chenkov was his neighbor on the property beside his, but he rarely saw the man or his "Family" that resided in the collection of trailers next to the man's four-bedroom house that was on a property half the size of Caleb's. Caleb's driveway ran past Victor's property and he always saw different cars outside the trailers that littered the field beside Victor's place.

Nate always joked that he thought Victor was either a drug lord or a gang leader because of all the riff raff that would be loitering on the property but after his recent unannounced visit Caleb wasn't sure those were so far fetched ideas.

FOUR WEEKS EARLIER -

Caleb swung the axe and it came crashing down splitting the log in two, sending the halves splintering off to the side. He picked up another block setting it on top of the stump that lay beside his gravel driveway. As he raised the axe above his head, he saw a car coming down his driveway. It was a yellow Camaro that belonged to his neighbor Victor Chenkov who rarely spoke to him.

The Camaro pulled up and Victor stepped out resting his hand on the car door. Caleb noticed the Russian Hammer and Sickle tattooed on Victor's hand between his thumb and index finger. Victor stood there looking around for a moment with the trademark solemn stone look the man always had then suddenly flashed a smile at Caleb. Victor was a short man with grey hair in a buzz cut all over. Victor had thick arms and looked muscular. Even though he looked to be in his fifties the man looked in shape. "Victor, what can I do for you?" Caleb asked the surprise visitor then Victor threw his arms. out.

"Caleb! Neighbor!" Victor said loudly, Caleb looked at the man's dilated pupils. Victor was no doubt probably high on something. He had heard rumors of Victor and his drug dealing from various people at the casinos in Amboy, but he chose to ignore it as Victor had never bothered Caleb or his girls but showing up here high could be the end of that.

"I wanted to come see you Caleb, I think we can help each other out, my friend" Victor said still smiling and walking over with his arms. outstretched.

"How so, Victor?" Caleb replied

Victor lowered his arms and put a knee on the picnic bench at the side of the driveway in a Captain Morgan like pose then lit a cigarette, "Well," Victor began then paused taking a big inhale. "back in my home country of Russia things are happening, things that may very well happen over here, not good things, my friend" Victor then went on about governments collapsing and things being in high demand in not just Russia but other countries that Victor had "friends" in.

Caleb just kept pretending to listen as the man appeared to be rambling on. Victor kept taking puffs of his cigarette between stories of how bad things could get then he finally got to the point.

"So, what I'm getting at Caleb is we're neighbors and your wife has a lot of fruit and vegetables and you have all these animals," Victor said sweeping his hand around in the direction of Caleb's fields. "In exchange for sharing some of that with me, I'll provide you with more than enough protection against anyone who comes looking to try and take it," Victor said tossing the cigarette butt into the gravel and squashing it like a bug with a big bulky boot. Caleb couldn't help but take note that Victor's "offer" was seeming more and more like a threat than a good deed.

Caleb looked out over at his fields with cows and horses grazing away without a care in the world. If anything as far-fetched as what Victor was saying was to happen, he definitely wouldn't let anything happen to his home and to get rid of this drugged out lunatic fast he just nodded his head in agreement. "Sure, Victor that would be great," he said with a forced smile and Victor walked over putting his hand out. Caleb shook Victor's hand, looking down at the tattoo. Victor smiled and turned his hand over so the full tattoo could be seen.

" I used to be in Russian military." Victor said then turned and headed back to his car. "I promise your family will be safe, as will you," he said without turning. Victor got into his car then honked his horn as the Camaro drove off down the driveway.

Ever since Victor had driven off that day, Caleb had tried to put the conversation to the back of his head. After all it had probably just been due to Victor bring high on drugs, some of the stuff Nate had come out with while high on weed had been paranoid comedy gold. The one thing had nagged at the back of Caleb's mind since that day was his curiosity of Victor's past, an ex-Russian military man now living in a farmhouse in Amboy Washington.

Now here he was, four weeks later, standing outside again with Victor's Camaro coming back down his driveway. Only this time Victor had company and most of what he had described about what

28

was going on in the world was beginning to appear on the news. All the information he had seen on the news had all been saying the same thing, that there was civil unrest all over the world. Here in the US, violent acts against police officers had increased and caused nationwide protests that appeared to be getting out of hand. Then there was some super flu virus that was hitting everybody hard. Caleb had a feeling any questions he had about Victor's stories last time he visited were about to be answered as he didn't have a very good feeling in his stomach.

CHAPTER SIX
Jake

"Okay! Attention everyone" Sandra got everyone's attention for the meeting to start, Jake looked around the room; there seemed more people missing than what Sandra had told him. He listened as Sandra gave her usual daily brief on lunch and dinner options for residents. She told them that there would be no patient therapy today which would definitely lighten the workload as not pulling people to take patients to and from therapy. This was probably so they could play catch up for an audit but then Sandra told them all that it was indefinite until further notice.

Sandra covered who would be covering the missing staff's duties then the dining room door opened, and everyone turned their attention to see the head of the facility Karen walk in.

She was a small red headed woman who was never at meetings but always scrutinizing things around the facility. Karen stood beside Sandra and looked around the room.

Karen was friendly enough if you did your job correctly but her being here meant something was wrong.

Karan stood beside Sandra like two parents about to give their children some bad news

"Good morning everyone," she began "First off, I want to thank you all for coming in, both I and the residents appreciate it" Karen paused clearly, she was upset and struggling to find the words she wanted to say. "I have received emails over the past few days on certain new procedures we have to implement, I have asked for clarification on these procedures as I'm very confused. I'm addressing this today in a conference call with several of the regional team who oversee other facilities and clinics like this one." Karen looked around the room

"If any of you have friends or family at other facilities and heard of these procedures, I would appreciate it if you could keep it to yourself. We will have another meeting in here after lunch as I will have clarification on what we're being asked to do"

He could hear Benny beside him mutter "What the fuck is going on?" as the room was filled with a lot of puzzled faces.

"See you all at one thirty, have a good day." Karen finished and left the room.

Sandra cleared her throat "As you probably all know by now, some of our residents passed last night. These were Mr. Glisan, Mrs. Walsh and Mr. Boyd, who a lot of you liked to call Frank"

Mr. Glisan and Mrs. Walsh were no surprise to him as they had been very, very sick with the flu and usually when people their age get the flu or a virus that bad it's hard to keep them hydrated but Frank... Frank was only sixty, he was in hall three with the other two because he liked to try and escape the facility in his wheelchair to try and "chase the ladies" as Frank called it.

Frank was a flirty old man who had flown a plane most of his life until he crashed his motorcycle five years ago and lost a leg. Frank's family dropped him off here but never collected him as they said they couldn't give him the proper care at home.

The usual cop out families used when they realized life was easier without the elderly members of the family to take care of. Sad sighs went up around the room as everyone loved Frank, Frank was the most popular resident that they all talked about, but the most surprising thing was that he hadn't had the flu the night before in fact he remembered Frank had been just fine.

Sandra continued " Mr. Moore was thought to have passed but when EMTs arrived it appeared he wasn't deceased despite the night

31

staff in hall 3 stating they called 911 after finding him deceased and non-responsive after performing CPR unsuccessfully. This will be investigated and so I urge you all to be very accurate and diligent when checking vitals"

Sandra was trying not to cry as she even had a soft spot for Frank. Blinking back the tears she continued "Unfortunately, however Mr. Moore did attack one of the EMTs and his roommate, they were both taken to hospital where Frank... Mr. Boyd later died due to his injuries." The tears could be seen on Sandra's face, she stopped to wipe her eyes and the sadness could be felt around the room.

This answered the question as to how Frank had died. Sandra breathed in and started again "Mr. Moore was taken to the hospital also, so please if you're in hall 3 don't talk about this near any of the residents," she closed the meeting with a thank you again and telling them all to be back at one thirty for the afternoon meeting with Karen. There was no mention of the state getting involved which was probably the only positive outcome of the morning meeting.

Jake spent most of his morning going around the rooms , checking on the residents in halls 1 and 2 who were all either engrossed in daytime TV or shuffling around between rooms. to visit their friends. The news of what had happened the night before hadn't reached them yet. That was good as these people were old and didn't need to be reminded they were on the last part of their journey that was life. Jake finished up in hall 2 and then headed towards the two large doors to enter hall 3. When a resident died the air always felt weird to him in the room they had been in and he would be heading to Ms. Long's room which was next door to Frank's and Mr. Moore's.

He punched in the key code, changing the illuminated pad from red to green. Glancing through the windows to make sure the coast was clear, he pushed the door open. People like Frank and Mr. Jones were always trying to escape into hall two to get to "the ladies" which had always made him smile, as he hoped when he was older Emily and him would be just as frisky.

The hall was empty like usual, unlike the rest of the facility where residents wheeled and buzzed around. This hall the residents mainly stayed in their rooms, so it was kept bare, a small dining room just for this hall's residents sat at the far end of the hall with some tables so they could sometimes do activities and a wall mounted TV. He approached the nurse's station at the foot of the long hallway and could see Travis sitting at the desk scribbling notes. Travis was hall three's daytime doctor who was solely on this hall. This must have been especially hard on him as he spent all of his time here. Travis had no family outside of work so the residents in this hall were his family. Travis looked up as he approached and nodded with watery bloodshot eyes. Jake passed one of his charts across the station to Travis to look at and sign off on.

"I gave Betty some valium; she was a little upset about last night so she might not seem herself." Travis handed the chart back "I also gave her a dose of cold medicine, she's seemed fairly healthy this week so I want to keep it that way" Travis turned his attention to his computer and Jake knew this meant Travis didn't want to talk about anything so he took the chart and headed down the hallway. It was very noticeable how silent this wing was from the rest of the facility, the thick walls and soundproof windows; all so these residents remained calm and whatever mental thing they had going on didn't get fired up by noises or distractions from the outside.

Ms. Long's room was at the end of the hall and lately she was asking the same questions.

"Do you have today's paper?" and "Is Charlotte here to get me?" someone asked about who Charlotte was thinking it was a family member, but it had turned out Charlotte was a friend of Ms. Long's in high school and would pick her up so the two could go out driving

33

around together. He thought it sweet that at such a pivotal point in her life she could only think of a happier time as it turned out she hadn't seen Charlotte in over 40 years. He was startled as he was walking down the hall a door beside him opened. A gaunt face peered out.

"Geez, David!" he said more to himself quietly than to David.

David's eyes were all milky and cloudy.

"You okay, buddy?" he asked but this was a rhetorical question as David had severe Alzheimer's and only cared and talked about a few things.

"Foooood?" David mumbled as he opened the door and shuffled out not lifting his feet off the ground. He looked down at David's feet that were red and trailing blood as he shuffled out into the hall. This often happened if David removed his socks and none of the aids had noticed.

David would shuffle his feet not lifting them then they would blister and bleed from being scraped. " David look at your feet! C'mon let's get some socks on you" He said guiding him back into the room. Then from inside the room a gruff voice called out

"Get that geriatric mother fucker out this room, I'm sick of his jokes and him asking me for food!" the voice belonged to Mr. Jones an elderly African American man in a wheelchair who reminded the staff of Samuel L. Jackson. As Jake walked in with David, he could see Mr. Jones was tinkering with something on his bed.

He liked Mr. Jones, he was old and ornery, always giving the nurses shit and trying to with Frank to flirt with the females. He had short grey hair and grey stubble that covered his face.

"Easy now, Mr. Jones, I'll get his socks on him and let him watch some TV out in the dining room," Jake said, sitting David down on his bed. He looked above Mr. Jones's bed at a photo which was of a much younger Mr. Jones in a navy uniform. He always imagined Mr. Jones to be a badass in his younger days. David stared at the picture too then back to Jake and asked "How...how many seconds are in...a year?" His speech was slow and slurred.

It was the same joke David told everyone every day, Jake laughed at it every day and people had told him he would get sick of it eventually, but he hadn't yet.

"I dunno, Dave, how many?" before David could answer, Mr. Jones threw what he was tinkering with across the room and into the wall, startling both Jake and David.

"There's twelve! Twelve fuckin' seconds in a year! The same joke every fuckin' day you stupid shit! Go fuck yourself!" Mr. Jones shouted as he wheeled himself out of the room and into the hallway. Jake turned to David who just stared up at him unfazed, "There's...Twelve seconds... January second.... February second..." David said chuckling to himself pleased with his joke probably like the first time he had ever told it. It wasn't like Mr. Jones to be so angry so he must have known about Frank. Jake stepped out of the room to see where Mr. Jones had wheeled himself to. Mr. Jones was reaching up from his chair to turn on the TV at the end of the hall, cursing under his breath.

The entrance doors to hall 3 opened with Benny and Michelle laughing as they came bouncing in. Benny nodded "You stealing my guys?" Benny asked holding up a chart. Both David and Mr. Jones were usually on Benny's route.

"I was taking David back in to get socks and Jonesy flipped out," he told Benny.

Benny let out a deep laugh "Yeah I guess he's getting moved." Benny told him that over the past few days Mr. Jones had been having more and more outbursts, so Travis had requested a room change. As Benny took over attending to David, Jake headed down to Mrs. Long's room.

As he passed by Mr. Moore's room, he looked in but there was yellow caution tape put across the doorway to deter residents from wandering in. He entered Ms. Long's room and caution tape had also been put across her bathroom door too. Both Mr. Moore and Ms. Long's had a bathroom they shared between the rooms. Ms. Long was bed ridden but other residents could wonder in and threw to Mr. Moore's room.

He looked at Ms. Long as she lay in bed silent. Usually she was awake this time of day, but he looked at the chart and was aware she was sick. He checked her vitals, noting she looked very clammy and sweaty. He looked at her wrists, noticing her veins seemed to be a purple color and were raised; it was on both wrists with some faintly on her neck starting to appear. As he was checking over her chart Benny slammed his hand on the door to the room startling him

"C'mon fucker, let's go get lunch" Benny said then disappeared down the hallway. He finished up his notes on his chart and took it to Travis as he left hall 3. He hoped Ms. Long would be feeling better and awake when he rechecked her in the afternoon.

CHAPTER SEVEN
Nick

Nick came out the shower feeling refreshed and ready to so some prep work on his presentation. It was still early, almost six o'clock, he figured he would run through his presentation on his laptop then head out for something to eat, then do some last-minute changes if any were needed before calling it a night. He put on some comfortable jeans and an olive-green shirt. He rolled up the sleeves as he walked over to the desk and opened his laptop, but it was dead. He grabbed the charger plugging one end into the laptop then looked for the outlet on the wall.

The other cables from the TV and lamp went down behind the desk so he got down and crawled under it. He was under the desk and his phone started to ring, it was a tight squeeze under there, so he reached his arm out and groped around on the desk above him for the phone, he felt it with his fingers and pulled it down answering it,

"Hi honey!" he said to his wife on the other end, but he was met with a child's voice.

"Hi, daddy!!!" squealed the voice on the other end, it was his daughter. His eyes lit up and heart began to melt. This was the first time away from his little Princess and she was his world, hearing her voice, it seemed like had been a lot more than a few hours since he had seen her.

The way the economy was going he knew if he wanted a secure future for her, he had to make more money and she was a big motivator as to why he had come to Seattle to pitch this idea that a lot of people had thought him crazy for. The cart he owned was doing great, but he needed to expand.

"Hi, Baby! How are you? You and mommy doing okay?" he asked, trying to hide his concern and guilt for leaving the two women in his life at home by themselves for the first time. The concern was that they lived right outside of Portland and there was going to be protests and even though they wouldn't be near the protests he was always thinking the worst. This is why he was always preparing for "the big one" so that even small things like protests that could turn into riots or a small power outage that could turn into a blackout lasting a few days his family would be ready.

"We're fine, daddy" he could hear the sadness in her voice, "I miss you already, I'm being brave and protecting mommy like you said" Hearing the confidence in her voice made him proud.

"Good! That's daddy's big girl" he replied back. Deep down he knew they would be fine, he had thought out every scenario in his head, he was anal like that. His wife laughed at him that he took his EDC bag with him everywhere he went in case he got stranded and had to make it home on foot to them. He would even google how long it would take to walk there. Ever since he had read the home survivalist book series it was always in the back of his head

What if shit hit the fan?

So, he had instructed his wife and baby girl what to do if anything ever happened. He knew his wife enjoyed all the training they did together, shooting guns, setting up traps in the garden, prepping bug out bags and first aid kits and prepping supplies.

Nick smiled to himself, his little girl was sounding all grown up "I miss you too, pumpkin, but it's important daddy does this and I'll be straight back" he slid out from the desk and rested his back against the bed looking at the spaghetti junction of wires under the desk.

"You promise, daddy?" she asked, and he could tell she was missing him a lot.

"Baby, I promise I'll be on the first train as soon as I'm done, the day after tomorrow. Can I talk to mommy?" he asked.

As he heard her pass the phone to her mom, he was distracted by a smashing of glass sound from outside and a long scream, he jumped as a body flew past the window with shards of glass then another. He dropped the phone and rushed to the window, just before he got to the window the screaming stopped and he looked out to see two bodies smashed on the concrete sidewalk below and a circle of people forming around them. He tried to look up, but he couldn't see straight up, some fabric and papers fluttered down. He stumbled backwards and picked up the phone on the desk by the bed to call the front desk, but it was busy. He could hear his wife from his cell phone on the ground

"Nick? Nick? Hello? Are you there?" he picked it up, still in shock and trying to calm himself but pacing from the bed to the window and back again.

"Hey babe it's me!" he said with a labored breath from what he had just seen trying not to panic.

"Nick, are you okay? What's wrong? You sound frantic!" Nick wasn't sure what to say he still couldn't believe what he just saw

"Yeah, I'm fine honey, I just...I just saw an accident outside of my window" he pushed his face against the glass to see what was happening.

"Seriously?" she asked sounding stunned, "What happened? Is anyone hurt" she asked.

Nick nodded to himself.

His wife had warned him about Seattle and how this would be bad timing that there had been a lot on the news about police brutality and possible protests in every major city. He knew of course with protests came the people who exploited them and instigated more violence.

"I'm not sure honey, I think people are waiting for the ambulances, it just happened as I was talking to Amber," he told her trying not to let her know the severity of the situation.

"Oh my gosh, well I'm sure they'll be fine, honey, we miss you," she said in her soft soothing voice then added, "I'll let you go, honey, but give us a call later when everything's settled, okay?"

Nick wiped the sweat from his forehead, he wasn't sure if he was clammy due to this crazy heat or from what he'd just seen. "Okay honey, I love you." he could hear Amber in the background saying bye and that she loved him.

"Speak to you later honey," she said, hanging up after they both exchanged goodbyes.

Nick threw his cellphone on the desk and ran his hands through his hair. He could hear sirens from outside. He walked over and looked out at the chaos below. He could see the crowd circled around the bodies. Some of them were looking up towards where he was and at whatever was above him. He was disgusted by how many people he could see with cell phones out. He put his hand on the window, the glass felt thick, He wasn't sure what had happened to make it break and these poor people fall but he needed to shake it off.

He stepped out of his room and into the hallway, it was quiet and he couldn't hear a thing as he walked towards the elevators, He took it down to the ground floor and as the doors opened he was on the ground floor and the chatter of people hit him. The lobby was packed with groups of people standing around all chattering and looking out at the crowds of people that were surrounding the bodies.

There was no sign of police or paramedics and Nick looked around at the shocked looks on everyone's faces. Then a hotel staff member stepped out from behind a small info desk. "Please! Again, everyone we need to clear the area! There is nothing to see outside, please go back to your room or about your business!" the small man shouted to the whole lobby; Nick guessed he hadn't been the only one with the idea to come to the lobby to try to find out what had happened.

He took the man's advice and turned to head back to the elevator. He got into the first one that opened. A group got in with him and there was an awkward silence. There were three Asian men and a girl. She was pale white, and her eyes were watery, one of the men an older Asian man with a flowing moustache held her and kissed her head muttering something Nick didn't understand. The other two Asian men dressed in slacks and dress shirts just stared at each other, then started to shout quickly at one another, Nick didn't speak whatever language they were speaking but could tell by the tones and facial expressions and hands waving they weren't happy with each other.

Nick stared closely at one of the men's white shirts, he could see red spray all on one side and the hand furthest from Nick was bandaged with red dots where the blood was starting to seep through. He glanced up and caught the older man looking at him, so he turned his attention to the floor display screen above the doors as it beeped, it was his floor. Walking out he turned, and he could see the look of concern in the older man's face as he held onto the young girl and looked at the two men still bickering with one another.

Nick turned and headed for his room feeling bad for the people going up in the elevator, he wasn't sure what had happened somewhere above him, but he didn't want to be anyone headed up that way. He definitely hadn't gotten any answers or were any calmer from going down to the lobby. His head was still mush and he couldn't think straight. He entered his room and walked over to the window, looking out the crowds were still down there but now there was some flashing lights. "'Bout time" he thought to himself as he shut the curtains. He wiped his head and there was a greasy film on it. He had just showered before this had all happened but headed into the bathroom and turned on the shower as hot as it could go, steaming up the room.

Whenever Nick needed a minute to think or center himself, he always took a bath or a hot shower as it seemed to calm his mind and settle him. He stepped in and the searing hot water hitting his back hurt but took his mind away from the racing thoughts that were going on in his head. The nervousness of his meeting tomorrow, what he had seen, his anxiety about being away from his wife and Amber at home, all of that started to melt away as he put his head against the wall and closed his eyes.

CHAPTER EIGHT
Jake

J ake walked into the dining room with Benny and Michelle to see everyone gathered around the 60-inch TV with a few residents watching, too. They made his way over to see what had grabbed everyone's attention. The news was on and there was an aerial view of rioting in a city then it changed to other views of the same thing happening in different places. Every couple of seconds, it would change to a different city. As the views changed, the city and state names appeared with them. There was information also being put up on the screen about symptoms , and if anyone had them to go to their nearest clinic or hospital. He was confused as to what protests and riots about police violence had to do with the symptoms of this super flu going around. From the symptoms he was reading on the screen this super flu seemed more like rabies than influenza.

Benny was talking to one of the other nurses then turned to Jake "They said a few minutes ago that Oregon as well as some other states have declared a state of emergency!"

As he pulled out his cell phone, he heard one of the other nurses say out loud to no one in particular what he had been thinking.

"What the fuck does this virus have to do with police brutality and protests?"

He walked away from the group so he could hear his wife, her phone rang, she picked up sending a wave of relief came over him

" Babe! Honey, I think you should head home," he told her.

His brow furrowed, he could hear the boys in the background, and she replied, "I left work about forty-five minutes ago honey, I

43

got a call from the school asking me to pick the boys up, are you on your way home?" she asked

"Headed home?" He was getting confused, "Why? What's wrong?" he asked.

She explained after getting the message from the school that other workers who had kids at other schools had been asked to pick up their children, too. Then while on the way in traffic the radio had been advising everyone to stay where they were, remain indoors and to not travel unless absolutely necessary.

"I'll get off as soon as I can honey and be home, I love you," he told her.

Benny was looking at him as he hung up the phone.

"Everything okay?" Benny asked him, he gave a nod then saw a few people turn to the doorway as Karen walked in.

"Thank you all for coming," she began, "this is a staff meeting only so I would like all residents to give us some privacy," Karen said authoritatively as she gestured to the door behind her.

This was unusual as Karen always let the residents stay in on meetings. Once the residents were out, she closed the door then turned the TV off, taking a deep breath in.

"As you know I told you I had to clarify a few things with home office," she lowered her head putting her hand against it as if she was trying to remember what she had planned to say.

"These were about things I didn't agree with...the email that I received and the information I was supposed to relay to you all and what was to be expected of us."

Karen was struggling to find the words she wanted to say and looking around the room, Jake knew he wasn't the only one noticing how difficult this seemed to be for Karen.

Karen continued "The email said that anyone sick or showing symptoms of the cold or flu were to be quarantined in their rooms and taken off all medications. Also, any staff wishing to return home

44

and not work their schedule would be allowed to miss their shifts with no penalties and as of 8:00 pm this evening, all current care methods to our residents will cease and new routines and procedures put into place." As Karen said this, sighs went up around the room. Karen just nodded biting her lip in obvious frustration then continued "There will be a FEMA aid station set up in the high school adjacent to this property, some of you might have noticed the trucks that have been arriving this week and parking in the school parking lot. For anyone who is still willing to work at this facility then a FEMA or CDC representative will be arriving to speak with you."

Karen then stressed the need to keep this from the residents and confused whispers were going off all around the room. This day was just getting more and more weird, Jake thought to himself. He could see she had been crying and was clearly not happy about any of this. Karen looked around the room at what staff she had "I appreciate each and every one of you and everything you've done but I urge you all to return home to your families with little or no further contact with residents." She bowed her head, nodding slightly as she tried not to cry and left the room.

The residents who were previously in the room now began returning but all the staff in the room were still in shock, just standing there confused.

Michelle spoke up "So that's what the trucks in the school parking lot were for." she said.

A few people headed to the big main window pushing back the curtain that gave a view of Battleground High School's overflow car park. A fence separated that car park from the rehab center and sure enough there were several unmarked white truck trailers. Jake had noticed them pulling in, but they were just off I-205 so no one had given them any thought but now they knew they were obviously

FEMA. This had clearly been planned which meant they knew something big was going to happen.

Benny got close to him "Something big is going down, man" and Jake nodded then looked at the TV which a resident had just turned back on. The scenes of rioting were still playing, the rioting and the virus were obviously connected Jake thought. Why was FEMA setting up a camp at a high school? Several nurses who were a little disturbed by Karen's speech or after being on their phones began gathering up their belongings from the nurse's station just outside of the dining room.

He looked at Benny who was texting on his phone "Marcus?" he asked, and Benny nodded,

"Marcus said there was fighting outside of the bar," Benny told him looking worried,

This was definitely weird as Marcus who was Benny's roommate worked at a bar that served mainly the older workmen crowd. So right now, it would be people on lunch from work and not the rowdy weekend crowd.

Jake looked around the room at who was still here. He wanted to get everyone's attention "We should at least stay here till these FEMA folks come in and we fill them in on the residents conditions!" he said loudly to the room and a few of the nurses nodded in agreement but some looked lost and confused. He knew the ones looking lost were probably more concerned about family members and were overwhelmed with all of this then Benny piped up.

"What Karen just said. That's some meteor hitting the earth type shit, something's up and these FEMA guys might be the best chance we have of getting clear answers on just what the fuck's going on!"

It was funny, he thought, as Benny said the weirdest farfetched funny stuff but usually always accurate and his last statement was serious and spot on. He looked at the people in the room all staring at him "Besides we owe it to some of these people, what if they were your family?" he said, hoping the added guilt would pressure them into staying. Kindness breeds kindness and some of the nurses looked like they needed something to focus on to take their mind off panicking.

"I'm going to go talk to Karan and try to get some more answers," he said turning to Benny but as he started to walk towards the door two EMT's ran past through the hall.

He looked back at Benny then followed them to see where they were going. They both stopped at the door to hall 3 and turned to him.

"Can you let us in? "one of them asked and Jake nodded as he walked over to the keypad

"Where's the nurse who let you in?" he asked knowing anyone entering the facility and was headed to hall 3 had to be escorted by the nurse on duty at the front desk.

"Your front desk's busy" the other one told him as he punched in the code.

The pad turned green and the door opened then as they entered Travis's voice crackled across the intercom "Attention, code white in hall three, all hall 3 staff please report immediately!"

Jake hurried in beside the EMT's with Benny, Michelle, and two nurses following them. As they entered, he saw Travis was shaking standing with the phone in his hand from just making the page.

Travis looked at them and filled them in "Room three is nonresponsive, that's who we called about and now room ten is going into cardiac arrest!" Travis blurted out in a panic.

Both EMT's split up with one entering room three with Travis which was just across from the nurses' station. While the other one raced down the hall to room ten which was Ms. Long's so Jake followed with Benny right behind him. Benny almost knocked over Mr. Jones who was wheeling his chair out of his room "Fucking retard!" he complained as Benny put his hands on the armrests to stop himself from toppling over it.

"Well, hello there, young lady" Mr. Jones said cheekily as Michelle came up behind Benny, but she just rolled her eyes following the group sprinting down the hallway and Mr. Jones let out a loud wolf whistle.

Once Jake got to the door, he could see Debbie pumping away on Ms. Long's chest. The EMT walked over to take over and moved Debbie's hands away. Ms. Long's eyes flashed open all milky white like no one was home and she jerked back and forth convulsing before lurching up and towards Debbie. She grasped onto Debbie's upper body and tried to bite her. Debbie put her arm out between them to keep Ms. Long away, Ms. Long groped at the air being held back by Debbie's arm before sinking her teeth into it.

CHAPTER NINE
Caleb

Caleb was standing outside in his driveway and again Victor's Camaro was coming down his driveway. Only this time he had company and Caleb didn't have a good feeling about who this company would be. Victor pulled up then got out smiling with his hands outstretched in his trademark air hug "Caleb! My friend! My neighbor!" Victor said smiling, "I come bearing gifts" Victor's smile got bigger and bigger, then he clicked his fingers. The doors to the Escalade opened as if on theatrical cue. Two large men got out carrying small machine guns stepped out.

Caleb heard Janice gasp from the balcony above him. One of the men stood in front of the Escalade in a sentry pose while the other walked to the back and opened the trunk. Both men were huge, well-built guys with the same short buzz cut as Victor, dressed all in black like stereotypical Russian thugs with small machine guns slung across their torsos. He wanted to burst out laughing it was so movie stereotypical, but he could see these men meant business. Trying not to seem too nervous he watched the man at the trunk. It closed with a thump then the man who had opened it stood there holding three big green ammo boxes. Victor looked at the man then nodded towards the picnic bench. The man walked over to the bench setting all three boxes down then opened each one looking at Caleb as he did. All three were full to the brim with ammo.

Victor walked up to Caleb putting his arm around him to guide him over to the picnic bench.

"As promised" Victor said looking up at Janice with a smile "I have one box of twenty two for those two rifles you have, a box of nine millimeter for your wife's pistol and also some thirty eight for your pistol" Victor clearly knew what firearms Caleb's family owned and this sent chills up his spine as alarms went off in his head.

Caleb shrugged his arm off "Why? Why would we need this much ammo?" he asked turning to face Victor.

Victor swept his arm around the property. "This! This is your home! And you will have to defend it!" Victor said firmly. Caleb just looked at Victor blankly.

"From who?" Janice asked from the balcony puzzled. Victor looked up at her smiling then sat down on the picnic bench.

Victor went on to explain that the virus that was crippling the nation in the last twenty-four hours had been crippling other countries for weeks. The virus was more than the mere common cold or Flu. Victor explained the US had just stood by instead of offering aid like the UN to other countries initially affected. The virus hadn't just been here for twenty-four hours either, the man calmly told them.

It fact, it had been here for weeks but there had been no large outbreaks or widespread infection until this week. Victor then informed them that Amboy had been pretty much untouched until this morning but now the town was in chaos thanks to the news. It would only be a matter of time before the infected or people seeking safety arrive out at their properties.

Caleb could see his wife eyeballing the two men and their guns.

"And what do we owe you for all this, Victor?" she asked.

Victor looked back at him before answering, "we're neighbors!" Victor said slyly with a smile then went on to justify his reason.

"My family and friends are not farmers or good with animals so when our food gets low, we would appreciate it if you could share some of yours with us," Victor said, looking around then up at Janice. "You have plenty of vegetation and animals, in exchange I agreed with your husband to provide ammo so you can secure and defend your property" Victor finished with raised eyebrows.

Caleb had thought Victor was just high the last visit, so he hadn't mentioned it to Janice at all. Victor nodded to the big guy by the car, who unslung his gun then tossed it to Victor. Victor stood up from the bench raising the gun at a tree then pulled the trigger. A bunch of shots rattled out loudly through the air and wood splintered from the tree in all directions.

Nate and the girls rushed out onto the balcony to see what the commotion was. Caleb raised his hand to assure them it was okay, and Victor chuckled "I know you don't have any fully automatics so here's an MP5, not very accurate but will do for crowd control if you get yourself in a jam or have to make a point." Victor said, tossing the gun to Caleb.

Victor nodded to both of his men and like before, on cue, they got into their vehicles.

"Stay safe Caleb" Victor said as he walked towards his Camaro. "We'll be in touch." Victor said as the man lit a cigarette then got into his car. Both cars started up and pulled away sending gravel and dust into the air.

Caleb looked up at Nate who was standing on the balcony.

"Come get these locked up," he told his son as he walked towards the house. He began wondering if Amboy was really like the rest of the places he had seen on the news.

He looked down at the gun Victor had tossed him and it scared him. He was good with guns, but he hoped he wouldn't need this. He knew Victor wasn't too much of a threat now because the man showed up armed with some serious muscle. Victor could easily have taken anything he wanted. So maybe if things were going the way Victor had warned him about, then this friendship with benefits would be a good thing.

Once inside the house Janice was waiting for him upstairs. She was standing in the kitchen with her arms folded. He walked towards her.

"Honey," he started, "everything's going to be okay," he told her, hoping to ease her worry which he could tell she had by the look on her face.

Janice's facial expression changed from worry to anger in an instant.

"Really? You think so? Our drug lord neighbor just handed you a machine gun and boxes of bullets...for what?" she blurted out angrily.

He shrugged his shoulders "I...I honestly don't know other than the food like he said because if he wanted anything else, he could have just taken it." He knew it but clearly had to convince his wife now.

"He doesn't seem the type of guy to do things for himself but has others do it for him, he knows we grow vegetation and livestock," he said hoping for her to see things from his point of view. The fact she wasn't cutting him off and arguing back meant she was actually listening.

He looked out into the living room and saw both girls were sitting on the couch listening.

He flashed them a fake smile then moved in close to his wife and whispered, "I don't trust him for one second, but he's given us resources to protect ourselves, against him if we need to." He looked into her eyes to let her know he meant it. She nodded and smiled back at him.

"Girls!" Janice barked not taking her eyes away from his. "I don't want you going into town." she said sternly. He could see both girls rolling their eyes, nodding, Janice looked back at him with a fiery look. "That man came onto our property and acted like he owned it," Janice spat.

Caleb knew this pissed off his wife to no end, but he looked her in the eye and again reassured her of the facts. They had enough supplies if they were cut off from town that if what Victor was saying was true. Then they now had plenty of ammo to defend themselves from Victor if need be. He kept the most important thing that was bothering him to himself. The fact that Victor must have been watching them for a while to know what firearms they had.

Well, not all of them, he thought to himself smiling at the edge this could give him.

Nate walked into the kitchen. "Ammos in the garage, Dad, but he didn't give us no twelve-gauge shells" Nate said, seeming ungrateful.

Caleb just nodded "He's been watching but we haven't used those outside for a minute." he told his son. Nate looked puzzled and Caleb knew it was because his son was high.

"Nate, I need you to focus right now!" he told the young man " Lay off the weed, get yourself straight, and I need you to run into town!" When he said this both Nate and Janice nodded.

If what Victor was saying was true and what was happening all over was happening in town then this could be a bad deal, but he had to know for sure. He turned towards the living room where both girls were still sitting. "You two! I know your Mother said no going into town, but you are not to leave the property either! Understood?" He said and both girls just nodded blankly again like scolded teenagers.

He stood in the kitchen while Nate disappeared downstairs and Janice headed into the living room. His wife walked through the living room and out the sliding glass doors onto the balcony.

He looked at her out there leaning on the balcony rubbing her head. He knew this was causing her a lot of stress. He walked outside to try and comfort her then stopped as something caught his eye. In the distance in the direction of town he could see two thick black plumes of smoke.

"Looks like it might be that bad," he said more to himself quietly. Janice turned to look at him but saw that he was staring past at something else. When his wife saw what he was staring at she let out a gasp.

"We should let them come here" she blurted out and Caleb was caught off guard for a second then she continued "If it is as bad as Victor says, we should help them." His wife's eyes were wide and teary. He loved her and her Native American heritage traits. So, when she got passionate about something her eyes got big. This let him know she was definitely serious. "If people are hurting and need help then we should let them come here, out of the way. If we can help Victor, then we can help our friends and neighbors and with numbers we don't need to worry about Victor." she finished.

He rolled this around in his head for a few minutes and she was right. Their farm had it all with the perfect location and sustainability. Anyone in dire need of help would appreciate it as well as defend it if need be but that also arose the question of Caleb defending it. He knew if anyone was there as a guest and wanted to take it for themselves this could be problematic. Then he realized this was where the "crowd control" would come in handy. He knew if people saw he had some serious firepower they might think twice about doing something stupid.

He wasn't as trusting as his wife of the people in town so knew he wouldn't fully trust any stranger around his girls or his farm.

He nodded, "You're right, honey, and I think I'll go into town with Nate to get a gander at things and get a better look at what's going on," he said, and his wife agreed. He knew they couldn't take Victor's word 100 percent and Nate was still very young, hot headed, and easily distracted.

Caleb kissed his wife then headed downstairs to meet up with Nate.

As he got down into the garage Nate was trying to wake up two of his buddies. The two boys were good friends of Nate's. Both were fast asleep on the couches they kept in the garage for the kids and friends to hang out. "Nate!" he barked as he walked in on the slumber party. Nate was startled, causing him to drop the bong he had in his hand. This startled the two boys who jumped from the couch. Caleb glared at them "You've got an hour to get your shit together then we're going into town!" He said looking them in the eyes one by one. All three nodded open mouthed as if in some zombie like weed state.

CHAPTER TEN
Jake

Debbie was screaming and thrashing trying to pull away from Ms. Long who was clamped on her forearm hard. Blood poured out around Ms. Long's face on the arm as the EMT grabbed her by the head trying to pry her mouth off. Ms. Long's head jerked as the EMT yanked and she let go only to turn and launch forward and bite the EMT's shoulder. Debbie fell to the floor clutching her forearm, screaming as blood poured from between her fingers.

Debbie's screaming was drowning everything out as Jake ran over to Ms. Long who was now falling out of bed and onto the floor on top of the EMT with blood starting to pool out around them both. She lifted her head snapping her jaws as Jake got closer. Looking at her he could see her eyes seemed empty and white, her face riddled with raised purple and blue veins, looking just like the ones that were on her wrist earlier. Ms. Long jumped toward him but he grabbed her wrists as she came flying forward. He knew this was insane as Ms. Long hadn't been able to get out of her bed for the last few years let alone be this strong. They both slammed into the wooden drawers behind him with the weight of her body then they fell to the floor.

Benny was above her pulling her off by the shoulders then wrapped an arm around her neck and pulling her up with a chokehold. Unfazed, Ms. Long she started thrashing then began trying to bite Benny. Benny lifted her clear off the ground "Ms. Long!" Benny exclaimed, " what the fuck!" as she tried clawing at his arm that was trying to restrain her flailing limbs. Benny turned and threw her across the room sending her body slamming onto her bed. Ms. Long bounced off it against the wall then onto the floor. Benny put out his hand to help Jake up while Michelle had helped Debbie out the room. Jake nodded over to the EMT who was convulsing on the ground. The floor was covered in blood and as they knelt beside him, they heard a growl. They looked round to see Ms. Long clambering over the top of the bed on all fours.

"Shit!" Benny muttered quietly. They both grabbed an arm of the EMT pulling him up as they dragged him towards the door, Ms. Long jumped from the bed towards them, dragging one of her legs that seem contorted and twisted at an awkward ankle. Jake didn't have time to look at it too closely though as they slammed the door behind them leaving Ms. Long who was inside growling and pounding on the other side of the door. As they fell to the ground against the wall on the other side of the hall from Ms. Long's room, they turned to see Michelle walking down the hall with Debbie screaming still holding her wrist.

"Help!" Michelle was screaming to anyone who could hear her.

"Let's go!" Benny said as they began to stand up pulling the EMT's arms around them and began walking him down the hall towards the nurses' station, where Michelle had sat Debbie in a chair nearby with her phone in her hand and was trying to tell someone what had happened but kept stuttering not being able to get it out clearly.

"Hey!" Jake shouted to the door of room three where everyone else had gone but the door was closed and there was no response. Benny looked at him and lowered the now unconscious EMT down in a chair beside Debbie. They both walked over to the door to room three and Benny pushed the door open and despite what they had just seen they were definitely not prepared for the scene inside.

"Holy shit!" Benny exclaimed as they saw Travis laying on the ground with one of the rooms occupants, Mr. Kraft on top of him

57

eating his neck and face while the other EMT was laying on the ground staring at the door. Blood was all around him as he lay lifeless on the floor with teeth exposed from missing most of his lips. Another of the rooms residents, Mr. Webster, was throwing himself against the window and pounding his bloody hands against the thick plexiglass.

Mr. Webster, hearing the door creak, turned around from the window with the same milky white eyes and veiny face Ms. Long had. He moved towards them snapping his jaws which were covered in blood and was making a gurgling groaning sound.

Mr. Kraft looked up from eating Travis, growling, then started to crawl towards them. The EMT on the ground began convulsing and thrashing around. Jake backed out of the doorway with Benny behind him as they slammed this room door closed, too.

Michelle was helping Debbie towards the exit doors of the hall when keypad beeps from someone entering the code in from the other side. Mr. Jones who was sat in his chair in the hallway had seen what had happened in room three and was looking at them.

"We need to get the fuck outta here, boys!!!" Mr. Jones exclaimed to them both. Benny looked at Mr. Jones and nodded. The doors opened and two nurses came in and began helping Debbie and Michelle out.

"We called 911 but no one's picking up!" one of the nurses told them. They all turned as they heard a clunking coming from another room then from the open doorway to that room, they could see someone slowly shambling towards the door. It was Mr. Birch; he was naked under his gown. There were brown streaks down his legs, and he twitched and shuddered as he came out of the room and turned towards them. His skin was a greyish tone with milky eyes wide open like the others had been. The clanging was his IV bag on the wheeled rack dragging behind him, he had the oxygen tubes still in his nose with dried blood all around the nostril connectors.

Benny put his hands out and began walking towards him "Mr. Birch" Benny tried to whisper but he just kept staggering towards Benny looking like a blind man gazing into the air for the sound of Benny's voice and as Mr. Birch shambled passed room six, David came out.

"Foo-" David began to say but was cut off as Mr. Birch flashed his teeth then lunged at David sinking them into David's neck and shoulders, sending them both toppling to the ground.

A shriek came from one of the nurses who was helping Michelle,

"Go! Go! Go!" Jake shouted as he waved the group back towards the doors as a police officer pushed in past the nurses and drew his gun. They looked on in horror as the officer fired three rounds into Mr. Birch who just shuddered as each shot hit him sending him rolling across the ground.

"What the fuck?!" Jake shouted out loud. Mr. Jones wheeled his chair towards Mr. Birch

" You mother fucker!" he screamed as he rolled towards the man covered in blood from eating Mr. Jones roommate David. The IV rack clanged to the ground as Mr. Birch writhed around now tangled in oxygen hoses. The milky white eyes were locked on Mr. Jones who was wheeling up beside the ghoulish frame on the ground. Mr. Birch grabbed Mr. Jones' legs, pulling him from his wheelchair and onto the ground. Mr. Jones fought and cursed as he tumbled out his chair.

The officer ran over to the two on the ground then turned to the group gathered at the doors

"Get out! Now!" he ordered them as they all backed up through the double doors closing them after they were out. Jake stopped once the doors closed and turned as more shots rang from the other side of the doors. He looked through the glass panels and saw Mr. Jones' chair sideways on the ground and a wheel spinning. Then the view

59

was obstructed as blood spattered across the glass panes then the shots stopped. It went quiet on the other side of the doors and

he wasn't sure how long he had been standing there as everything sounded like his head was underwater. He was snapped back to reality when a hand grabbed him by the shoulder pulling him towards the dining hall. Then more chaos hit him as he could see residents being herded into their rooms by men in white jumpsuits with FEMA armbands on. Three of the men came over and began pulling their collars down checking their necks and wrists.

"Any of you injured?" asked one of these men standing in front of him, an older man with grey curly hair and glasses. The two men behind him just stared at the group, examining them up and down with their eyes

"No!" Benny said aggressively looking at the man with grey hair and glasses who was doing the talking

"What's going on? " Benny asked the man "You guys need to get in there! They need help!"

The older man in charge stepped past them and stared at the blood on the window panes. He shook his head "No, there's nothing we can do for anyone in there," the man said coldly then turned around to them and gestured towards the dining hall "I'm going to have to ask all of the staff to head in there," he said, pointing them into the dining hall.

Still in shock, the group did what was asked but Debbie was taken off down hall 2 by one of the people in a jumpsuit. Jake walked slowly into the dining hall with Michelle and Benny behind him and the rest of the staff were already in there minus Karen.

The man who appeared to be in charge looked around the room then raised his hands.

"I apologize for the rash entry and change of plans, but the virus is escalating more quickly than had been predicted and until we're sure you're all completely clear of symptoms we're going to keep you all isolated here while we conduct our tests." The man said this, and objections went up around the room.

The man raised his hands higher as if that was going to calm the room "I understand how you feel and the urgency to get back to your families, but this is safer for them! You were all given the chance to leave, right?" he looked around the room then continued. "If you leave now without knowing if you're infected you could risk the chance of infecting loved ones and the way things are going, they'll probably be headed to one of our camps anyway"

The staff was still objecting, and Jake could feel the tension rising in the room, a scream came from behind a FEMA man standing at the entrance to hall 2. They all looked as Mrs. Schaeffer, one of the residents ran into the dining hall with blood on her shirt. Out of breath she pointed out into the hall where banging and crashing could be heard. Two more FEMA entered the room walking over to Mrs. Schaffer. They pulled her collar down looking at her neck then they pulled the dining room's large double doors closed. The man in charge pulled a radio from his pocket.

"Simon? What's going on" he asked into the radio as it crackled then a voice answered back. "We're getting it under control now, sir, the guards are on their way in"

The man in charge nodded then the radio crackled again "The nurse from hall 3 was put in a room and the occupant of the room was in the final stage then turned, we have it contained now." the voice said but chaos could be heard in the background and from behind the double doors.

Benny looked at him "Contained? Turned? I call bullshit," Benny said then nodded towards the fire exit. Michelle caught onto the nod and ran for it.

"Wait!" Jake shouted knowing they should wait for the right moment, but she pushed the double emergency doors open setting off the fire alarm.

"Shit! Go now!" he shouted to the room and all at once they rushed to the door spilling out into the car park.

CHAPTER ELEVEN
Caleb

Caleb was putting his pistol in the glove box when the trio of boys came rambling out the house. "You boys all set?" he asked. The three boys all nodded wearily. "We'll drop Tim off on the way to town, Mark you can head home soon as we get there," he told them. They all clambered into his Jeep. He turned the key and the Jeep growled to life. He looked up at the balcony to see Janice leaning over looking at them. He gave her a wave then pulled out from the front of the house. As he drove down the long driveway, he couldn't help but think what if what Victor had said was true. What if it was as bad as he said? The fact he'd given them free ammo and a semi-automatic machine gun said a lot.

They drove along the dusty road leading from his farm to the main road. As they passed Victor's place, he squinted through the trees to get a look into the Russian's property. He could see Victor's big three-story house pretty clear with men bustling about. The men seemed to be unloading boxes from some vans parked. There were also several cars parked out on the grass along with two large RVs. *Victor's place was packed, that's for sure,* he thought to himself. Then looking at the roof of one of the RVs he could see a man standing with a rifle. The man looked at them turning his head in sync with them as they passed. "Creepy," Nate commented.

At least he knew the road to his farm was being defended and monitored he thought to himself. Turning onto the main road they would hit a gas station before getting into town. This is where they would drop Tim off and he could ask one of the guys who worked there if they knew of anything going down before heading into town. Mark muttered from the back seat then when he looked at him in the rear-view Marcus held up his phone. "I'm still not getting any service," Mark said, annoyed.

His girls had been complaining about spotty service all morning, too. Right before Victor showed up, they had lost their cable and internet connection.

As they neared the gas station there was a bunch of cars at the pumps and he could see it was pretty busy inside.

"Man, it's packed," Nate commented.

He pulled over just outside of the gas station forecourt to avoid the congestion at the pumps and they all got out. "I'll see you guys later," Tim said with a wave as he took off. The boy only lived a block away from the gas station. Walking onto the forecourt he could see all six pumps were being used with a couple of cars waiting, too. This gas station was right off the freeway, but he'd never seen it this busy on a weekday. He noticed an orange truck parked at one of the pumps, it was an older Ford flatbed that belonged to Bill Chalmers.

They entered the gas station and saw the line at the cash register that was being staffed by one guy. The news was on a TV behind the counter. Looking at it, he could tell there was definitely something big going on. There was a red banner along the bottom that said "News Flash" then directions scrolled along the bottom detailing symptoms.

One of the employees who Caleb recognized came out of the back room carrying a case of water. "Hey, Josh!" Caleb said waving to the boy. The boy nodded as he headed towards the cash register counter. "What's up, bro?" Nate asked the boy.

The boy set the case down on the counter for the man at the front of the line then turned towards them. Josh walked over wiping the sweat from his forehead. "Man, this fucking virus has people spooked! They think they're going to declare a national emergency and that'll mean martial law," the boy blurted out to Nate.

"We're running out of everything and more and more people are coming in from the freeway bulk buying up all our stock wiping us out," Josh said, out of breath.

Caleb looked around the store for Bill, he knew Bill lived with his wife who wasn't doing too good.

"So, what's the deal, bro, what are they saying's going on?" Nate asked Josh.

Josh looked around then leaned in towards Nate. "A sheriff came by early this morning," Josh started to tell them in a low whisper, "said they were being ordered to block the freeway entrance and exits while more had to go to the high school to help set up a shelter," Josh's pupils were huge and the boy stunk of weed. This whole situation was definitely weird and getting weirder, he realized.

"They said this virus was released by the Koreans and was engineered to turn us into rabies infected zombies," Josh said. The boy's imagination was clearly on a drug infused rollercoaster Caleb thought to himself.

"Hey, you guys only got one register open?" A man near the front of the line complained, glaring at Josh. Josh puffed his chest out but before he could say anything the static of the gas station's speaker came to life. The cashier was looking out into the forecourt and leaning into the microphone.

"Mr. Chalmers," the attendant said into the intercom "Mr. Chalmers, you okay? Do you need someone to come help you pump your gas?" the boy at the register asked into the microphone.

Caleb walked over to the window and looked out at Bill's truck but didn't see anything.

"Hey, Josh!" The cashier shouted "Go check see if the old guy's okay, would you? His gas is paid for but not pumped yet."

Josh nodded then headed out the door onto the fore court.

He could see Josh walking over to Bill's truck but there was no sign of Bill. Then his attention was grabbed by a woman screaming. It was a high-pitched shriek that cut through the chatter and talking of the other patrons inside the gas station. He looked over to a lady who was standing outside the bathroom door with her hands over her mouth. The lady was staring down at the bottom of the door. He moved closer to see what she was staring at as did a few of the other customers. The cashier pushed through to the front and the boys jaw dropped. Caleb was taken aback when he saw what they were now all staring at. A pool of blood was coming from under the bathroom door. The lady had her hands covering her mouth and was starting to get hysterical.

"Lady!" a man in a trucker hat and red flannel said stepping up to her. The man grabbed her by the shoulders "Calm down! Do you know who's in there?" the trucker asked.

The lady was shaking and nodded nervously "My... my son and his cousin" she said.

Caleb watched the cashier fiddling with a set of keys trying to find the right one. The boy's hand was shaking as he put them into the handle to unlock the door. When the door clicked signaling it was unlocked, he could hear everyone holding their breaths. The tension in the air could be cut with a knife as the door opened. Gasps went up from the group gathered around the restroom door. On the ground was a teenage boy laying against the wall with a younger boy sat on the lifeless boy's chest. The younger boys face was buried in the older boys shoulder with blood pouring out. The boy was making snarling noises like a rabid animal feeding. The young boy stopped then looked up at the onlookers flashing his blood-stained teeth. The boy then pounced for the person closest which just happened to be the child's mom. She fell to the ground with a shriek and the little demon climbed on top of her. The boy began tearing shreds of flesh from her forearms with his teeth as she tried to defend herself. The

66

guy in the trucker hat tried to pull the boy off. Caleb knew this situation was not going to end well. The kid was fast and turned, biting the man's hand then growled, turning back to his mother.

"Oh shit," Caleb heard Nate muttered.

"This must be the virus the news is talking about?" he said.

Then he looked down to see the boy who had been lying on the ground lifeless as his eyes flashed open.

"They're infected!" someone screamed. As if on cue the group that was standing shocked by what had just happened erupted into chaos.

Caleb could hear shelves and things being knocked over by people rushing for the door.

He was frozen in place staring at this boy whose eyes were all milky white. The boy's body began spasming and he turned over onto all fours like an animal. The boy rushed over to the trucker sinking his teeth into the man's leg.

"Dad!" Nate yelled "We gotta get out of here!"

Caleb could feel himself being pulled by Nate and Mark as he looked at the lady who had stopped screaming and the small boy sat on her chest munching away at her insides.

OUTSIDE HE LOOKED over at Bill's orange truck and could see Josh hanging half inside the passenger side window. Mark let go of him and wandered over to the truck

"Josh! Josh!" Mark shouted to get the boy's attention.

The boy just hung in midair lifeless with his legs hanging down as the top half of his torso was inside the truck. "Dad! You okay?" Nate asked walking him towards their Jeep. Everyone was scrambling to their vehicles. Screams could be heard from inside the gas station from the people still inside who couldn't tear themselves away from what was unfolding. Nate got him to the Jeep, but something clicked inside him. He looked over at Mark who was shaking Josh.

Josh spun round pulling himself out of Bill's truck window. Josh had a huge gash in his neck where someone had taken a bite. Josh jumped at Mark, snapping his jaws sending them both to the ground as they collided.

Mark tried to push Josh off, but Josh's teeth found Mark's forearm then Mark let out a scream. As Nate sprinted over Bill's truck door opened and Bill slumped out onto the cement. Caleb realized Josh must have been trying to get Bill out the truck and was bitten. Bill was a gaunt white color with red rings around his nose and eyes with blood soaked around his mouth. The old man crawled towards the two struggling on the ground with jaws snapping like the others. Caleb ran over to help Nate getting Mark free. Josh turned as they approached, snapping his jaws at them. Caleb didn't slow down at Josh looking at them. Instead he brought his foot up slamming it into Josh's chest like he was kicking a door open. Josh flew off Mark, tumbling onto the ground. They both helped Mark up, carrying him to the Jeep. They laid him in the back as the boy breathed heavily groaning.

"Hold on, Mark! Hold on!" he exclaimed, grabbing a rag and throwing it in the backseat for Nate to use to put pressure on the wound.

He jumped into the front seat firing up the engine and the Jeep screeched as they peeled out sending dust up into the air. He looked in the rearview to see Nate sweating and putting pressure on the huge gash on Mark's arm. Behind them out on the road was Bill crawling after them dragging his body along the road at a snail's pace.

CHAPTER TWELVE
Jake

The fire alarm was ringing and the FEMA man in glasses was screaming into his walkie-talkie.

"Shit! Go now!" Jake shouted as the group gathered in the room rushed out the fire exit. Everyone ran into the parking lot scrambling to their vehicles. Once Jake got outside in the parking lot, he could see on the other side of the fence there were FEMA tents getting erected in the high school parking lot. There were several bigger white trucks with trailers pulling in.

They sprinted towards Benny's truck. Several FEMA people were running over to the parking lot from what was being set up in the school grounds. The fire alarm going off was drawing a lot of attention.

FEMA and Red Cross workers were waving their arms at the people getting into cars, but it didn't stop people from trying to leave.

The man in glasses came out the fire doors pointing at them "Stop them!" the man barked.

As Benny got to the truck Jake could see a soldier coming from the other side with a rifle pointed at him. Benny put his hands up and Jake did the same as he saw another soldier with a rifle coming from behind another car.

They were marched over to the fire doors as the alarm was turned off. "You idiots," the man in glasses began. "Do you know what you've done? We were keeping people here to safeguard their families. They have already been exposed to the virus" the man's veins on his temples looked like they were about to pop out.

A scream came from inside the dining hall and a resident came out shambling towards the man in glasses. It was Patrick, a resident, and there was blood all around his mouth. Patrick lunged for the man in glasses and they both began struggling. "Get him off me! He's infected!" the man in glasses said panicking.

Jake could tell both soldiers looked scared, the one in front of him lowered his weapon and rushed over to the two struggling. The soldier beside Benny was starting to slowly lower his rifle also as he was staring at what was happening. Jake knew this was his chance and went for it.

He tried to grab the rifle from the soldier's hands, but the soldier was too quick and instead they both began struggling for the rifle falling to the ground.

Jake was on the bottom as they wrestled with the rifle between them. Benny hit the soldier on the back of the head with his elbow. The soldier let out a groan as he slumped to the ground releasing his grip on the rifle.

Shots rang out and both of them looked over to see the man with glasses lying on the ground clutching his neck with blood oozing between his fingers. The other soldier was standing, aiming his rifle at Patrick who was rolling on the ground groaning. The soldier let off two more shots which thumped into Patrick's body but still the man groaned and began getting up.

Looking at the fire exit, Jake saw two more residents come stumbling out. They too had blood around their mouths and fresh wounds on their bodies. The soldier fired at them, but they just kept coming forward. Jake watched as the soldier rushed toward the man in glasses and grabbed his coat and dragged him away from the residents.

"We need to get the fuck out of here!" Benny said.

Jake nodded and both headed towards the truck. Jake turned and looked back when he heard a man let out a cry. It was the soldier dragging the man with glasses. The soldier was now struggling with the man in glasses who was biting down on the soldier's wrist. Benny jumped into the truck and turned the key. Jake wanted to go help the soldier but there was now four of the infected. More soldiers were coming through the gates from the high school so they would help Jake told himself. He raced round the other side to climb in. He opened the door then looked across the other side of the truck's cab. The soldier Benny had hit on the back of the head was at Benny's door.

The soldier pulled open Benny's driver side door then started to pull Benny out. Benny kicked at the soldier, but he grabbed his foot and pulled him out. As they hit the ground, Benny punched the man then tried to stand up. One of the infected residents came up to the two men struggling. Jake dropped the rifle in the truck as he scrambled across the seats to help Benny. He reached out to grab Benny to pull him back into the truck away from the soldier. The soldier head butted Benny then took off as the infected tried to grab him. The resident clumsily fell onto Benny who was halfway back inside the truck.

Benny put his arms out to hold the former resident at arm's length. Jake froze as he saw even more residents coming stumbling out of the fire exit with faces covered in blood and the milky white eyes.

Benny fell back out onto the ground with the resident snapping his teeth. Jake jumped out and grabbed the back of the resident's shirt. He pulled who he remembered to be a frail old man off Benny. Something wasn't right as Jake threw the man onto the ground. The man's face was all white with the same milky white eyes as the other infected. The man's name was Brad; Brad was seventy-nine and weighed one hundred and twenty pounds. As Jake pulled him, though, the man felt like way more. Jake looked at Brad who was on the ground looking up at him with those empty eyes. There was blood all around his mouth and coming from his nose. Whatever this was it definitely wasn't Brad anymore.

Jake was mesmerized staring at Brad then at the other former residents all shambling towards them. All with the same gaunt look and milky white eyes. Patrick, who had been shot multiple times, walking like he was half asleep, Brad who had just pulled Benny from the truck. *This virus is impossible to believe*, he thought to himself.

"Hey, Brad!" Benny shouted from behind him. The thing that used to be Brad turned its head in Benny's direction. Benny was holding and was aiming straight at Brad. All Jake could think was *holy shit* at the situation. Benny squeezed the trigger and the rifle stuttered in Benny's arms.

Benny fired a three-round burst into Brad. Jake looked at Benny then nodded towards the truck. The other residents were all shuffling faster now towards them. The soldiers from the high school all stayed on the other side of the fence.

Benny jumped into the truck throwing the rifle on the seat then started the truck up.

As Jake raced around to the other side of the truck to get in his arm was grabbed. He turned to see a soldier who was clearly infected. The man had a hole in his cheek with teeth exposed. The man's milky white eyes seemed to look above Jake. Jake tried to shrug the man off, but his grip was unbelievable. As they struggled, he looked over to see Brad, who was groaning, getting pretty close. The soldier seemed to have a death grip on Jake's scrubs as he couldn't push the man loose. The man was pulling Jake close with his mouth wide open and ready to bite into Jake's neck.

Jake put his hands on the soldier's chest which was freshly soaked in blood from a gaping wound on the man's neck. Blood was pouring all over his hands as he gave an almighty shove. The soldier staggered back then froze as the front of his head exploded with blood, "Hurry up and get in!" Benny yelled.

Jake wasn't sure who fired the shot or if it was meant for him, he didn't care right now, his only thought was getting the fuck out of there.

Jake ran to his side of the truck another resident pounced as he got to his door. He grabbed the man and slammed him against the truck bed. He was holding the man against it with his right forearm while he groped inside the bed of the truck with his left. The man was thrashing and reaching for Jake's face. Shots echoed as Benny was firing at the oncoming group of former residents. Jake grabbed a hold of a handle and lifted it up, it was a tomahawk. He brought it down on the residents head. The skull made a wet cracking noise as it caved then the resident went limp. The man crumpled to the ground in a heap. He looked down feeling sick.

"I'm so sorry...Mr. Parsons" he said quietly, shaking as he stepped away from the body getting into the truck.

He was still shaking as he closed the door and Benny put his foot down on the gas. The truck roared as they screeched out of the parking lot.

As they turned onto the main road more gun shots could be heard behind them. Jake looked behind them and saw the group of residents heading for the FEMA/Red Cross set up. He saw two more infected stumbling towards the gunfire, too. He realized they must be attracted by the noise.

The truck roared more as Benny shifted gears trying to get them away from there as fast as possible.

Jake fumbled in his pocket for his cell phone. Pulling it out he frantically dialed his wife.

"Baby!" he exclaimed out of breath still as Emily picked up "I love you! Are you and the boys okay?"

"Yeah, they're here playing video games," Emily told him "Honey, are you okay? You sound out of breath?"

He wanted to throw up and blurt out what had happened. He looked over at Benny who was staring at him shaking his head. He got control of himself

"Yeah, I'm okay, honey, we're on our way home…listen, don't let the kids out and don't answer the door," he told her.

"Okay" she said hesitantly.

"I'll be home soon, honey" he told her. He was relieved that she and the kids were okay.

"Gotta go, honey" he said as he looked out ahead of them.

"Fuck" Benny muttered. Benny was staring ahead of them at the entrance to the freeway. It was blocked with police cars and military trucks.

"Backroads" he said to Benny, both of them not taking their eyes off the group of officers who were standing by the cars as Benny put the truck into reverse. The officer's attention, however, was focused on the freeway. There was a line of cars all stopped. They turned off the main street onto the back roads which would get them home a little bit longer but with definitely less people. Benny put his foot down with no intention of stopping for anyone. They both wanted home to their loved ones.

Jake sat back in the chair, his hands in front of him dripping blood from Mr. Preston. He blinked his eyes as they started to water and sting. He started to zone out as tears welled up behind his eyelids. The road changed from city concrete to a bumpy back roads riddled with potholes. He noticed every bump and jolt as he sat there sinking   into   his   seat   zoning   out.

CHAPTER THIRTEEN
Caleb

Nate was looking at him in the rear-view mirror from the back seat. He could see Mark writhing about uncomfortable sweating profusely.

"He doing okay?" Caleb asked his son.

He could see Nate biting his lip looking at the blood-soaked rag on Marcus's arm. "Yeah, he'll be good after a few good bong rips" Nate said, and Mark let out a chuckle.

This made Caleb smile, Mark was one of Nate's oldest friends since they were in kindergarten together. He would hate for him to turn into one of those things.

As if reading his mind Mark piped up, "I don't wanna be a zombie" Mark said, strained.

"Don't worry, buddy, zombies ain't real, we'll get you better" Nate reassured his childhood friend.

Caleb wanted to agree with his son but knew better. From what he'd seen zombies were exactly what this infection turned you into.

It didn't take long for them to get to the road leading past Victor's place to theirs. Mark had passed out and he wasn't sure if this was due to pain or the virus. The bite looked gnarly and even Nate winced every time he looked at it. As they passed Victor's place it still looked pretty lively and the same guy was on the roof of the RV. They pulled up to the garage doors and Janice came out onto the balcony. He looked up and wasn't looking forward to her reaction. He got out and opened the garage door so Nate could just take Mark to the couch there. As the Jeep doors closed and Nate was helping Mark out, he heard what he had been waiting for.

"Oh my god! What happened?" Janice screamed from the balcony.

Caleb took a breath trying to figure out what to say without scaring his wife.

"It's bad darlin', town's real bad. We have to try to get the news on TV to see how bad it is."

Janice stormed back in the house, his wife got mad at things she couldn't control, and this was definitely out of their control.

He entered the garage and saw Mark lying on the couch with Nate beside him. Nate looked over at him "Dad he's getting worse, his fever is crazy!" Nate said, worried.

Caleb went over and looked down at the boy. Mark's small beard was glistening in sweat as was his forehead. "I'll have your mom bring him down some Tylenol," he said reassuringly to Nate.

Nate nodded and began packing his bong. He didn't say anything as he knew his son had just seen a lot. He had too and he needed to figure out what to do next.

Upstairs Janice was in the kitchen messing with an old radio when he walked in. "Hey," he said to get her attention. "How's the girls?" he asked.

"How are the girls?" his wife replied, surprised "How is Mark? What happened?" she asked walking towards him. He opened the fridge and pulled out a beer.

"Darlin'" he began then took a swig from his cold one "I think we'll need the ammo Victor gave us and then some." he told her. Janice's face dropped.

"What do you mean? Is it that crazy? We still haven't got the cable back on, so I was going to try the old radio we used to have here after I saw the smoke from towards town." she told him.

He gulped down more of his beer, "It's pretty crazy, old Bill Chalmers...he's dead," he said.

"Dead? Oh my gosh!" she said, shocked "He was friends with my father when he was alive, they were like best friends" His wife had tears in her eyes as she said this. She would always talk to Bill and his wife for what seemed like forever when they bumped into each other in town.

"What happened?" she asked, trying to hold back the tears.

"He turned into some kind of crazy person, a few people did and started attacking and biting people. That's how Mark got bit," he said realizing saying it out loud how ridiculous it sounded.

"Bill bit Mark?" she asked.

"No, Bill bit that Josh kid who's Nate's friend," he took another long drink of beer, "Bill bit him, he went crazy then when Mark tried to help him, then Josh went crazy and bit him" He finished and downed the rest of his beer. The look on his wife's face was how he felt at the gas station when the bathroom door had opened. Janice staggered back then sat on a kitchen stool with her hands on her head.

He walked over and put his arms around her "I'm not sure what's going on, honey, but we'll get through it us, the girls and Nate," he reassured her.

After what he'd seen, though, he knew he needed some reassurance himself. Looking out the window there were plumes of smoke in the distance. "And why didn't you take him to the hospital? That's probably where he needs to go," Janice asked.

Caleb rolled his eyes slightly "Honey, I think going to a hospital right now would be a very bad idea," he said. He'd thought about it when they'd put Mark in the back seat but knew a lot of people would probably be headed there and if what Victor had said was true then he knew he had to get back to his farm and the girls.

"C'mon, honey, let's go put the radio on in the Jeep" he told her as walked with his arm around her towards the stairs leading down to the front door.

Once outside, the plumes of thick black smoke dotted the horizon. Whatever was happening was getting worse and not just in one area. The radio crackled as he turned it on and twisted the knob trying to find a clear station. Reception was spotty at best up here, but he hoped he would get something. He looked at the scared look on his wife's face. He could tell she was terrified.

Hopefully whatever news they got from the radio would calm her a little bit.

After a few minutes of tuning, he finally got something, and both their eyes widened.

"This is an emergency broadcast for Clark county! Please remain where you are and do not attempt to travel. If you are not a resident of Clark county and have nowhere to go, please head to the nearest FEMA or Red Cross relief shelter, where you will get further instruction. Please remain indoors and limit contact to people only in your immediate vicinity. If you or anyone you know has been in contact or injured someone showing symptoms of having aggressive outbursts, please isolate and avoid further contact. Symptoms of a sign of infection include high fevers or muscle spasms. FEMA and Red Cross shelters are being set up locally at schools and large venues. Please make no attempt to travel unless absolutely necessary. Local law enforcement will be conducting wellness checks for their areas."

"It's an automated message," he told his wife as it began replaying. There was a noise of someone on the gravel and they both turned to see Nate standing.

"What are we going to do about Mark?" Nate asked

"Where is he?" he asked his son. Nate pointed over his shoulder back into the garage.

"He's in there, Hayley's with him…why?" Nate asked.

His expression must have told Nate what he needed to know as his son turned and ran back towards the garage. Janice let go of his arm as he took off towards the garage, too.

He caught up with Nate at the door and they both walked in. Hayley was sitting beside Mark with a glass in her hand with a straw in it. The look on their faces must have took her by surprise.

"What's wrong?" she asked putting the glass down "I wasn't going to smoke anything Dad," Hayley told them.

"Honey, just go upstairs okay, help you mother get dinner ready," he told her, and she got up and handed the cup to Nate. After she walked upstairs, he turned to Nate, "It said on the radio if you're hurt by someone who's infected to isolate them" he said sternly to his son.

Nate looked at him and shook his head a little "Dad, I know how zombies work okay, I'm a stoner and I've seen a lot of zombie movies" Nate said sarcastically.

'Nate, this isn't funny, it's not like TV or movies we know nothing about these things other than they like to try and eat people," he said.

Nate widened his eyes, "Liiiike zombies, right?" Nate said again sarcastically.

His son was right, and he knew it, but he hated admitting it. "Okay, yes, these things are like zombies but we don't know anything about how this virus spreads or how long before he turns into one of them and that's if he even does," he said even though he knew saying the word zombies and calling them that sounded so stupid.

"Just keep your eye on him, okay?" he told Nate.

Nate nodded as he left to go upstairs and check on the girls.

Upstairs, Janice was in the kitchen talking to both the girls. "You girls know I love you and I promise nothing's going to happen to you or our family" he told them.

Both Hayley and Madison looked worried still then Madison spoke up "We're just worried about friends, Dad," she said meekly.

He hugged her. "I know, honey, we are too, and we can go check on everyone soon as we're told it's okay but for right now the radio says to stay where we are," he told them, emphasizing the point to not leave.

"What about Mark?" Hayley asked, "He was bitten by someone, right?"

He nodded somberly "Yeah and we can't take him to a hospital so we're going to have to care for him as best we can," he said looking at both girls.

Janice looked at him. "What about Victor, you think he knows more about what's going on?" she asked. He shrugged his shoulders

"Honey I want to avoid contact with that man as much as possible but at least we know we're pretty safe," he reassured them all, "on the way out and he has guys overlooking the road so I don't think any unwelcome visitors will be coming our way." He knew that was definitely a good thing. Hopefully anyone infected who tried to make their way down the road to his farm would be stopped by Victor's men.

"Dad! Help!" Nate yelled from downstairs.

Caleb darted towards the stairs grabbing a knife from the knife block as he past it. He heard the girls gasp from behind him. "Stay up here!" he barked.

Downstairs, Mark was thrashing around on the couch and Nate was trying to hold him still.

"I think he's having a seizure or something, Dad" Nate said in a panic. "What's the knife for?"

It had been automatic to grab it, but he wasn't sure if he could really use it on his son's friend if it came to that.

Before he could explain himself Mark's eye flashes open and they were all milky white and glossed over. Nate screamed, letting go of Mark then jumping up. Mark rolled off the couch onto the floor and was groaning and snarling.

"Oh fuck" Nate muttered backing away from Mark.

Caleb put his hands out "Mark! Can you hear me?" he asked, and Mark turned to him as if following the sound of his voice. "Mark...we're trying to help you," he said but the drool was pouring from Mark's mouth and his head was glistening with sweat. He began getting up and was still snarling. A scream came from the stairs behind him and he turned to see his wife standing there. Mark started coming towards them and his wife began screaming more. He stepped in front of Mark with the knife out. "Mark, if you can hear me please sit back down," he asked but Mark was oblivious and was focused on getting to Janice. Just as Mark was about a foot from him a chair came crashing down on his head. Nate hit him a second time with the chair and he fell to the ground. Mark rolled and tried to get up, but Nate brought the chair down again and again.

Mark was still trying to crawl towards Janice who was still screaming hysterically.

Mark grabbed a hold of his leg and opened his mouth exposing his teeth. He panicked and brought the knife down into the back of Mark's neck at the base of his skull. He pulled his foot away as he did. As soon as he drew the knife out Mark started snapping his teeth again. Nate slammed the chair onto the top of Mark's head and finally Mark went limp. Nate threw the chair on the ground then slumped down with his back against the couch. He looked around at his wife to tell her to go make sure the girls were okay but both girls were standing there behind his wife. "Girls go...go back upstairs, please," he stammered.

The girls, both shaken, helped their Mom back up the stairs. He looked over at Nate. "We gotta move him, you okay?" he asked, and Nate just nodded with wide eyes not blinking but filled up with tears.

"You think he's dead?" Nate asked without looking away from the body.

Biting his lip he wanted to tell his son no but the fact they had hit him that many times then stabbed him and probably smashed his skull it was a definite yes "No, Nate, we didn't kill him, Josh did," he told his son, "That wasn't Mark son that was something else."

CHAPTER FOURTEEN
Jake

They pulled off of the dusty back road they had taken from Battleground past the quarry. The rock quarry was on the corner. It was usually bustling with trucks hauling rock and machines smoking but it was all closed up. Across the street the Walmart parking lot was just as busy as usual.

He could feel Benny looking at him as they turned into the park. "You'll be okay?" Benny asked him.

Without looking up from the blood on the floor mat he nodded. The truck came to a stop at his driveway and Benny put his arm on his, "Tell Emily and the kids I love them"

He smiled nodding again, he knew after the day they both had just went through that this kind of statement meant something different now than it would have before.

"Let me know you get home safe," he asked Benny.

"Will do," Benny replied.

He got out taking in a deep breath. The truck pulled away, horn honking. He looked down at his scrubs to see the blood splattered all over them.

Looking up Emily was standing on the porch looking at him. Emily's eyes got wide looking at him then she looked back to the house to see if the boys could see.

"Oh…my god" she gasped. He nodded, pulling his shirt off over his head then put it in the trash.

He climbed the steps to their front porch to his wife. He wanted to wrap his arms around her and tell her how much he loved her.

"I'm going to go around back and in the door. I don't want the boys to see me" he told her.

Emily just nodded staring at him "Are you okay?" she asked.

He looked down for a second trying to hold back the tears "I will be…I love you," he said.

"Oh, honey, I love you, too! We all do. You're scaring me" she said brushing a hand across his cheek.

Once in the back door and unnoticed he headed into the bathroom. He pulled the trash can out from under the sink and began removing the blood-stained clothing he still had on, throwing it in there. Turning on the sink tap, he put his hands in to soak the blood off. Looking up at the mirror and wiping off the condensation he looked like shit. The steam from the shower was filling the room and it felt good. He stepped into the shower and turned the water as hot as it would go. The water seared his skin, but he just zoned out thinking the day over wondering if he could have done things differently. It took him a minute, but he realized he was crying but knew he had to get himself under control. All the people and what had happened; how could things turn around from that? He realized no matter how bad things got he had to protect his family. If whatever infected those people and turned them into crazy cannibals reached them, he had to do whatever it would take. He knew inside that would probably mean taking another life if he had to.

Stepping out of the shower and into the bedroom, he put on some crisp, clean clothes. Despite not having the blood-soaked scrubs on, he still felt dirty like he was still wearing them. As he walked into the living room both boys were sitting focused on the TV.

"Hi, Dad!" Paul said not taking his eyes off the TV.

"Hey, buddy," he said as he walked towards his wife who was in the kitchen.

"I made you some tea, honey," Emily said, forcing a smile. He could tell she was trying to act as normal as she could for the boys' sake. He walked over to her and wrapped his arms around her, squeezing her tight and smelling her hair.

"I love you so much," he said and started to kiss her.

"Get a room!" Jeff shouted from the living room. This was the boys' favorite phrase lately.

Emily chuckled and he smiled "Hey, you boys have a room, why don't you go play in it till dinners ready?" he told them. Both boys got up grumbling and walked into their bedroom.

"So, you want to tell me about your day?" Emily asked, putting an arm around him. He was trying to act like he was okay but clearly, he wasn't doing a very good job. "I guess this virus that's been on the news…it's worse than they're saying. A lot of people died today at the home." He wanted to go into detail, but it was hurting too much. He didn't want to cry in front of his wife or scare her too much with what he'd seen or done.

He kept glancing towards the hallway to make sure the boys weren't listening as he definitely didn't want them scared by any of this.

"Outside of my work there was a guy who the police must have been trying to arrest…" Emily's voice started to crack as she spoke. He could tell she was trying to hold back emotions too and not get upset. "They kept shooting him, but he kept trying to get to them like he was possessed," Emily's eyes started to gloss over as she teared up. He pulled her close and hugged her.

"I got a call from the boys' school asked all parents who could go and pick up their children, so I did and drove them straight home," Emily said wiping her eyes, "They were still shooting him as I left the parking lot"

"It'll be okay, honey," he reassured her. He decided not to tell her about the FEMA people trying to round them up or the police blockade. Especially not him killing Mr. Preston, at least not yet.

Later, as he was helping Emily make dinner, he finally decided to put the TV on. He'd put it off to try and keep some kind of feeling of normality in the house. He knew something this big and crazy would change a lot and like Benny had said it was huge for FEMA and Red Cross to get involved. He knew he had to at some point though so picked up the remote and turned on the TV.

The news was on, but it was some kind of emergency announcement. The news anchor was reading from a paper on the anchor desk.

"Do not travel if you do not have to, please remain indoors, isolate anyone who is infected," the anchor said. There was information bulletin on the screen listing symptoms.

- Aggressive behavior
- Fever
- Lesions
- Discoloration of eyes and skin
- Rapid dehydration

The anchor continued to speak while the symptoms still remained on the screen,

"The authorities have declared a state of emergency in the following states," the anchor said while the states scrolled across the bottom. The anchor continued "Emergency services are asking you to follow these steps." The information changed to huge capital letters A,D, and D, beside each one an instruction appeared which the anchor also read out.

- A - avoid "Please avoid contact with anyone showing symptoms or anyone not in your immediate location."

- D - Deny, "Deny access to anyone trying to enter your property or immediate location,"

- D - Defend "If people try to force their way into your property, defend yourself by any means necessary but avoid contact with the bodily fluids of your assailants. If contact is made isolate the persons who came into contact with the fluids and await medical response."

The screen changed again to a list of schools and facilities. Beside each was either Red Cross/FEMA help center or the words "ON STANDBY" Battle ground high school had "FEMA Center" next to it but the boys' school had "ON STANDBY" next to it. The news anchor continued "Due to displacement and congested travel routes, the Red Cross has set up temporary shelters at schools and facilities where you can stay until it is recommended to travel. Local authorities are working to secure your county and make it safe to travel again. They will be making every effort to make this happen as fast as possible," The anchor said in a monotone voice, obviously reading a script.

He looked at Emily who stood at the sink gaping at the TV. Paul and Greg walked out from the bedroom. "Is dinner ready yet?" Paul asked.

Then Greg chimed in, "They said school was off tomorrow and the next day, hopefully it'll be off for a few the next day so we get a long weekend," and Paul laughed in agreement.

Before he could say anything to them the screen changed to a live feed and a news anchor in a street. The lady looked terrified and there was a car on fire in the background.

"We're still awaiting the arrival of the National Guard! The rioters have begun setting vehicles on fire and people carrying firearms have opened fire on each other" The lady was shaking and standing close to the camera. Behind her silhouettes could be seen walking through the flames.

The anchor continued "We've seen people be brutally injured and continue fighting and attacking each other! The police and emergency services are being stretched very thin! I have never seen anything like this before! Arrgghh!" the anchor screamed then the feed was cut off.

Returning to the news studio the presenter sat silent for a few moments. "I'm sorry...we will try and get back to our anchor Sophie as soon as possible to make sure everything's okay."

The presenter touched her earpiece, "Again we will update information as soon as we receive it but until then please follow the guidelines that we'll keep cycling on screen"

The screen cut back to the list of symptoms.

Jake turned and headed to the kitchen window. It was getting dark outside, but he could see a red glow in the sky and several plumes of smoke in the distance somewhere. "I don't think you boys will be back at school for a while"

CHAPTER FIFTEEN
Nick

Nick opened his eyes when he heard a loud thud that startled him. He wasn't sure how long he'd been laying there been in there, but it was getting dark outside. Realizing he had lost track of time he got up. He walked over to pull the large curtains closed and was tempted to look down at the ground below but stopped himself.

He wondered what the loud thump had been that startled him. After what he had seen earlier, he hoped it wasn't anything too crazy. Maybe it was from people repairing the window or the room if it had been damaged too, he thought. Nick's stomach growled, he realized he was pretty hungry. His hunger subsided though when he looked at the room service prices. He grabbed his jacket deciding he would venture out to eat. Seattle was known for its fresh food and wide variety. On his way out he was going to stop by the front desk. Getting more info on what happened would ease his anxiety. He grabbed his phone from the charger so he could call his wife. It would be nice talking to Valerie as he took in the sights of downtown Seattle.

Stepping out from his room into the eerily empty hallway was a stark contrast to how busy the lobby was earlier. As the door shut behind him, he heard a loud thump much like the one earlier. He turned to look at the door next to his. He swore it came from in there, but it was gone. After a few minutes of standing in silence he walked over to the door. Not something he would do every day but due to present circumstances, his gut giving him a weird feeling. He pressed his ear against it and waited. Nothing. He turned and walked towards the elevator shook away his sense of paranoia.

It wasn't every day two people fell from one of the top floors of a hotel so he knew this would be on the news soon enough. Calling his wife to fill her in on the details before she saw it on the news was a good idea. The way the lobby had been earlier he could only imagine the groups feeding into it for a small slice of media attention. He was surprised when the bell chimed, and the doors opened. The lobby was completely empty except for the person manning one of the check-in desks. He could see through the window the yellow caution tape that had sectioned off part of the pavement was there but no crowds or any news crew.

Nick walked over to the service desk. "Hey, a lot quieter than earlier, huh?" Nick said trying to make small talk. "I was wanting to go get some food, is there any stores or anything near here?" he asked. The receptionist gave him a weird look and pointed at the wall behind her.

"If you go outside and follow the sidewalk to 6th and keep going there's a Target, it's after nine, though, most restaurants are closed already" The receptionist told him.

Nick nodded, turning to walk away then stopped and turned back, "Hey, so earlier-" he began but was cut off.

"I'm afraid hotel policy is I can't discuss it, but we can email a discount voucher for a future stay for any inconvenience caused," The receptionist said. He could tell she was trying to sound as professional as she could. Nick could see the cloudiness in her eyes like something was wrong, so he didn't push it further.

"Thanks, have a good rest of your night" he said walking out of the hotel lobby, puzzled. He must have been lying on the bed for longer than he thought.

As he stepped out into the fresh Seattle air the cold crispness hit him immediately. Definitely a big change from the heat and humidity he had been subjected to earlier. He saw a couple walk by the caution tape and peer at the blood-soaked ground, the only evidence that anything had happened was the caution tape and red stained pavement, which surprised him.

The couple was looking up at the hotel. Nick did too as he past the scene. He couldn't tell which room was his, but he could see a gaping smashed window. The rooms curtains were blowing in the wind. The window still hadn't been boarded up since it had happened. Obviously wasn't a priority he thought as he turned and continued walking on his way.

He followed the receptionist's directions and could see the Target logo in the distance. It was maybe six or seven blocks. He could hear sirens again. *Does this city ever sleep*? he thought to himself. He could hear shouting from the other side of the street. He looked over to see some tables and chairs that was some kind of restaurant's outside patio. A group of people were jumping on the tables while others kicked the chairs swearing and shouting. Nick shook his head and just kept on walking.

As he got closer to the Target store, he could see red and blue lights bouncing off the buildings.

He could see a large gathering of people in the street which seemed to be where the police lights were coming from. As he got closer, he could see several police cars and police bikes with officers. They were on both sides of the streets controlling the large crowd. Traffic was stopped and there was an ambulance in the middle of the street at the four way stop. The four-way stop was the only thing between Target and him.

He crossed, making his way slowly through the crowd. He told himself not to look and be drawn into more craziness. He could hear the people on the street throwing insults at the police. The crowd was so big it spilled onto the road. He could feel the tension as he waded through.

Cars were slowly passing around the people and honking their horns. The people just shouted and threw up angry fists and made rude gestures. Curiosity got the better of him as he was just about to enter the store. He turned around trying to peer over the heads in the crowd. The side he had just crossed onto was filling with more people. The street on the other side was, too. He could see caution tape on both sides with police and EMT's on the road. His first thought was that someone had been hit by a car. There was constant honking here in Seattle with pedestrians walking across the road anytime and thinking cars would stop. Drivers weren't much better as they seemed to think pedestrians didn't exist.

He turned and walked through the Target's revolving doors. He picked up a basket as he entered. He overheard two ladies who were standing inside watching through the huge glass windows. He heard one of them say "He must have been on drugs!"

It was what the other lady said made him realize it wasn't an accident. "He was shot so many times!"

Nick froze for a second and pushed it to the back of his head. This is what he had been hearing on the news all week. This is why they were protesting in Portland and all across the country.

This along with the incident earlier wasn't anything he wanted to dwell on. He walked around the store grabbing the essentials he needed. Nick was a survivalist so always thought of worst-case scenarios. Even when grocery shopping, that played a big part in what he bought. Everything he put into his basket didn't need refrigeration and had pretty far out expiration dates. All very high in protein like nuts and jerky. For dinner he grabbed a salad with a pack of cooked chicken breast. Then he grabbed some bottles of water as he got into the checkout line.

He looked past the cashier at the view outside the window. The crowd gathered looked like it had gotten bigger, but the police presence remained the same,

As he left the store his phone started to vibrate in his pocket. He knew it was his wife before he answered.

" Hi honey!" he said, answering. He knew hearing his wife's cheery voice would take his mind away from the worst-case scenarios running through his head.

"Hi, babe," she didn't sound so happy, however.

This let Nick know something wasn't right, "Honey, what's wrong?" he asked.

"Nothing, just miss you," his wife was hesitating but continued. "Have you seen the news? They're telling everyone not to travel." Valerie said with a jab. His wife had asked him to wait to travel for the food cart meeting. She had told him all the stuff on the news was making her worried. He wanted the ball rolling, so he'd insisted he had to go, that she was just being paranoid.

He stepped off the curb to cross the street to move away from the crowd. Away from the noise so he could hear his wife better. He wanted to give her his full attention without worrying her more.

"Really-" He began to ask about the news reports when a loud gunshot interrupted him.

The loud shot was followed by screams. He froze in the middle of the street and turned around to cars stopped in the street. The doors of the cars that were stopped at the intersection started to open. In the middle of the intersection, lit up by head lights of the cars was a homeless looking man. The man was standing in the headlights swaying. Nick squinted then his jaw dropped as he realized who it was. It was the rowdy homeless man from earlier that he saw while in traffic.

The man was just standing there in the middle of the road. Some officers stood with guns drawn, pointed at the man. Beside them on the pavement he could now see several black body bags. The gunshot had caused most of the crowd to move back. Two more gunshots rang out as two of the officers fired. Blood erupted from the man's chest as he staggered back then fell, two more officers moved around him with their guns still trained on him.

There was a groan and the homeless man rolled around on the ground. The man started convulsing then began to get up. A hush fell over the crowd.

The man fumbled around like a baby trying to get up on its feet. After a few tries he got up looking like someone who had just climbed out of a car wreck. There were blood stains all over his ragged clothes. The officers were screaming orders at him then they let off more shots as he lunged towards them. Protests and cries of objection came from the crowd. People were screaming in shock and disgust at what was happening.

Nick could hear his wife on the phone asking what was going on, but he couldn't reply. His voice was stuck in his throat as he stood there in shock. The man staggered and shook with every shot that hit him. Then as a burst of blood erupted from his head the man dropped to the ground. This time the man didn't get up and the officers circled   around   him.

CHAPTER SIXTEEN
Alice

Alice sat in her patrol car scrolling down the list of active calls on her computer. She stared in disbelief the amount of open calls. She couldn't believe what she was seeing. Even on the busiest nights there hadn't been this much going on. It seemed like the whole of Vancouver was in trouble tonight. Clicking on a call then grabbing her radio. "Control! This is Boy 32 taking the 126th street call," she released the button waiting for the dispatchers reply.

"Affirmative, Hayward, paramedics just arrived on scene and subject is non-compliant," The dispatcher answered. The radio crackled off. She started up the engine then turned on her lights.

"One down and a whole lot more to go," she thought speeding up. She was only a few minutes away; she knew now this was going to be a busy night. Tomorrow there was definitely going to be overtime in Portland to help with the protests. Looking up, there wasn't a full moon so that didn't explain the craziness. The last couple of weeks there had been more and more acts of crime around town. Not just Vancouver but according to the briefings all across the county and state. People seemed to be going crazy, losing their minds. She knew it was happening over in Portland with the protestors blocking roads. The violent acts against police, emergency responders, and even the other members of the public. Still, by looking at the number of calls coming through the craziness had apparently hit Vancouver.

Alice slowed down as she neared the scene. It was a residential call about an attempted break in. The suspect looked badly injured from what she could see. She pulled up behind the ambulance. The driveway was lit up by the ambulance lights. Both paramedics seemed to be struggling with a man on the ground. She got out slamming her door then rushing over immediately taking charge. "Sir! I'm only going to ask you one time to be compliant with these gentlemen!" she ordered.

The man, who was lying on his back, was struggling and thrashing around.

One of the paramedics grabbed the man's feet to stop them from thrashing. The other had the man's shoulders pinned. The man just looked at her, it was nighttime and dark, but she could see his eyes were sunken in and all milky white. The man's face was covered in blood and he just started snapping his teeth at her like a rabid animal.

She slammed her hand on the man's forehead. The man's head was now pinned to the driveway. "Calm the fuck down! These guys are trying to help you!" she shouted. In her peripheral vision, she saw people in the house doorway. The man was still trying to thrash and get free. The paramedic on the guy's legs shouted to her, "Here grab his legs! I have something in the truck I can give him," The paramedic told her smiling. She nodded, letting go of the man's head. Then she put her hands on the man's legs while the paramedic ran to the ambulance.

After fumbling around in the back, the paramedic jumped out. The paramedic was still smiling as he popped the cap off a syringe. "This'll calm our friend down" The paramedic said to her. The other paramedic pinning the arms nodded in agreement. She didn't envy the paramedic holding the man's arms.

The man struggling reeked and his breath was foul. The paramedic slammed the syringe into the man's thigh. Within seconds the struggling ceased as the man's body went limp.

"Works every time." The paramedic chuckled removing the syringe. The other paramedic let go of the suspect's shoulders laughing. The paramedic opened his EMT case and began inspecting the suspect. There was a huge gash on the suspects shoulders.

"Oh my god…" The paramedic said. The other paramedic knelt down to examine the wound, too.

Both were talking about the gash and how badly rotten it was. Not a discussion she wanted to be part off. "How long will he be out for?" she asked them.

They didn't even look around at her but one of them answered "Oh about an hour, which is good cause trying to clean this up is going to be a bitch," The paramedic told her.

They started to remove some of the clothing that was stuck in the gash. The smell was getting to be too much. She got up and headed towards the people standing in the doorway of the house.

"Sorry about that," she started, "So could someone explain what happened?" she asked. There was a man probably in his late 50's standing slack jawed. A woman was beside him holding onto him who looked around the same age. The lady pointed at the suspect who was now being strapped down into a stretcher. "He was wandering up and down the street…for about an hour," the lady began. "He was going up and down the street. He was going into yards and even pounded on that window," she said pointing to a house across the street. "Then when he saw us outside looking, he headed to our house."

The man then chimed in, "Once he started coming over, we could see he had blood all on him, so we came in the house. We locked the door then called you guys. We could see he was hurt and when we tried to talk to him through the door he started growling. Like he was on drugs or something," the man said, not taking his eyes from the paramedics.

Alice nodded as she took details in her notebook.

"Well you guys did the right thing not coming into direct contact with him, if he is on drugs then it's possible he could have something. By the way he acted with the EMT's trying to help him, he probably wasn't going to be too friendly." She turned as the EMT's shouted to her

"Hey! We're good to go, you want to meet us there?" The paramedic asked. She nodded as she still had some details to get.

One of the paramedics hopped in the front of the ambulance, starting it up. She watched as the other one was in the back. The doors were still open. This one was checking the straps they had put on the suspect. The man was lying lifeless and calm. Then as the paramedic was checking the suspects vitals she jumped. The suspects eyes darted open and he turned biting the EMT"S wrist. "Fuck!" the EMT yelled trying to pry the suspects mouth from his wrist.

Alice ran over and jumped into the back of the ambulance. She grabbed the suspects head trying to squeeze his cheeks to loosen the bite. The EMT broke free falling against a drawer of medical tools sending them clanking to the floor.

"What the hell?" the other EMT said from up front. Alice stared at the suspect writhing around on the stretcher. The wheels were locked but the suspect was thrashing about so much they were jittering about. "Few hours, huh?" she commented hopping down out of the ambulance. She walked towards her cruiser, opened her trunk, and pulled out a bag. The EMT driver got in the back of the ambulance. She could hear them talking.

"You okay?" the driver asked. The EMT was cradling his arm and nodded.

"Fuckin' dick bit me! Hurts like hell, too!" The EMT said.

Alice hopped back into the ambulance wrapping a mask around the suspects face.

"It's to stop the spitters, hate getting saliva all over the back of the car or my head," she told them smiling. The two people were still in their doorway watching.

"We're good," she said giving the old couple a thumbs up. The suspect was still thrashing around on the stretcher. As the driver was bandaging and cleaning the other EMT"S forearm he looked at her. "He should have been out for at least forty-five minutes" The driver said in disbelief.

The other EMT chimed in "Whatever he's on, it must be pretty strong."

She nodded in agreement looking the suspect over. The suspects eyes were all white even the pupil. The veins sticking out on his face were purple and green. She looked down at the man's ankle.

It was twisted and contorted at a weird unnatural angle. She'd gotten emails at work about individuals who had these same symptoms attacking people. They were extremely violent and hard to restrain. They were still looking into it, but officers had been warned in the email to have as little contact as possible. To avoid bodily fluids from these individuals as whatever they had taken could be transferred. They could exhibit extreme tolerance to pain and seemed incoherent.

"We've had emails about cases like this" she said staring down at the suspect who was still flailing around.

The EMT with the now bandaged arm looked up at her. "Yeah so did we, I have to go get tested and monitored now," the EMT said disappointedly, giving the stretcher a kick.

"I'll finish up here and catch up with you guys at Southwest," she told them, getting out of the ambulance.

She headed back to the couple standing in their doorway. The woman started to walk towards Alice.

"Is he okay?" the lady asked, Alice nodded and forced a small smile, looking back over her shoulder she watched the ambulance drive off.

"My sister was in the dollar store today and said she saw a man bite a small boy," the old lady told her.

Alice raised her eyebrows. "Yeah there seems to be some new drug or something going about, let's get this wrapped up and I'll let you folks get back to enjoying your night," she said, whipping out her notebook.

After she was done getting the couples info, Alice said goodnight. She sat in her cruiser checking the computer. Dozens more calls were now active. Taking a few gulps of her energy drink she knew it was going to be a long night. She had agreed to a second shift in the AM which she was now regretting. Officers from her precinct had gone over to Portland to help with riot control.

She still needed to go to Southwest for the suspect's info. She needed that before she could actually charge him and close the call. She'd stop at any active calls en route to Southwest she thought as she started the engine.

Alice turned off 126th and headed down Mill Plain Boulevard. It was a straight shot down to Southwest that was on 86th. As she was driving past a strip mall lot that had a Safeway, she looked over and there was a group gathered. They were kicking someone on the ground. She fired up the lights and did a U-turn, driving over the median in the middle of the road to get to the other side. Her cruiser flew into the lot then pulled to a halt. Alice turned on the spotlight on her wing mirror. Aiming it at the group they paused and backed up from the man on the ground. The man on the ground was spasming and convulsing. The man slowly started to get to his knees. He looked right at her car and she froze. This man had the same vacant spaced outlook the last guy had. His eyes were all milky white with red stains around his mouth. The man's clothes were all torn and covered in blood.

CHAPTER SEVENTEEN
Nick

Nick stood there with his phone against his ear. Fighting started to break out in the crowd. There were more sirens in the distance getting closer. He turned heading back the way he came to the hotel. Before he could explain to his wife what had just happened, more shots rang out. He didn't turn around but could hear screams. Instead he picked up his pace to get as far away from this chaos as he could.

"Honey, I have to call you back once I get back to the hotel," he stammered.

"No! I can tell something's happening and I'm not getting off this phone until you are safe in your room" she disagreed.

He could hear the concern in her voice. "Okay I'll keep you on the line," he said, nodding.

"Honey, you have to come home as soon as you can! It's on the news! People have a disease!" his wife sounded scared.

"Val, it'll be okay," he said, trying to calm her down while trying to remain calm himself.

"Amber and me have been watching it all night! The Portland protests turned into riots. There's outbreak everywhere of a disease making people act like they have rabies!" His wife wasn't even taking breaths and was just working herself up. Nick quickened his pace away from the noise behind him.

"The people with the virus are becoming violent and attacking people, honey! Not just strangers but neighbors and family members," she said, scared. He could tell his wife was on the verge of crying.

"Honey!" he said sternly "I need you to try and stay calm, Amber needs her mommy focused until Daddy gets home" he said calmly.

Nick was almost halfway back to the hotel already, listening to what his wife was telling him was on the news. It made a lot of the crazy stuff he'd seen today make sense. A lot of people had been acting erratic all day. Nick didn't watch the news, or he would have pieced it together already. These weren't all coincidences so he would have taken better precautions. Nick could hear shouting from up ahead. It was people outside the restaurant he saw on his way to the store. This time however they were on his side of the street.

"Are you almost back to the hotel?" Val asked.

He put the phone down by his side as he approached them cutting her off. There were six of them throwing the outside patio chairs at the small window panes of a jewelry shop. As he approached the group, Nick moved slightly towards the road. He didn't want to be between the group and the windows. As he was passing them one turned to him.

"Hey!" one of the men barked.

"The po-po still all down there?" another asked.

Nick looked back the way he came then back at the men. "Yeah," he said softly.

The man's face lit up then the group of men all started laughing. The man slapped Nick on the shoulder then got back to vandalizing the jewelers.

As Nick walked away from them, he put the phone back to his ear, "Sorry, honey, streets are getting pretty rough," he told her. Even though he was trying not to worry her, he knew she wasn't stupid. Amber was probably staring at her mom wondering what was going on.

"I'm almost there though, honey" he reassured his wife. He had only one more corner to turn to be on the same block the hotel. As he did a bunch of police officers were standing outside of the hotel putting on riot gear. One of them turned looking at him as got close to them. The officer looked down at Nick's Target bags. Another officer gave him an up and down look then nodded at him to pass. Nick hurried with a forced smile and looked further up the street. There was another group of officers getting into their riot gear, too. This was going to be a long night and clearly what was happening in Portland wasn't just happening there. He walked into the hotel lobby which was still empty minus the girl manning the check in desk. She smiled as he walked towards the elevators as if oblivious to what was happening. He raised the Target bags and smiled a thank you.

"Almost there," he said stepping out of the elevator, letting his wife know he was that little bit closer. He knew if he didn't her anxiety would kick in. He could tell by her awkward silence how worried she was for him to get back to his room safe. "Here!" he said, swiping his key card.

Once inside the room he dropped his bags then threw himself on the bed.

"I love you, honey," he told her softly. He could tell she was smiling on the other end of the phone.

"I'm going to catch the first train home in the morning and say fuck the meeting, shit has just got too crazy here and if shit's starting to hit the fan down there too, I need to be home with my girls," he said with a smile. Not forced, this was real. The thought of being back at home curled up on the couch with those two was everything. All hell could be breaking loose outside, and he still wouldn't care.

" Oh, Amber will be so happy, honey! You have your apocalypse bag, right?" his wife asked with a fake chuckle. He could tell she was being strong, and this was good for Amber. He knew if what was happening here was a sign of what was happening in other places, too. Then something big was going down and shit probably

103

was hitting the fan. He needed to be back there ASAP, his sense of preservation and the survival of his family was kicking in.

"Yup, got my EDC get home bag," he told her.

"I'll let you go honey; I'm going to carry Amber to bed and snuggle up with her" she told him.

"Honey…" he started calmly "Listen, tomorrow I need you to pack some bags, enough for a week and go into my shop and load up on some supplies then if I'm not back by 5:00…" he paused for a second thinking about how to say it. He needed to word this as to not worry his wife any more than he could tell she already was. "I want you take Amber and head to your sister's." he said. There was silence and he could tell she was about to object. He continued, "At least I trust the people in your sister's area, she's out of the way in the country with Mark and it'll be easy for me to get to you there if the freeways are busy," he said.

Her sister Roslyn and her husband Mark lived out in the Oregon country. With the only thing for miles being wineries, he had a good paying job in a paper warehouse in downtown Portland with an hour commute every day. It was a scenic drive so the roads should be clear. The lack of people where they lived was worth it.

"O-okay… I love you honey…I'll see you tomorrow…before 5:00." she emphasized.

He nodded smiling to himself. "Kiss Amber good night for me."

"Honey…do you think things will really get that bad?" she asked him.

Nick laid on the bed looking out the window at the night sky, silhouettes of blue and red bouncing off the buildings still. He thought carefully about his next few words. If she knew he was worried she would start panicking and that wouldn't be good for anyone.

"Honey, I think it might get a lot worse before it gets any better and honestly, if you went to your sister's I would know where you were, and I could walk to you if I had to. Those are safe country roads and hills," he took a deep breath. "All that stuff you made fun of me for buying, in my end of the world bag… that's what it's for," he told her smiling, hoping she was smiling, too.

He turned on the TV as he lay there, and the emergency broadcast system was on the hotel's main screen. It was informing hotel guests that there was Martial law being declared. It listed states that were officially in a state of emergency. Oregon and Washington were on the list.

Nick sighed to himself looking at the screen, "Tell Amber I love her, and daddy will be home soon, if I can't get home in time on the first train or they stop I'll meet you at your sister's." he said.

"Honey, I need you to not stop for anyone, no matter who they are or how much help they need." He told her. In times like this he knew survival came down to making split second decisions. To ensure your survival, you couldn't second guess yourself. As things got worse, the worse people got and the fewer people could be trusted,

They said goodnight and Nick put his phone on the charger. Looking at the TV's menu screen it scrolled "hotel advisory" across the top then changed to info bulletins. It advised guests to stay in their room. If they have to leave to go straight to their destination. Then it said after checking out to go to one of the listed FEMA shelters. By pressing 1 on the remote you could be given a list of local help and relief centers. Nick knew how the government worked. He wasn't a tin foil hat wearing kinda guy. He knew in times of natural disasters no matter how much notice the US Government had they still didn't notify the public in time. This resulted in way more casualties that could have been prevented.

It happened at Katrina in New Orleans, and Harvey in Texas. That's why when seeing the FEMA info on the hotel station when he turned it on, he'd tried to calm his wife and make a bug out meet up location. He knew they weren't giving the public all the information. It was definitely bad, but this told him it was about to get much worse....

CHAPTER EIGHTEEN
Alice

Alice turned on her loudspeaker, "Vancouver PD! Everyone on your knees with your hands on your head" she ordered. The group had already stepped back once she'd turned the spotlight on.

There were six of them, all teenagers. Four looked at the man then took off. The two left did as she ordered. A wave of relief came over her. When there was more than one person involved in a call, officers were required to call for additional units. She knew by how busy it was that there was next to no chance of getting back up. The man who was being assaulted was struggling to stand up. Alice got out her car and walked towards the two on their knees. One of them was a young girl. The girl was crying and wouldn't take her eyes off the man. Tears were running down her face.

"Please! Please! Make him stop! He already bit me and tried to hurt me!" the girl begged.

The girl looked at Alice. Alarm bells were going off in Alice's head. This girl was terrified, so she nodded drawing her gun. She had already seen enough biting for one night.

"Sir! I am asking you to put your hands on your head and lay back down on the ground!" She asked. The man stood upright with blood dripping from his mouth. The man's face was contorted and severely beat up. The man just stared at her vacantly then started snarling.

"Now!" she ordered.

The man just kept snapping his jaws then turned his head to the girl, who was sobbing. The man was only feet away from the girl. Alice began walking towards them with her gun trained on the man.

She could make out what looked like gunshot wounds on the man's chest. He had the same milky eyes and red swelling around his nostrils and eyes as her last suspect too. The girl shrieked, jumping forward from her knees as the man got closer. The girl was crawling towards her. Alice stopped but kept gun on the man. She didn't want this girl getting too close to her either.

The boy jumped up from his knees punching the man. They both fell to the ground struggling.

The girl rolled over looking back at them. "Scott!" the girl screamed.

Alice stepped past the girl hoping to get a clean shot if she needed one. There was no chance as these two were to close for a clean shot. "Fuck!" she muttered to herself holstering her Glock.

Alice turned on her taser and it crackled as she stepped above the two. Before she could say anything, the boy let out a scream. The man was tearing into the boys shoulder with his teeth.

Alice grabbed the boy's shirt, pulling him free. The boy scrambled to his feet holding his shoulder. "Stop!" she barked. "Get back on the ground!"

The man was oblivious and lunged towards her. The taser crackled as she stuck it into the man. Thousands of volts ran through the man as he tried to get up.

The man was shaking as the current ran through him. As if not phased, the man's jaws still snapped at Alice, arms outstretched towards her. This wasn't normal. She turned the taser off stepping back from the man. She turned to the two youths.

The girl was still crying holding onto the boy. Blood was pouring down the boys arm from the bite on his shoulder.

"Shoot him! Please!" The boy begged. The look of terror was evident on the boy's face.

She quickly drew her gun, "This is the last warning I'm going to give you! Stop!" she warned. Whatever was wrong with this man he wasn't listening or feeling any pain. She dropped the aim of her gun to his left leg. The gun recoiled in her hands as she pulled the trigger. Chunks of the man's thigh flew out as the bullet tore through the leg. The man reeled then fell to the ground.

She stepped forwards slowly as the man lay on the ground, a gurgling growling noise coming from his throat. Alice couldn't believe it as the man started to get up again.

She was able to get a closer look now at the wounds on his chest. Aided by her patrol cars spotlight they were definitely gunshot wounds.

The man was pulling himself towards Alice, dragging his newly shot leg behind him. Alice looked into the man's eyes. There was nothing there…nothing. She aimed her gun for his head. Then said to herself softly, "Stop...please...stop." She was shaking but trying to stay composed.

"Shoot him again!" the boy screamed in Alice's ear coming up behind her. This startled her and she squeezed the trigger. The man's head rocked back as the bullet connected. The man's arms went limp. The lifeless body fell forward with a thunk. This time the man didn't get back up. Alice holstered her gun turning to the two behind her.

"Why didn't you stay back?" she asked the boy. She was angry at how the situation had ended. More annoyed that she was rattled and fired. She was usually better at staying composed than that.

The boy was looking at her with tears in his eyes. "You saw him!" The boy said waving his hand at the body lying on the ground. "He'd already been shot by some guy who took off and when we went to see if he was okay, he attacked Lilly!" The boy explained holding the girl close.

Alice could see they were both pretty shook up. She nodded "Okay, why don't you both go wait over there by my patrol car," she told them. She approached the body looking the man over.

He was wearing nice clothes she noted and appeared in his mid-twenties.

She rolled him over to check over his injuries. She looked at the gunshot entry wounds on the chest. There were bullet holes but also a couple of other wounds. They looked like defensive scratches. There was blood around the man's mouth. Alice pulled some latex gloves out from her belt so she could examine the face even closer. She wanted to get as much information as possible. This needed to go in her report so they could identify just what this was. An autopsy would give more accurate detail. If this was something new, then any details she could get now would help.

Pulling open the man's eyes, it was like he was blind. There was a milky white film over the pupils. This made sense as the light from the car didn't seem to bother him. The jerking of his head when hearing people speaking was something blind people did. So, it seemed like the sound was a trigger.

The face wasn't as veiny like the last guy. Pulling his lips apart he definitely had flesh in between the teeth. This made Alice's stomach turn. It was definitely similar to something in Florida she'd heard about. She remembered a few years ago there was a man on bath salts.

A homeless man got attacked and his face chewed off. The assailant had to be shot multiple times after attacking the officers before he stopped. This had been brought up the other day because there had been similar cases recently. Now it had been her second similar case of the evening. Alice peeled the gloves off and put them in an evidence bag, knowing she might need them later as further evidence. She tried to radio dispatch but there was no reply.

She walked over to her car to try the dash mounted radio. There was just dead silence then static. So, she tried radioing another officer but the same thing. She could feel something was wrong as this wasn't normal.

"You two get in the back," She told the two kids. After zipping the body up inside a body bag, she got into the car. As she sat there looking out at the body bag in the headlights her stomach turned. If there was no contact with dispatch, there would be no one to come and collect the body. This meant there were two options: leave the body here or take it with her. There was no reply on the radio for over an hour. An ambulance was pulling into the parking lot, so she fired up her roof lights to get their attention. It worked and the driver pulled up beside her.

"Hey" she said rolling down her window.

The ambulance driver leaned out his window "Hey what's going on? Your radio working?" the driver asked.

She shook her head. "I need to head to Southwest to wrap up my last call and just going to take these two with me. Would you mind getting the CoD done on that body?" She asked the driver.

This driver was a regular who must have been on the same shifts as her.

The driver looked over at the body bag. "Uh sure, I'll do the Cause of Death and fill in the paperwork then meet you down at Southwest and you can fill me in. Sound good?" The driver said.

"Thanks, Stefan," she nodded, thanking him. She looked at the two kids still sitting in the back seats.

"I'm headed to Southwest anyway. You need your arm seen to and I want you both checked out in case that guy had something,''she told them. They both nodded from the other side of the steel cage between her and the back seats. She waved at the EMT's getting out the ambulance as she drove off.

Turning back onto Mill Plain she put her lights on but not the siren. She wanted to get to Southwest as quickly as possible. "Thank you," the girl said softly from the back seat. Alice shot her a smile in the rearview mirror.

"You're welcome," she replied.

Being a police officer was mostly a thankless job. People were always seeing you as the "bad guy", the "imperial stormtrooper" for the government. Alice hadn't been thanked many times in her four years of being a cop. Something about this girl and tonight it meant something. She had definitely never been thanked for shooting someone in the head before, that's for sure.

There was a bright flash from out the left side of the car. The boy in the back let out a "whoa!" They all looked out the car to see what it was. There were flames from a neighborhood licking up in the air. Alice's heart missed a beat. That was the direction of her neighborhood. It was also roughly where her precinct was.

She looked back at the kids, "We're taking a detour," she told them, turning the cruiser sharply. Putting her foot down and changing gears, the car raced down some side streets. She was going way too fast she knew that. The cruiser was lifting off the ground every time they hit a speed bump. She was looking up above the houses to try and judge where the flames were coming from, trying to map out in her head just how close it was to her home. She was so fixated with the flames she didn't hear both the kids in the back warn her before it was too late.

A truck slammed into the side of the cruiser. The car was filled with the sound of screams and crunching, twisting metal. The cruiser was sent rolling off the road and into a small field. Alice's head bounced off the dashboard and the cage behind her. She closed her eyes and her teeth. The girl's screams were the last thing she heard as everything went black.

CHAPTER NINETEEN
Stefan

Stefan stepped out of the ambulance as Alice's car took off. Rob, his partner stepped out the back of the ambulance. They had been EMT partners for three years now. Rob was looking at him, "You ever going to ask her?" Rob asked. Stefan shrugged his shoulders as he knelt down beside the body bag. Rob chuckled "Stefan Lear! I have known you for just over three years and never known you to be this shy" Rob said laughing. He was about to let out a laugh himself when he got a whiff from the body. Alice had told him the guy was dead but hadn't said for how long.

By the foul smell he got as he unzipped the bag it seemed like it had been a good few days.

"Wow… this is definitely the nastiest thing I've seen this week," he said.

"Holy shit," Rob said.

As he shone a light on the dead man's face, Rob knelt beside him. "Hey, you think this could be the virus?" Rob asked. This thought had crossed his mind, too. They'd gotten emails this week about a potential super virus. The emails were pretty vague but included advanced necrosis which would account for the smell. The emails stated that it could be very contagious. That anyone exhibiting symptoms of extreme anger or outbursts should be isolated. Those were for people admitted to the hospital. There was only one email about if encountering a deceased person who would be infected.

He looked at Rob. "Well if it is this mysterious virus we've been hearing about, then we need to get him to Southwest and isolated for transport," he said zipping the bag up.

"That also means Alice and those kids she had in her car need to be isolated and quarantined, too" Rob replied.

"With the radio down, we should head to Southwest now and catch up with her before those kids leave" He said nodding towards the gurney. He would need Rob's assistance lifting the body onto it. Rob was a big guy towering at six foot five. The man was nothing but sheer hulking muscle. Everything he wore he looked like he would tear through if he flexed. They both grabbed an end and lifted the body bag onto the stretcher. After it was loaded in the back, they both got into the front. Stefan turned the key looking at the body in the rearview mirror. He was hoping Alice was fine and not infected.

"So, you going to ask her when we get there?" Rob asked, looking at him with widening his eyes.

"If she's not infected then yeah course I will… just to shut you up." He laughed and Rob chuckled with him. As they drove towards the hospital cars were speeding past them. Something was definitely in the air. He remembered watching the news today when he was at home. The protests in Portland were turning ugly. Taking Alice to Portland for a date was probably a bad idea.

As they arrived at Southwest there was a line at drop off. There were three other EMT crews taking people in. "Wow it's busy tonight" Rob said. They both stared at the people being walked in by the other EMT"s. Luckily, they were headed to the side entrance to take the body in. Once they dropped off the body, they could find Alice. Finding out what was going on with the radios would be next. Stefan looked in through the huge glass windows of the ER lobby as they drove past. "Holy shit it's packed in there!" he said. EMT's bringing people into the ER was normal but the packed ER lobby was a first. They drove round to the side loading doors where a hospital security guard was at the door with a nurse. They slowed to a stop and rolled the window down.

"We got a deceased one, possibly infected with the new virus we got the emails about." Stefan told the nurse. The security officer stepped towards them undoing the stud on his holster. Rob leaned over towards the window.

"It's okay chief…he's dead." Rob said sarcastically.

The guard just stared at them. "Were either of you bit or hurt?" The guard asked. Stefan could feel the tension.

"There something we need to know?" he asked the officer.

The nurse looked in and shone a flashlight into both their eyes. "Things have changed." the nurse said, turning the flashlight off. Stefan was intrigued and wanted to know more. "The radios went down so we weren't updated on any changes of procedure" He told the men.

Getting out of the ambulance, he walked round to the rear where Rob opened the doors. He couldn't help noticing and Rob had noticed, too. The guard was standing at the door to the hospital and hadn't taken his hand off his gun the whole time. "There something wrong?" Rob asked the nurse.

The nurse was a small, frail, red headed guy with glasses and looked like a Weasley. "Umm, no, just precautions. We…we've been asked to make a hundred percent sure they're dead before taking them into the hospital" The nurse stammered timidly.

Rob let out a howling laugh. "A hundred percent dead??? How much fucking deader can someone be?" Rob said laughing. Neither the nurse nor the security guard were laughing.

"Okay, what's going on?" He asked looking at the nurse.

"Head inside and you'll be briefed by your superior, but we're not allowed to give out any information," the guard said.

He bit his lip and nodded then looked over at Rob who shook his head in annoyance. "You two take this one in then, we'll go get briefed then be back out," Rob said angrily.

Tossing the ambulance keys to the nurse he looked over at the guard. "What if he's not... 100% dead?" Stefan curiously asked.

The nurse looked round at the guard obviously anxious to hear the answer, too.

"I'd have to shoot him in the head," The guard said in a low dull tone.

Stefan nodded somberly then turned and headed with Rob in the direction of the ER entrance.

"What the fuck you think's going on?" Rob asked.

"Not sure but with the radios down and how busy it is tonight I'm starting to get a bad feeling," he said. Rob nodded then they both paused for a second in awe. The line of people waiting to register at the ER check in desk was out the door. He couldn't believe it and gave people quick once overs as he passed them on his way in. They all seemed to have gashes or large wounds.

Once inside he waved to the girls at the check in desk who were clearly overwhelmed. He stopped to survey the scene in the ER lobby. There was a janitor handing out masks to everyone after they checked in. Every seat was taken with some chairs having more than one person squeezed on. There was old people sweating profusely with rags on their heads. Young people holding fabric or clothing over wounds. The air smelled like a mix of copper pennies and disinfectant. This couldn't all be from the super virus he thought, or could it? If the virus was the cause of maybe half of these admissions, then they were going to be in for a very rough time.

"Stefan! Head through!" Brandi, one of the admission nurses shouted to him. The large double doors leading into the hospital from the ER waiting room buzzed open. Brandi met them as they walked through, and the two heavy doors closed behind them. He could still hear coughing and groans coming from the lobby.

The admission nurse Brandi had a huge crush on Rob. "Hey" Brandi said, blushing.

"Busy night tonight, huh," Rob said putting his hands on his hips like a catalog pose. Rob may have the looks and muscle but lacked charisma. Every time Rob did something cringe worthy like this Stefan couldn't help but try not to laugh out loud. He noticed Brandi was starting to blush like some high school girl.

"Yeah it's nuts! We're waiting on the National Guard to get here," Brandi said not taking her eyes from Rob. Rob must have been just as surprised by this as he was as the model pose dropped.

"The national guard?" Rob asked.

Brandi nodded looking at him. "All of the radios are down and there's been a national emergency declared," Brandi said.

"Do you know what exactly it is they're coming here for?" Rob asked.

Brandi shook her head and looked just as confused as they were.

"Hopefully they'll help us deal with the overflow in urgent care as we've been told not to let anyone leave," Brandi said, looking puzzled.

This was really strange but made sense, he thought. If there was a new super virus going around then they should be here, not out infecting other people. The fact it had happened so suddenly was what scared him. There had been vague emails about symptoms for about a week now. Nothing to suggest an outbreak like this or the severity of the virus.

"We've also just been told to tell any units that come in to stay here, too, until they get here," Brandi said.

"Figures," Rob said, "our radios aren't working maybe they have better ones and can give us more info on this virus before we go back out," Rob said, sounding positive.

He knew what Rob was saying made sense but until the National Guard got here, he wanted to find out as much as he could about this virus. The security guard at the side doors seemed to have newer information.

"Hey if we're stuck here for a bit maybe you can ask Alice out on that date," Rob said with a huge shit eating grin.

"You're trying to get a date, Stefan? Is she here?" Brandi asked, smiling.

"Yeah, she's a cop but brought in two kids, probably a little bit before we arrived," he began before Rob cut in.

"Yeah, we have to get some more info from her about the body we brought in and since she won't be leaving either this is perfect!" Rob said clapping his big hands together.

"Could you find out what room they're in?" he asked Brandi.

"Sure, but I haven't seen any cops, not in the last couple of hours," Brandi told them.

This wasn't a good sign he thought to himself as Brandi disappeared into the admission office. He peered around the corner to see her skimming through the admissions on the computer. He looked up at the large plexiglass windows that separated the admission nurses from the patients. The place was packed and the line of people waiting to give the nurses their info had only gotten bigger.

"What was the name?" Brandi asked.

"Her first names Alice, last is Hayward, but it would have been two kids she was checking in," he said.

Brandi was staring at the screen shaking her head. "Nope she's not here," Brandi said. Suddenly a gurgling noise came from the line of people waiting. The admission nurses let out gasps jumping out of their seats. A small child at the front of the line began vomiting blood. Blood was getting splattered all over the plexiglass with some coming through the slot that people slid their ID and information through. People began screaming and shouting as the ER lobby erupted into chaos.

CHAPTER TWENTY
Alice

Alice's eyes fluttered as the pounding in her head got louder and louder. She tried to assess the situation by looking around. The car was on its side, she was being held in place by the seat belt. She tried to focus but her vision was groggy. Her face was wet and throbbed.

Trying to move around was hard as she ached all over. The last thing she remembered was hearing the kids in the back scream. Her head was touching the door window which was against the ground. She lifted it from a sticky pool of what must have been dried blood.

She tried to look out through where the windshield had been. Her vision cleared up a bit when she narrowed her eyes. The car seemed to be in a field. There was a truck in the field, too, with a crumpled in front end. There was smoke coming from the front of the truck. Taking a guess, Alice decided this was what had hit them at the intersection. She tried to turn her neck to see in the cage behind her. The grogginess quickly snapped away as she saw the girl in the back. The girl was covered in blood and eating the boy! The boy had a huge chunk of glass going in his left eye socket.

Either the crunching of broken glass or Alice's labored breaths got the girls attention. The girl threw herself against the cage separating the front and back of the car. Bloody fingers poked through the mesh cage. The girls blood stained teeth were grinding on the cage as the girl tried to bite her way through. The girls eyes were all milky white and vacant. The same soulless gaunt look she had seen twice tonight already.

Alice had no clue how long she's been out. The seatbelt release wasn't working so she reached over to pull open the glovebox. Its contents all spilled out onto her. It was so much harder trying to do things suspended sideways. Add to that the throbbing all over her body and the crazed cannibal trying to gnash her way through a steel mesh barrier.

She looked for the seatbelt cutter that was on the multi tool. It was kept stowed away in the glove box for just this kind of accident. Slicing through the belt, she fell hard against the door which was now the floor.

She elbowed the cage hard, "Shut up!" she snarled to the girl who was growling and hissing. Alice pushed on her shoulder radio but found nothing. She reached over for the cruiser's radio. The frustration inside her was building. The radio was busted into pieces probably thanks to the crash. She decided to climb out through the broken windshield. The inside of the car was stuffy and humid. Once outside the car the cool night air hit her. This gave her a little bit of comfort and relief.

Once outside the car she stood up and stretched. It was still dark, but the sky was dotted with red glows. The smell of smoke was thick and heavy in the air. Holding her head as it throbbed, she walked towards the truck. She could feel where the gash was on her head. Blood was still trickling down her head. Suddenly she stopped in her tracks and stared at the truck driver. Despite what she'd seen this evening she still couldn't believe her eyes. Was she concussed? Was she delirious? She looked at the driver in disbelief or more, what was left of him.

The drivers head was halfway through the windshield glass. Skin torn from his face and hanging. The front of his skull was exposed and bloody, revealing deep eye sockets with milk white eyes. There was smashed bloody teeth and dangling tissue.

Alice pulled out her gun as she slowly started to walk toward the truck again.

Hey!" she shouted. As she expected, the driver reacted like a blind animal caught in a trap. All riled up, the head poking through the glass began moving. Side to side it was thrashing against the glass. She could see the arms flailing inside the truck through the spider webbed glass.

She turned looking towards her patrol car lying on its side. The girl was still in the back banging the cage like an animal. That's when she realized…these weren't people anymore. She aimed the gun at the truck drivers head. Her hands were shaking as she was about to squeeze the trigger, but she lowered her gun. Her head was throbbing, and she wasn't a hundred percent sure this was the right thing to do right now or not.

She looked up at where the flames had been that had distracted her before the crash.

They weren't there anymore but the smell of burning was. Judging by where the glow had been before she wasn't far. It was about five to six blocks away and pretty close to her house.

Alice hobbled out of the field and looked down the road in either direction. No cars, so she crossed the road, still holding her head. Heading the direction of home sounded like a good idea. She stopped and turned around to take one final look at the scene behind her. The sight of a smoking truck with some kind of demon stuck in the windshield. A police cruiser on its side with some kind of cracked out cannibal in the back. Any other day this would be nuts and a major crime scene. From the way tonight had been however this looked like a nightmare. One Alice hoped she would wake up soon.

Alice had been walking for a few blocks at a pretty slow pace. Her right leg was hurting pretty bad from the crash. The blood had finally stopped dripping down from her forehead.

There hadn't seen a single person in sight while she'd been walking. Plenty of houses she had passed had lights on but no signs of activity. She'd tried her cell phone, but it was all cracked, not even turning on. A door creaked open as she passed a gate leading up to a house. An elderly bearded man came out with a shotgun raised. She put her arms up and looked him in the eyes. Slowly the man lowered his gun.

"S-sorry" he stuttered "I didn't realize you were a cop and those things don't put their hands up, but you were walking like one," The man said in a scared tone. Then he gave a whistle and a thumbs up to a house across the street. Alice turned and looked over at a garage attached to the house. Squinting, she could see a man lying on top with a rifle trained on her.

This confused her even more. "What the fucks going on?" she asked.

The man's eyes widened as he looked at her in disbelief, "Are you serious?" he asked.

Before she could give a smart ass reply he continued. "Some disease, the news says, making people go crazy and act like maniacs," he said.

Another man appeared from behind the house. "'Bout time the cops got here," the new younger man said matter-of-factly. The man walked over to the shotgun toting homeowner and Alice. The look that both the homeowner and her gave the man let him know she wasn't here to help. She looked at them both "I was in an accident and just trying to head home," she told them.

The man with the shotgun nodded solemnly, "We've been calling 911 all night, figured you guys would have your work cut out for you with all the fires and gunshots we've been hearing."

The other man cut in. "Why did you ask us what's going on? You're a cop? Aren't you guys on top of this?" The man said getting himself worked up.

Alice didn't know what to say. "Look," she hesitated, trying to tread delicately. These men were obviously scared, and she didn't want to make them worse. The next person passing might not be as lucky as her to get a courtesy question first, shoot later.

"I work nights, I clocked onto my shift at eight and on my first call I got into an accident, I have no idea what's going on or what my colleagues are doing, I lost my radio in the crash." she told them honestly.

Gunshots rang out from somewhere in the distance that got their attention. "Honey, it's bad, you better get to where you're going, we've had kids racing up and down these streets. Two of those things tried to get in our houses and there's no help in sight." The elderly man told her as he glanced at her holstered gun. Something got the man's attention from inside the house. The man turned heading back into his house. The other younger man followed him in.

She took a step towards them, "What's the news saying?" she asked.

The elderly man stopped in the hallway and looked at her.

"They're saying it's a virus, like rabies…making people go nuts, get violent, not be themselves" the elderly man explained.

The other man cut in, "Says that emergency services will be stretched and to avoid traveling unless absolutely necessary while local law enforcement and medical staff get the situation under control."

"Which I guess are nonexistent right now," The elderly man finished.

Alice nodded somberly. "We'll see, I'm sure not every cop in Vancouver is in as bad shape as me," she said. Both men nodded but didn't seem too convinced.

Alice waved her hand as she turned and continued in the direction of her house. The man on the garage roof gave her a wave as she left.

Walking along the street she couldn't help but wonder. The only things mentioned at the pre-shift briefing were that there had been a higher volume of calls all day and a spike in violent crimes. All of the officers thought this was due to the protests. The anti-police stance was becoming more evident all over. Activist groups were taking some extreme measures lately.

The next few blocks she walked through were quiet. There were new red glows in the sky coming from fires, she guessed. There hadn't been any more gunshots. She wasn't sure if this was a bad sign or a good one. As she turned onto her street, she got excited. She couldn't wait to see Max, her dog. She knew she needed to get her wound looked at soon by someone as it was starting to throb more. Her neighbor's yellow truck was in his driveway. It belonged to Benny who lived with another guy. Benny worked at an elderly care facility so maybe he could take a look at her head, she thought.

Stumbling up to the front door she rang the doorbell. Weird she thought as she hadn't heard Max bark. Max always barked when she was home from work.

The door opened and it was Benny "Alice!" The dark skinned Native American exclaimed. Benny wrapped his arm around her and guided her into the house. "Marcus!! Come help!" Benny yelled staring at her head.

Marcus came running down the stairs with a hatchet in his hand.

"That in case of a home invasion? That all you got?" she asked, smiling trying to joke.

The way Marcus was looking at her she could immediately sense something wasn't right.

"What's wrong?" she asked.

Before either of them could reply to her she started to see dots. Then her legs felt like spaghetti as she felt herself fall to the floor.

CHAPTER TWENTY-ONE
Stefan

The admission nurses all pushed past Rob and Stefan to get out of the office. Brandi pushed him as he stood staring the blood covered plexiglass. Once out she slammed the door and locked it.

"Why are you locking it?" he asked puzzled.

Rob had already darted to the two large double doors to get into the lobby to try and help.

A senior nurse came out from one of the triage rooms and was shaking her head "I'm sorry but the new protocol is that we've to lock down the lobby" the big lady said matter-of-factly.

Rob glared at her, "Are you fuckin' joking? There's a kid in there throwing up and it's full of people! Open the damn door!" Rob said getting heated.

Before the nurse could reply the intercom crackled, "Medical emergency in module E, male" a female's voice said. The nurse looked at Rob then at Stefan, "If you two want to help someone there you go," the nurse said not taking her eyes off Rob. Stefan knew he had to break the tension that was building. "Look we'll help as best we can but what protocol?" he asked gesturing towards the double doors. The nurse broke her gaze from Rob and looked at Brandi.

"No…no…no, don't look at her! You tell us!" he insisted.

Before the nurse could answer the intercom crackled again, "Medical emergency in module D, male" the same female voice said only this time a different module.

Nurses rushed past them further into the hospital with IV racks and defibrillators. Rob shot him a look and then stormed past the nurse. "We'll head to module D, but we'll be back!" Rob spat.

He started to follow Rob but stopped at the nurse. "Look, just tell me, we're here on lockdown not going anywhere. If we're helping at least give us some information about what we're helping against." He pleaded with the nurse. The nurse bit her lip and sighed. "The orders came from the CDC and FEMA who are on their way. They should have been here hours ago. Security has been told to seal the lobby from outside, but we have kept the quarantine on this side until help arrives," the nurse said.

He nodded but this gave him more questions than answers. "Thank you, I appreciate it," he told her. The nurse nodded.

"Don't get bit or any blood on you, you'll be treated as infected when they do get here," the nurse said. She gave a sympathetic look towards the double doors then turned, walking back into her triage cubicle. As he headed after Rob, Brandi was on his heels behind him. "I'll…I'll help, whatever you need," Brandi stuttered.

The girl was obviously a little shook up from what she had just seen. The other admission nurses were still back there freaking out, but Brandi seemed to be hanging in there pretty good.

"Sure, just stay close and do what we say," he told her, not turning.

Rob was stopped at the end of a hallway. They caught up to him and in front of him, several nurses were around an elderly man who was laying in the hall. As Stefan was about to walk round Rob a doctor put his hand out. "We'll need you guys to stay back and slowly vacate this area," the doctor said.

Rob shrugged his shoulders and turned to him. "What the fuck are we doing let's get out of here, they don't want our help," Rob said, and Stefan nodded in agreement.

"Actually how 'bout we head to the morgue and try to chat with the security guy to try get more info?" he said, and Rob nodded. They headed through the hallways, passing nurses every couple of minutes rushing to get somewhere. There had been three more pages of medical emergencies since they had headed in the direction of the morgue. What really got to Stefan was that there had been no clear pages. Usually once there's a page for a medical emergency as soon as the emergency had been seen to, they would page emergency in module whatever cleared. There hadn't been a single one. This worried him as did the fact that the CDC was supposed to be here which meant it was a serious virus that probably wasn't easy to cure, if at all. Then there was FEMA, he knew they provided mainly disaster relief. They were at the morgue and about to open the doors when they heard Brandi behind them.

"Oh my god...what's happening?" they heard her say. They both stopped and turned to see what had gotten her attention and it was a TV in the morgue waiting room. They walked over to see what she was watching that had shocked her.

It was the news, it had a list of states declaring a national emergency, Washington was right there along with Oregon and most of the other western states.

All three of them stood there for a few minutes reading all the other info on the screen.

The A.D.D. instructions, the symptoms of someone infected and the FEMA shelters. The morgue door opened and the security guard who had met them at the side door walked out.

"We were just coming to see you," Stefan said to the security guard.

"Why?" the guard asked giving him a puzzled look.

"You knew FEMA was on the way? So, you know more than most people here," he said.

The guard looked a little nervous. "We just got briefed that we were to keep any infected as isolated as possible until the relief team and experts get here, they shoulda been here by now," the guard said nervously.

"Then what? You think they're just going to let you clock out and go home to your family? They've locked down the ER lobby and no one's allowed to leave." he told the guard who looked in shock.

The guard started shaking his head, "No..no, I was told by my supervisor that soon as they get here and I do a hand off briefing on infected bodies I put in I could go," the guard said worried.

Brandi piped up "I wouldn't bet on it, we were told no staff could leave until after we had been tested and cleared and even then, we would have to wait to be cleared," Brandi told them.

"I hope not, I've got a family I need to get back to," the guard said, worried.

"Sounds like you two were both fed a load of bullshit, so sounds like we need to get the fuck out of here," Rob said.

The guard looked up at the TV as it was now showing footage from a helicopter. They all turned and looked as the info on screen had changed to a live stream. The footage showed a bridge blocked by black vehicles and people running towards the barricade. The footage said, "Live from Portland" The people on the bridge were attacking the officers at the barricade.

A female presenter began talking, "There is still no sign of the national guard who are supposed to be on scene by now! But we have had reports of them being sighted on I-5 and 205 so hopefully the officers in Portland trying to keep the peace will get the backup they need, and this situation will be brought under control!" The female news reader narrated as the view on the TV still showed the bridge and barricade.

Their attention was taken from the TV by the sound of gunshots. They were loud! Lots of them! "That's coming from outside!" the security guard said.

"Told you! We need to get the fuck out of dodge!" Rob said.

Stefan thought about how to get through to the security guard, "You said you had a family to get to? Help us get out so we can all go home, that's obviously where we need to be," he pleaded. Stefan didn't have a family but wanted out of the shit show this was becoming. It was clear no one had been told the correct information. The guard nodded and pointed down a hallway.

"Those shots came from the front of the building, we should take the fire exit at the rear of the parking lot and cut across the field," the guard suggested. Stefan knew they didn't have much of a choice as the other fire exits led out front where the commotion was coming from.

"Let's go," he said, leading the way.

They could hear screams and shouting coming through the air ducts from other parts of the hospital. As they got to the fire exit leading out into the parking garage, there was a group of three nurses already at the door. The nurses turned as they heard them running down the hallway. One of them was covered in blood and another was cradling her arm.

"Whoa, hold up," he told the group as he looked at the nurses. They stopped as the nurse covered in blood walked towards them. "We're not going back up there," the nurse said, holding back tears.

Stefan could tell she was terrified, and he didn't want her getting any closer to him in case she was infected. "We're not trying to keep you here, we're getting out, too," he reassured them.

The nurse gave a half smile and put her arm around the nurse who had the injured arm. The other one pushed the door setting off the fire alarm. They all rushed out into the garage and the coast was clear, there was no one there. As they ran towards the exit leading onto the road, they heard a growl. A man with blood around his mouth stepped out from behind a car. "He's infected!" one of the nurses screamed.

The man burst into a fast hobble towards them, but he wasn't very fast at all. As they reached the exit a soldier grabbed the first nurse to reach it. The soldier was in green with a FEMA armband on.

The soldier tackled the nurse to the ground while two more appeared with rifles drawn. The group all put their hands up in the air. Stefan was still worried about the infected who was behind them. He turned to look at how far away the man was. "Hey! You! Face forward!" One of the soldiers ordered. Stefan opened his mouth to explain but the other soldier must have already seen the man. Two shots rang out echoing inside the garage. The soldier walked towards the man letting off three more shots. The man staggered back as they slammed into his chest. The soldier on the ground finished zip tying the nurse's hands then looked at the soldier firing.

"It has to be the head!" The soldier on the ground shouted to his colleague.

The second soldier, who still had his rifle trained on the group, turned to fire at the man also. Stefan wasn't sure what came over him but as the soldier raised his rifle, he pushed the soldier over. Stefan then sprinted out the exit away from what was unfolding behind him. As he stepped onto the road something big slammed into him. He felt his feet lift on the ground and the feeling of weightlessness came over him as he spun through the air. The concrete rushed up to meet him as he met it with a wet thud. He felt warm fluid coming down his face.

He knew it was blood and couldn't feel his legs. He put his hands on the ground to try and lift himself up. Just as he got his chest lifted, he felt the sharp cutting pain of teeth sinking into the side of his   arm   on   the   bicep.

CHAPTER TWENTY-TWO
Rob

As the group burst out into the parking garage, Rob felt in his gut something wasn't right and he should have listened to his gut. As the group had headed towards the exit that led cars out onto the main road three soldiers had rushed them and were now zip tying the nurses up. An infected who must have been lurking in the garage was now behind them. Shots rang out as one of the soldiers fired at the oncoming ghoulish man. A soldier on the ground zip tying a nurse shouted to his colleague to aim for the head. This made sense to Rob, every zombie or horror movie he had seen with diseased people had the same parameters when it came to dispatching the infected. Somehow, he couldn't help but laugh in his head of the irony that here in real life it stood the same.

He stood with his hands raised, frozen in place, too scared to move for fear of being shot. Stefan somehow lost it, though, and tried to make a move. He watched in slow motion as Stefan pushed one of the soldiers over then sprinted out the exit that cars used. Then his stomach lurched in shock as Stefan ran out onto the road outside of the parking garage. A car drove straight into Stefan with a shuddering thud as metal hit flesh and bone. Rob had always arrived on car accident scenes after they had happened but always imagined the person being hit to fall straight over. This was the first time he had seen it in person and that wasn't the case. Stefan's whole body lifted off the ground and cartwheeled through the air in awkward angles then hit the ground with a wet slap.

Stefan's body lay there at a weird contorted angle as he groaned and tried to lift himself up. Robs hands were still raised but he walked forward slowly towards his friend who was in a position where he could drag himself along on his arms. Rob stopped in place though as the muzzle of one of the soldiers rifles was pushed into his chest. "That's far enough, big guy," the soldier said, glancing over at Stefan who was in the middle of the road trying to pull himself up. Out of nowhere a man can stumbling into the middle of the road and slumped himself down beside Stefan and sunk his teeth into Stefan's arm.

The soldier shook his head, "See, too late for him, fucking idiot!" the soldier muttered seeming agitated. Rob noticed that all three of these men who were seemingly trained soldiers were awfully on edge.

"Let's pull back," a soldier said patting the one who was in front of Rob on the shoulder. It was the one who had initially shot at the infected that had appeared in the parking garage. He turned and looked around, he'd been too focused on Stefan and had failed to see the soldier put down the man who was lurking in the garage. Rob's hands were zip tied behind his back and all he could hear were screams coming from inside the hospital and the nurses all sobbing as they were zip tied, too.

His attention was turned back to Stefan as a shot rang out! He looked over to see the man who had bit Stefan on the bicep lying on his back on the road with a soldier standing over the body with smoke coming from the barrel of the rifle.

Stefan was lying face down on the road with a pool of blood around him. Stefan's eyes were wide and empty staring in their direction. The car that had hit him was stopped and the two people who were inside were now being zip tied also. "Let's go!" The soldier said who was holding him at gunpoint and motioned towards the parking exit. Outside there was a camo flatbed truck with some people already in it. Rob stepped up into the truck bed looking around at the half dozen people already up there. They were all sitting zip tied at the wrists also seemed like regular normal people. Rob looked over at Stefan whose body was left in the middle of the street like it was some piece of roadkill. The soldier next to him must have sensed his despair and shouted to one of the other soldiers in the street.

"Hey! Put that one down," the soldier said pointing at Stefan. For a minute Rob swore he could hear Stefan muttering as one of his friends arms twitched but the amount of blood around his body said that was impossible. Maybe he was shock or maybe this was the start of the infection, he thought. Rob sat down in the bed of the truck not saying a word then turned to look again at his friend as a soldier stood above Stefan and fired two more shots. He then watched as the soldiers got a couple more people into the truck. The engine started up with a growl and the truck moved slowly down the road.

As they moved away from the lifeless body of his good friend, he couldn't help but feel overwhelmed with sadness and helplessness. The truck turned a corner then stopped in front of the hospital. He could make out some kind of cordon that was set up around the hospitals front entrance. He had seen this before in training videos of disease quarantines. Only instead of doctors and nurses around the perimeter there was soldiers and police officers. This was even more confusing to him as this was a hospital and the people going there needed help. Yet all of these men and women standing around the outside perimeter had guns drawn. People sitting in the truck bed began to stand up to try and get a look at what was going on. It seemed like a standstill with everyone's attention directed towards the hospital that was emanating an eerie silence.

The police and soldiers had crude barricades up and were standing on point with nothing coming from the hospital. It was crazy as only a little time earlier when they had arrived at the front

ER entrance was alive and busy as ever. Now it was quiet seeming like a graveyard with even the screams he had heard while trying to get out now stopped. The ER itself was a large glass windowed lobby well-lit from the inside.

He could only see a few bodies moving around inside yet he knew when Stefan and he had entered earlier there had been dozens of patients.

"What do you think they're waiting for?" Brandi asked from across the truck bed. He shook his head without taking his eyes off the hospital.

"I don't know but I don't think it'll be good for anyone who's still in there" he said quietly.

A bull horned made a loud ear-piercing high-pitched noise as it was turned on then crackled as a man's voice came across it.

"DO NOT MOVE ANY FURTHER! TURN AROUND AND GO BACK INTO THE HOSPITAL! MORE MEDICAL AID WILL BE ARRIVING SHORTLY! PLEASE BE PATIENT!" The voice said authoritatively.

Rob began to stand up looking around to see if he could see where the voice talking was coming from. He couldn't see so he looked towards the hospital to try and see who these commands were being directed at. Squinting, he could woman in a hospital gown walking across the grass coming from the hospital's large tower. They were quite a bit away from the tower, so she was hard to make out with all the lights being on around the entrance of the hospital. The woman was stumbling slowly across the grass then another person came into view behind her then another. The voice came across the bull horn again. " PLEASE! THIS IS YOUR LAST AND ONLY WARNING! THIS AREA IS UNDER QUARANTINE! ANYONE WHO TRIES TO LEAVE WILL BE MET WITH LETHAL FORCE!" The man on the bullhorn cautioned.

The people coming towards them didn't seem to hear or acknowledge the warning at all. One of the soldiers aiming at the hospital looked round towards the truck.

"Sir?" The solder shouted.

Obviously, this was a threat or an order that the soldiers weren't sure if they were to follow.

A soldier walked towards the barriers and had a bull horn in his hand, but he couldn't see the man's face. He wanted to see it as this was obviously who was in charge right now. The number of people coming from the hospital was growing as now he could make out at least eight shapes in the distance. "FIRE AT WILL!" the man shouted only this time the bull horn remained at his side.

A chorus of shots rang out, filling the air with muzzle flashes as both the soldiers and the police officers manning the barricade let loose with gun fire.

The truck bed started to fill with sobs and shrieks of objection, but he just sat there fixated by what was unfolding before him. Shot after shot was being fired towards the people coming from the hospital. These people didn't seem to care or be bothered by the hot lead being thrown their way.

The truck bed was slapped twice by a soldier walking past. Brandi almost fell over the side trying to get the soldiers' attention. "What the fuck's happening?" Brandi asked and the soldier stopped looked at the people in the truck bed.

"You don't need to worry about that, miss! Your safe and we're getting you guys out of here to a safe distance where you'll be released." the soldier said.

Rob swallowed as his throat was dry and looked over at the soldier who seemed uneasily calm despite the crescendo of gunfire going on. Brandi stepped back and sat back down then burst into tears.

"Seriously, man, let us go, what are you going to do with us? Why are we zip tied?" Rob asked the soldier. The soldier walked towards the truck bed looking him dead in the eyes.

"I already told you, we're taking you to a safe distance where you'll be released. You're restrained for your own safety. We can't risk you getting infected and unfortunately we had to draw the line and the line was this barricade" The soldier finished gesturing at the makeshift barricade of police cars and Hummers set up.

"So that's it? Everyone in there is "infected" to you?" Rob spat.

The soldier gave a half smile with pursed lips. "Trust me, you'll thank me later," the soldier said.

"I doubt that," he said back bitterly.

The soldier slapped the truck bed again. "Come on! Get these folks out of here!" the soldier ordered. The truck revved up then took off down Mill Plain which was a straight road that led from the hospital straight to downtown. It passed a lot of freeway access points and big neighborhoods, so he wondered where this "safe perimeter" was.

Rob looked at Brandi and her eyes that were swollen with tears. The nurses were all huddled together and the other people in the back of the truck looked terrified. He turned and looked back to see the men and women at the barrier still firing away. The "infected" from the hospital were still making their way to the barrier. It was a sight Rob knew he'd never forget.

CHAPTER TWENTY-THREE
Alice

Alice felt the two men's' arms around her helping her up onto a stool. Her vision started to come back into focus again. Benny was in front of looking into her eyes. "Alice! Alice! Can you see me?" Benny was saying to her. She nodded and went to touch the gash on her head, but Marcus stopped her by slapping her hand.

"Nope I don't want you touching that, you look like you've been through hell so not sure I want it getting infected," Marcus told her. She could see him pouring something onto a cotton ball. "What are you doing?" she asked.

"I'm cleaning that nasty cut," Marcus told her. She looked at Benny who was grimacing at her head. The expressions Benny was making let her know it must have been bad.

"Sorry, I wasn't sure where to go but knew you guys had medical training," she told them.

She could see Benny looking her over and she knew she should say something.

"I was in a car crash," she said. They both gave her funny looks, so she shrugged her shoulders. "What?" She asked.

"Um, why didn't you go to the hospital?" Benny asked.

"The radio went down before I crashed and there's some kind of virus that's probably got the hospital swamped so I didn't want to add to their burden with my little cut." She told them, rolling her eyes. Benny was looking over at Marcus and that's when she remembered the expression Marcus had when he saw her at the door.

"What's going on? There's something you guys aren't telling me" She could feel it now that they were keeping something from her.

"I killed your dog!" Marcus blurted out.

Her heart sank as since her kids had gone off to college that dog had been her roommate and best friend. That's when the anger filled her.

"You fucking what?!" she yelled, jumping from the stool swinging a fist at Marcus. She felt her feet lift off the ground as Benny wrapped his arms around her and lifted her up so she couldn't get to Marcus. The scared man had backed himself into the kitchen sink knocking over dishes.

"It's not what you think! I had to! He was attacked wasn't going to make it!" Marcus explained. It took a few minutes to register but she could feel her heart slow down.

"I'm good," she let Benny know.

Benny put her down gently, "Marcus did you a favor," Benny said.

"What do you mean attacked?" she asked but she had a feeling what the answer would be.

"One of those things...an infected person, it was eating Max, I...I...froze and Benny saved me but Max he was whimpering, his insides were all strewn across the grass...so...I put him down," Marcus had tears in his eyes. She thought as much, that it has been because of one of these things...these infected. She'd known these two men for years and knew Marcus didn't have a malicious bone in his body.

"I'm sorry Marcus, I know you wouldn't hurt Max on purpose I just haven't been thinking right. It's been a rough night," she apologized. "What happened to the guy who attacked Max?" she asked looking at Benny.

She could tell the Native American was nervous as he was biting his lip. She was good at reading people as it was part of her job. "I...um...I put him down, but you have to understand Alice, these aren't people...not anymore" Benny said trying to justify himself, but he didn't need to.

Alice had seen so much tonight she knew something was up. "It's okay I've seen them tonight too. And put one down myself," she said sadly.

"So, you definitely had a rough night," Marcus said with a half-smile.

"Yeah you could say that, seems like the whole world's gone crazy," she said with a fake chuckle. Even though she meant it partly as a joke she knew she was right. The way things were going down it definitely looked that way.

"They're definitely not people, that's for sure" Marcus said in a sad tone.

"I heard there was a virus but didn't think it would be anything like this," she said.

"Benny said FEMA showed up at the old folk's home and took charge..." Marcus said handing her a water.

"Thanks" she said taking it and cracking it open. She was thirsty and wasn't sure if it was due to shock or if she had been infected with whatever these cannibalistic crack heads had. She knew she was just being paranoid, well, at least she hoped she was just paranoid.

"I think we all need one of these," Benny said pulling a bottle of vodka and some shot glasses from a cupboard.

"Really? Do you think now's the time Benny?" Marcus argued.

She could feel a little tension as Benny glared at Marcus. "Tell me we've all not had a day? A fuckin' bitch of a fucking day!" Benny said loudly.

"I'll take one...maybe two." Alice nodded.

"Fine! I'll take one, too, I guess" Marcus said squinting his face. They took a shot then another then Alice stood up as she knew it was all getting too much.

"Be right back, need to use the restroom," she told them. She didn't really need the bathroom but wanted some space. Alice could feel it swelling up inside her and needed some privacy just for a few minutes to compose herself. Once inside she locked the door then sank to the floor crying. Max was all she had, and her kids were miles away and despite how tough an act she always put on what had happened tonight had finally wore her down. Wiping away the tears with her grimy sleeve she knew she was tough. She always had been, not just at work but at home as a single mom raising two kids and all that life had thrown at her.

When she walked out of the bathroom the two guys were still sitting at the table. Benny looked at her, "You okay?" he asked getting up from his stool.

She'd cleaned her face, but it must have still been obvious she'd been crying.

"Yeah, I'll be fine," she told them reassuring herself as well as them. Sitting back down on the stool she couldn't help but let out a laugh.

Marcus already had more shots poured. Benny sat back down, and they didn't ask but for some reason she started talking, reciting her day and didn't know why.

"I slept all day," she began. "I had my usual pre-shift meeting but there were a lot of my colleagues missing, some were over in Portland, but others just didn't show up…I figured running late," she said then took the shot. It burned as it went down but was definitely helping the pain both physical and emotional.

"We were all told that the call volume had been a lot higher and they we were to just to deal with the load as best we could." She got angry as she said this. It hadn't seemed at the time, but her superiors must have had some kind of idea of what was going on.

"My first call of the night was dealing with an attempted home invasion by a man who seemed crazy then a group of kids were attacking a man...or something but he definitely didn't seem human" She said her shot glass towards Marcus nodding at the bottle.

Marcus was looking worried and staring at her head.

"Maybe a bad idea with the shots if that's a concussion and with the situation right now..." Marcus began saying apologetically. Benny grabbed the bottle and she noticed the glare Benny was giving Marcus.

"Are you kidding me! I've seen zombie movies. Those are fucking zombies out there, shit's got real and hit the fan real hard!" Benny blurted out to Marcus as he poured more shots.

She could feel the tension between these two but wasn't sure exactly what it was.

"What about your work? Did they give you any more info about the virus? Other than what's on the news?" Marcus asked. She felt a bit embarrassed as she didn't really pay attention to the news. It was all pretty much bullshit political agenda, she thought, but now wished she had.

"Umm, no, I just got up then went straight to work. Why? Is there info on what's going on?" she asked.

Marcus shook his head "It's been getting worse all day and night; the news has been telling people to avoid travel and to follow the instructions of emergency services and law enforcement in their area" Marcus said meekly. She could feel disappointment of the last part of what he had said. She was a cop and knowing less of what was happening then he mustn't have been very reassuring.

"Cell service went off around ten," Benny chimed in sliding another shot over to her.

"When I woke up my radio was smashed but I knew before then something was up with the signal, there was no reply from my precinct which meant there was no one there," she said.

"There was an explosion over near the police precinct on Mill Plain, maybe a transmitter or tower went out," Marcus said.

Alice shook her head knowing that wouldn't happen. "Nah, ever since Katrina, Homeland Security put things into place so that our communications went through satellites and used wireless technology so we wouldn't have to rely on things like those in extreme disaster situations," she said and could feel how dire this must have sounded about the situation.

Benny got up. "I think we should try to get some rest, one of us stay on watch at a time," Benny said as he walked towards the window and looked out towards the street. "The gunshots and noises have calmed down a bit and when it gets light, it'll be easier to see what's going on and figure things out from there," Benny said, looking at her then to Marcus.

She knew that sounded easier said than it was as she had so much going through her head.

Marcus got up and walked out of the room. She didn't want to go home and be alone but didn't want to ask to stay. A sigh of relief came over her when Marcus came back into the room with some blankets and a pillow. "Thank you" she told him. Marcus nodded then looked over at Benny who was still looking outside.

"Benny, Alice can have the couch. Do you want me to keep watch first?" Marcus asked.

Benny didn't even turn around "Nah, I got it, you go get some rest," Benny said.

Alice got herself situated and all comfy curled up on the guys' couch. Sleep wasn't coming easy though between the pounding of her head and what was racing through her mind. The vodka had definitely dulled the pain a bit. She squeezed her eyes tight at the thought of her dog being eaten by one of these crazies and her having shot someone. She was a mess, but she knew she had to pull it together.

She thought back to how things had been so normal that day. She replayed it over in her head, hoping it would make sense. The roads had seemed a little busier than usual, there was the increased volume of calls that they had been warned about. It started to make a little sense to her now. It hadn't just been tonight; it had been building up for days. All the increased reports of violent acts and police shootings all around the country. If officers had been in the situation Alice had been in tonight, she totally understood why they would shoot these people. Virus or not, these guys felt no pain and were just plain crazy. She could feel herself relaxing and nodding off then was snapped out of it by a blood curdling scream coming from what sounded like a female outside.

CHAPTER TWENTY-FOUR
Benny

T he high-pitched scream came from right outside and chilled him to the bone. Benny had been sipping a coffee to try keep himself awake. He had been dozing off, staring out the kitchen window at the moon in the sky outside. The last hour or so had been quiet and with what he'd been through, Benny could feel his body wanting to turn off. That's when the scream had come from the front of the house and it made him jump, instantly awakening his mind and body. The coffee cup fell into the sink as he turned and ran for the front door.

"Benny!" Marcus shouted throwing a hatchet from halfway down the stairs.

Benny caught it in midair then stepped into the living room where Alice was sitting up on the couch staring at the window with the blanket pulled up and wrapped around her. He crept over to the window and peered out from behind the curtain.

"You going out there? With that?" Alice asked him from the couch. He nodded, trying to focus on the street outside. It was dark with only two dim street lights lighting up the road. He saw some movement right in front of the house in the middle of the road. He could make out some shape on the ground moving slightly.

Opening the front door slowly to not make too much sound he then crept low outside making his way to the street. As he got to his gate his could see two dark shapes on the ground. He could hear a wet, grunting, slobbering sound. Looking closely, squinting his eyes he could make out two different shapes. One looked like lady laying on the ground not really moving. The other appeared to be a man with his back to him crouched over the lady. Benny knew he had to make this quick, quiet and couldn't hesitate. In one fluid motion Benny leapt over the small gate then sprinted towards the two. The man on top of the woman must have heard him as the slobbering stopped.

Benny could make out the woman's face pretty good as he ran towards them. Whoever this lady was she was dead with a lifeless gaunt look twisted onto her face. The empty eyes were looking in his direction but hadn't moved since he'd got to the gate. As the man's head turned mid feast towards Benny it was too late. Benny didn't change direction or hesitate to swing the axe as hard as he could. The man's face was empty and covered in blood with glassy white eyes staring at Benny as the axe came slicing across the man's temple. It felt like hitting a baseball with one of those mini bats Benny thought to himself. It sliced through the man's temple, sending blood and pieces of bone flying in all directions. It made a wet dull sound as it took out the corner of the man's skull. The man fell at an awkward angle towards the ground and landed with a wet slap on the asphalt. Benny just stood there breathing heavily with blood dripping from the axe.

He was waiting for the man to move or try and get back up. Instead the man just lay there next to the women both lifeless, only the man was missing a corner of his face and skull.

Glancing down at the woman he hoped he could get a better look and maybe recognize the lady, but he didn't. He knew most of his immediate neighbors and recognized the rest that lived in the next few streets, but he didn't recognize this lady. He felt a kind of relief that she wasn't someone he knew then at the same time this also worried him. Since coming home from the rehab center, the only immediate neighbors he'd seen had been Alice.

148

He looked over so see Marcus and Alice both in the doorway. Marcus began walking out of the house towards him, but he put his hand up. Stopping in his tracks he could tell Marcus was looking at the bodies at his feet. Luckily the lighting outside wasn't great so he could see any of the gruesome details he had.

"Marcus...go back inside, I'll be in in a minute. There could be more of them," he said trying to hold it together. Alice walked down and put her arm around Marcus's shoulder to pull him back towards the house. As the two headed back inside he turned and looked down the street but there was nothing just eerie silence. He wasn't sure if this was a good thing or bad thing. He knew the best thing they could do was just follow the steps that had been on the news and hold out till morning. The news had stated that FEMA and local authorities would be stepping in to restore law and order. He knew firsthand from the old folk's home that FEMA weren't here to help. If anything, they were here to contain this thing by any means necessary.

After a few moments he walked back inside to find both Marcus and Alice in the living room. The TV was on, but it was just the same message now with no news presenter narration or change in image. AVOID, DENY, DEFEND were still in big bold letters on the screen with a message at the bottom saying the local authorities are working hard to get the situation under control.

Benny was beginning to sense Marcus's frustration at the situation but before he could say anything Marcus blurted out, "I don't understand?" Marcus began looking around the room. "We're supposed to just sit here and wait... all this has happened so fast and we're just stuck in limbo with no more information that what we're getting," Marcus's face was red with anger.

"We just need to get some rest and tomorrow if we don't get answers, we'll go find some ourselves," Benny said reassuringly but saw Marcus roll his eyes.

"How are we going to do that? Where should we go? Because according to you those FEMA guys aren't really that friendly," Marcus said like a bickering spouse.

"We don't need to go to Battleground, the news said there was a FEMA camp being set up at the school over by Jake's" He fired back.

"Good idea, we can check on Jake and his family too...they're probably just as freaked out as us" Alice said worryingly. Alice had been friends with Jake longer than he had.

"One thing though, if we go, we agree we're not going with FEMA anywhere or letting them try and take us" he said looking at them both in the eyes.

Marcus nodded but he could sense apprehension from Alice and could understand why so he tried to explain his doubts about FEMA's real intentions.

"Look these people will kill us if we don't cooperate and today it seemed like they were more concerned with quarantining everybody than helping anyone sick or needing it," he said, hoping to get how he felt across.

Alice nodded, "We're not going to do anything against our will...I agree...so before we go, we're getting all the ammo and guns from my place." Alice said.

Benny nodded feeling confident in what they had planned. "Sounds good, let's get what sleep we can and then pack up early," he said.

CHAPTER TWENTY-FIVE
Nick

Nick lay there exhausted, staring at the ceiling of the hotel room. He'd been awake all night just lying there. He originally wanted to get some sleep maybe just a couple of hours but that didn't happen. Not with everything that was going on inside of his head. So much had been running through his mind all night. From his wife and baby girl to how crazy people had been last night.

The homeless guy being shot and seeing the two bodies on the ground below his hotel had really disturbed him, what was the world coming to?

The noise of what was going on in downtown Seattle had kept him awake, too. Sirens had been pretty much a constant all night then there were gunshots. He'd heard glass smashing, metal grinding as cars hit each other. It had been a long night, but Nick forced himself not to go to the window as he knew there was nothing he could do.

He hadn't heard any sirens in a little bit, and it was starting to get light outside. He knew the first train was around 7:00 am. So, he figured he should probably get to the station before it opened. He needed to get in then exchange his ticket as quickly as possible. The sooner he was on his way home to his girls the better. He sat up and swung his legs off the edge of the bed.

Nick had laid in his clothes all night and still felt a groggy from his lack of sleep. Getting up, he walked over to the window rubbing his tired heavy eyes. Opening up the blinds, he looked outside to check for any signs of what had gone on last night. What he'd heard all night definitely hadn't prepared him for what he saw outside. There was a haze of smoke lingering between the buildings with dark plumes of smoke rising up in the distance. He looked down and saw the street below littered with trash, glass, and even a car had mounted the sidewalk. The car's hood was smoking but there was no one around it. There was no traffic at all, and he laughed to himself.

He pulled out the business card of the cabby who'd brought him here. The streets were a mess, so he didn't want to risk getting swept up in any rioting or protesting. The only focus he had was getting home. He dialed the number; it rang then someone picked up.

"'Ello?" boomed the loud familiar cabby's voice.

"Hey! Hi, it's Nick the guy from yesterday, are you working?" he asked, not sure if it was just the immediate downtown area in tatters or the rest of Seattle, too.

"I always work, my friend, no matter how much shit storm it is..." the cabby said.

There was a pause "-but I still don't know who you are?" the cabby asked.

Nick thought to himself, he had not given the cabbie his name.

"It's the grilled cheese guy!" Nick said with a small smile to himself. He could tell the cabby knew who he was when the man let out that big deep laugh.

"I'm at the hotel and need to get to the train station as soon as possible," he told him.

The cabby was still laughing to himself "Of course, Mr. Cheese," the man laughed. "It's pretty crazy right now but I will be there in ten to fifteen minutes, I honk horn." the cabby told him then hung up.

Nick pulled some jerky out and started to snack on it. As he did, he gave his duffle bag a once over, then his EDC bag. He knew if things got sticky the EDC bag would get him out of a lot of situations and keep him safe. It was good, he thought, as after laying there all-night hearing what had been going on outside, he knew he should be ready for anything. It was good, so he buckled the one strap over the front of his chest. Grabbing his duffle bag, he headed for the hotel room door. Opening the door, he almost took out a housekeeper. The small lady was pushing a housekeeping cart past his room,

"Sorry!" he exclaimed as he slipped past the cart raising his arms to avoid hitting it. The small Hispanic lady give out a sigh, glaring at him. The lady muttered something in Spanish then turned to knock on the door next to Nick's room. He walked towards the elevators and pushed the call button.

As he waited, he could hear the lady go from a light knock to pounding on the door. *Wasting your time,* he thought as the lady called out, "Room service!" Then as he heard her opening the door, she let out a horrific shriek. Startled, he turned to see the woman backing up with her hands in the air screaming in terror!

He moved away from the elevator towards the rooms so he could see what was scaring the housemaid so bad. He reached out his hand to grab her shoulder as he walked towards the room. Then he saw him or it in the room lying on the ground wrapped in a shower curtain thrashing about. It was a person laying halfway through the shattered glass bathroom door and into the hotel room. The maid fell to the ground hysterically screaming. Nick could tell it was too entwined in the curtain and caught on the glass in the door frame to get to her. Torn flesh was caught and ripped from its abdominal area in the bathroom door frame. A huge spike of glass was impaled through its leg and shower curtain. He bent down and put his hands on the housemaid's shoulders.

"C'mon, get up!" he barked, helping her up. Looking at the person entwined in the shower curtain he was shocked. It was a guy who must have been in his thirties or forties. Even though the guy was wrapped in the curtain he could see dried red splotches of blood that had bled through. These looked like they were from the cuts all over his body from the glass.

The man's face was lacerated open with dried blood all over his face. He had obviously been in there for a while. After a few snaps of its jaws and grasping at the air with splintered glass covered arms, its head fell to the ground, Nick recognized this as the thump he had been hearing which meant this guy had been like this for at least twenty-four hours.

Nick helped the maid towards the elevator, the door was opened and they both got in. The maid was standing with her hands over her face crying and talking hysterically in Spanish, Nick put his duffle bag on the ground. As he began hitting the "L" for lobby button he wiped a film of sweat from his forehead.

"What the fuck was that?!" he shouted out in the elevator pounding his fist on the elevator wall. He was prepared for a lot of things but not for what he had just seen…that man had been in that shower curtain stuck in that door frame for over twenty-four hours! The guy should have bled out from all those cuts from falling through the glass, but he was just lying there like a possessed, half dead zombie trying to get to the maid.

The elevator dinged as the doors opened to the lobby, grabbing his bag he put his arm around the maid and the two walked out into the lobby. It was deathly silent with not even anyone at the check in desk.

The maid darted away from him, heading behind the check-in desk pushing a door open to what must have been a staff only area. Nick was about to call out to her when he saw his cab pull up at high speed and screech to a halt. The cabby pounded on the horn; it was loud with how silent the street was outside. He turned and headed out and as he stepped out into the city, he couldn't believe how quiet it was. There were no cars honking or sirens filling the air. He wasn't sure if this was a good or a bad thing. The cabby got out and flashed Nick his big pearly smile.

"You miss me, Mr. Grilled Cheese, huh?" The cabby chuckled before opening the passenger door for Nick. The cabby looked around then got back in the car.

"You know what's going on?" Nick asked him to jump in the car. He was hoping to get more answers on what was going on downtown, but the cabby shrugged his shoulders.

"I told you, man" the cabby began. "People are going crazy, says on news to avoid people who are acting nuts," the cabby laughed.

Nick wasn't sure what the man found so funny, but he was shaking. The cabby's attitude kind of calmed him a bit.

"Train station?" the cabby asked, and Nick nodded staring back at the hotel. "Might have to go the long way, the army and police are blocking off parts of downtown but will try get you there in time for train," the cabby said with a wild look in his eyes. Then the cab pulled out with an ear-piercing screech of rubber on asphalt.

As the taxi drove up the hill, Nick was looking down the side streets. He could see people scurrying across the empty roads. There were broken windows here and there but nothing that gave away how dire the situation was. As they got to the top of a hill and turned, Nick looked at the view overlooking downtown. It looked trashed; he could see some plumes of smoke but there were no sirens so who was fighting the fires?

"Fuck ass!" the cabby blurted out as the cab slammed to a halt. The road was blocked ahead with barriers and two armed soldiers waving at them to turn around. The cabby turned and looked past Nick out the rear window. The cab was slammed into reverse and it spun around, causing Nick to slide in the seats. As they headed back the way they had come, he gripped his EDC bag tight.

As they headed back down the hill, Nick was noticing signs he'd missed when they drove that way.

They looked like the ones used on the freeway with lit up instructions, as they passed one it read:

"FEMA Shelter & Emergency Medical Services located by waterfront aqueduct," they had gotten on the scene fast, Nick thought to himself. Usually FEMA is late to the party, but they seemed to be on top of it this time. As they got closer to the train station and nearer the waterfront, the streets were starting to get busier. There were homeless people pushing carts and families with cases heading towards the waterfront like rats fleeing a sinking ship.

"Wow! Worse than earlier," the cabby said, honking the horn at people who were walking in the middle of the street. They turned off to a side street and Nick could see the train station a couple of blocks ahead of them. As they pulled up there was a crowd at the doors with security guarding the door pushing people back. He could see people waving cash at the security, trying to push a way through. He watched as the guards just pushed the people back, keeping the entryway secure. There must be thirty or forty people, Nick thought to himself. The cabby mounted the sidewalk with the right side of the taxi. Nick looked at the cabby in the rearview mirror then nodded his approval.

"That was a quick trip, Mr. Grilled Cheese! I hope you make it home safe, hopefully all this will be over soon, and you'll be back to visit Seattle again," the cabby said, upbeat, tapping the meter.

"It's Nick and I kinda doubt that," he said looking at the fare. It was more than double what it had been the day before. The cabby must have caught the expression on his face.

"Hazard pay! Been a crazy morning…Nick."

Nick smiled "Yeah, I get it, thanks," he said, throwing him the fare plus an extra fifteen.

"Good luck, Nick," the cabbie said smiling as Nick got out. Nick half smiled then some people from the crowd came rushing towards the cab pushing past him.

Nick got to the back of the crowd at the train station entrance and noticed a sign on the door; "ticket holding travelers only!" Not to draw too much attention to himself Nick stepped back, pulling his ticket out and waving it. One of the security guards saw it and waved him through. Nick had to push through, clutching his bags tight. As he got to the front of the crowd, a security guard pushed some people out the way. Flashing his ticket up a guard opened the door for him while the others held the crowd back.

CHAPTER TWENTY-SIX
Mason

Mason closed his eyes to try to get some sleep now that his wife had gotten Abby, their baby to sleep. Abby was their youngest daughter had been restless most of the flight from SeaTac airport in Washington. He figured now he could close his eyes and get some rest. The plane's intercom speaker crackled as an announcement came from a male who must have been part of the crew in the plane's cockpit.

"Attention ladies and gentlemen! This is your captain speaking, unfortunately due to events out of our control we will not be making our scheduled layover stop in Minsk. I will keep you all updated as soon as I receive more information. Any passengers with Minsk as their final destination will be given transfers from the airport we touch down at. Thank you again for flying British Airways,"

This stirred up quite a bit of excitement in the cabin as people began waving their hands around to attract the flight attendants attention. A lot of people began whipping out cell phones frantically trying to make calls. Mason just smiled to himself as he looked over at his wife Alex who was sleeping peacefully with their baby, Abby, on her chest.

"Daddy!" His other daughter said tugging at his arm to get his attention. "Why are you smiling, Daddy?" Sarah asked.

Sarah was his other daughter and was very, very smart for a four-year-old. Mason just smiled more.

"Well, we were supposed to stop at Minsk for a three-hour layover before the plane took off again for Edinburgh. Now

158

hopefully we'll get there sooner as your little sister isn't having a good time," he whispered to his little girl. Sarah nodded like she fully understood then got back to coloring her book. This trip had been eye opening for both Alex and him. He'd wanted to take his girls to Scotland to visit his home. They had planned to go long before now, but the girls had put a stop to that. Both girls were a little bigger now so they figured they would give it a shot. They had assumed both girls would be restless maybe with a tantrum or two. They thought they had planned ahead accordingly with snacks and distractions. They hadn't helped Abby at all who cried most of the first part of the flight. The surprise had been how good Sarah had been at acting like a big sister.

Mason's heart had melted when Abby had started crying when the plane took off and Sarah immediately came to her little sister's aid. Sarah had offered Abby some candy then a crayon to help color which had calmed the baby for all of about two minutes

He'd thought that was a nice surprise and now they were bypassing the Minsk stop. Hopefully this would get them to their vacation destination sooner. If there were more pleasant surprises with this trip, then he'd be okay with that. He could hear some people in the seats behind him complaining to a stewardess.

One guy about the missed stop then another guy that they weren't getting any Wi-Fi signal.

Pulling out his call phone Mason unlocked it to see for himself. Sure enough, there was no service on his phone. The last thing he saw on Facebook was his news feed filling up with both Pro- and Anti-Police posts. So not having Wi-Fi___33 wasn't too much of a problem for him at all.

The intercom chimed again causing most of the cabin to go silent, waiting to hear more from the Captain.

"Hello again, ladies and gentlemen. This is your captain again. I wanted to let you all know that shortly we'll be landing at Brest

159

International Airport. For those of you who had Minsk as a final destination you will be transferred from here. I will keep you updated with info as I receive it," The captain finished then the intercom chimed off. This seemed to set a lot of passengers at ease which hopefully meant it would get a little quieter again.

"What's happening?" Alex asked rubbing her eyes trying to wake up.

"It's okay, honey, you can go back to sleep. We're not laying over in Minsk anymore, instead it'll be another airport in Belarus," He told her brushing the hair away from his wife's half open eyes.

Alex smiled then closed her eyes drifting back off to sleep again he thought.

Two flight attendants rushed down the aisle past their seats towards the front of the plane. It must have caught his daughters attention, too, as Sarah was looking up from her book down the aisle. A man came through the curtains at the front of the cabin pushing past the two attendants. They were trying to talk to the man who was well dressed in a suit. The man shouted past the attendants into the cabin.

"Please! Does anyone have a phone I can use?" the man asked looking around.

The man flapped his arms in disappointment then a male attendant grabbed the man. The man spun, pushing the attendant over into some seats then pointed a finger at the female attendant.

"Why won't you let me use the plane's phone?" the man asked frantically. Another man dressed in jeans and tight white t- shirt walked up to the man in the suit flashing a badge.

"Is he a cop?" Sarah blurted out.

"Nah, honey that's an Air Marshal, they're on every plane," he told her, rubbing her head.

"Marshall like from Paw Patrol?" Sarah giggled.

"Yeah, kinda, does the same kind of job, now go back to coloring, sweetie" he told her trying to keep her calm.

The Marshal pulled the man back through the curtain towards the front of the plane. This had been where the man had come from, near the front. Mason settled back into his seat then Sarah cuddled into his arm making him feel suddenly at ease.

HE WAS WOKEN up by a loud overhead announcement telling everyone to prepare to land. Yawning, he looked over to see Alex feeding Abby. He must have been more tired than he thought as he hadn't even been woken up by them. He helped get Abby into her car seat to prepare for the landing. He wasn't sure how long they'd have to wait at the airport to reboard the plane or if they'd even have to get off this plane.

A flight attendant began walking past checking seat belts, so he waved her close.

"Hey, you wouldn't happen to know if we'll be changing planes when we land would you? Or are we just staying on this one?" He asked.

The stewardess smiled at him and he could tell it was forced. "Yes, everyone will have to disembark the plane then head into the main terminal sir, from there you'll be directed what to do next," The lady told him, checking his seat belt.

"Okay, thanks," he replied back with a forced smirk of his own.

Once the plane came to a full stop, they grabbed what carry-on luggage they had brought on. From the plane to the main terminal building it was a short walk on old beat up asphalt with planes parked everywhere. As they entered the main terminal, Mason was surprised how packed it was with people. Everyone was standing looking at either TVs showing the news or the huge flight information boards up on a wall. He was holding Abby's car seat that she was in, asleep, seat with one hand and his other had their two carry on duffle bags. He looked at Sarah who was stuck tight to Alex's leg. Normally Sarah would always want to be independent, walking beside them everywhere they went, refusing to hold either of their hands. He could tell Sarah was overwhelmed by the amount of people crammed into the terminal.

"Let's go check the information board see if our flight is on it," he said to his wife.

Alex didn't reply, his wife was staring at the TV's on the walls along with most of the other people around in the terminal. He looked up to see news broadcasts on all of the TVs that were scattered around the terminal. They weren't all showing the exact same footage but definitely all of this was happening here in Europe. He could tell even though he didn't speak Russian which is what the native language in Belarus was, that the people around him were worried.

He also couldn't read any of the writing that was appearing on most of the TV's, but he got the point that something big was happening. There was footage of planes getting loaded with missiles. Another had footage of riots in the streets of some European city with a name he wouldn't even try to pronounce.

"Oh my...that's Kiev," a man standing behind him said in English.

He could tell the man was referring to footage being shown of protesters clashing with police.

Alex must have heard the man too.

"Where's that?" Alex asked whispering to him.

Looking at his wife he replied "It's a city in Ukraine not far from Minsk"

Granted it was across the border so the riots happening there probably weren't the reason the plane had been diverted. There were similar protests happening back in America that hopefully weren't turning into riots like these.

It seemed a bit of a coincidence that they were having problems this side of the globe, too.

He'd hoped after showing his family the place he grew up that they would want to move to Scotland. He loved America but the political extremes and increasing civil unrest had made him think of a fresh start for his family. Just as he was about to reassure his wife that the riots and the diversion from Minsk was just a coincidence, shouting filled the air. They looked over to where all the angry sounding voices were coming from. They weren't speaking English, but the anger came through all the same. As did the gestures of closed fists that he was glad his wife and daughter were too short to see. The people were crowded round the flight information boards that had security guards holding rifles standing at the bottom. The guards were signaling people to get back.

"What's going on?" His wife asked scared.

Looking at the information boards he could see what everyone was getting so angry about.

Every outgoing flight said "SUSPENDED" next to it. On the arrival screen theirs was the last plan scheduled for some reason and it was still early.

Their flight along with the other incoming flights listed all said "LANDED"

He was confused as to why the plane had been diverted from Minsk only to be grounded here. The shouting coming the people wanting to know about their flights was getting louder and more intense. With his lack of fluent Russian, it could definitely become a problem if things escalated quickly.

"C'mon" he said to his wife nodding towards the far end of the terminal.

As they moved through the crowded terminal, he noticed more and more soldiers. He'd never seen so many armed men in an airport before. Granted, he hadn't been to many European airports, but the number of armed soldiers just didn't seem right. The soldiers were setting up barriers throughout the terminal which seemed the size of a pitch with the same big arching roof overhead.

Looking up, he saw a sign with an arrow, it wasn't English but seemed like a universal sign for exit which told him they were headed in the right direction. He noted that as he caught sight of another universal sign that he was looking for.

As they approached the circular Information kiosk there were three female staff members manning the booth. They seemed to be struggling, trying to help the small crowd of a dozen gathered around. Looking at them, they were dressed in black slacks, aqua blue polo shirts with the Belarus flag embroidered onto the chest pocket. This was something he'd expect tourist information workers to wear, not airport information officials.

He was about to tell Alex to wait with his daughters near the kiosk while he found an airport employee, but he froze. The noise was deafening, he wasn't sure if it was echoing or repeating as more shots were being fired. The gunshots drowned out the sea of people who were fussing and complaining seconds before. Those same people were now a sea of screams and crying as the airport terminal erupted   into   chaos.

CHAPTER TWENTY-SEVEN
Nick

Inside the Seattle train station, the atmosphere was completely different than the chaos going on at the entrance. The station was pretty full, but he couldn't see any staff walking around. The big board above the door leading out to the tracks only had seven trains up for the whole day. Usually there would have been almost two dozen. Nick looked at a poster on the wall, it was a "germs info" poster about covering your mouth when you cough or sneeze with some advice on washing hands. Nick made his way to the bag check in where the ticket desk was so he could hopefully exchange his ticket.

He hadn't thought this far ahead and was just winging it at this point. Entering the room where the ticket help desk was, he greeted with an empty kiosk. Nick looked at the guy at the next kiosk which was for checking bags in. The guy seemed a little distant, coughing and sweating profusely. The man's face was dark red with beads of sweat dripping down onto whatever the man was zoning out at on the desk. The bright red face reminded Nick of someone who had a drinking problem and were a natural flushed. Nick walked up to the window, tapping it gently to get the man's attention without startling the guy.

"Hey, can you help me? I need to change my ticket," Nick asked.

The guy wiped his forehead with a rag that was on the desk. "No," the man said blankly.

"There's no ticket alterations today, we may be closed tomorrow and looking like the next few days," the man said before going into a coughing fit.

Nick looked the man who obviously wasn't in the best shape, the guy had sweat beads all over his face. Nick knew that was enough information for him. "Okay, okay thanks" he said nodding as he slowly walked backwards away from the glass.

He saw the long line of people waiting to head out to board a train. Nick looked up at the board to check the platform for the Portland train: G6 it read to Portland. He knew he had to get to G6 and get on that train. There's no way he could afford to be stuck here for a few days not with how bad the situation was getting. Nick looked around the room to see if there was maybe someone, he could buy a ticket from. Nick's brain felt like it was going to explode with questions on what to do if no one would sell him one. He walked as if on autopilot towards the line that was formed of people waiting to board trains.

"Portland!" a man shouted from the front of the line. Nick looked towards the doors leading out to the platforms. There were two men in safety vests standing at the front of the line. One of the men was talking into a walkie-talkie while looking between the platform and the line. The other man was checking tickets of people at the front of the line.

All he had was his over the shoulder EDC bag and the duffle which could be carried. As he inched his way closer to the front of the line, he heard the man's radio crackle.

"Brian! Let them out! Let them get on the trains we have to leave now," a male voice said. The man with the walkie didn't reply but instead started checking tickets, too. Another railway worker came over and opened a second set of doors to let people go out and began checking tickets, too. All he needed to do was just make his way past the ticket checker to the doors.

He could hear angry shouts coming from behind him at the station entrance. Then suddenly shots rang out from outside the station. Nick looked towards the entrance where the shots had come from. There was something going on outside he couldn't see. The security guards were blocking the view through the huge glass doors. Then two of the guards came inside locking the door behind them. The other guards outside still seemed to be holding people back. The crowd inside the station started to panic as more shots rang out. At the front of the line, Nick could see the guy with the walkie was focused on the front doors. The guy wasn't even checking and was just waving people past. Nick moved through the line knowing this was his chance. As he neared the front of the line, he moved towards the guy just letting people through. Almost at the front the sound of glass shattering seemed to slow down time. Then screams mixed in with more gunshots filled the air.

The line Nick was in turned into a wave of people rushing the doors leading outside to the trains. Turning as he passed through the door, he saw a security guard lying on the ground surrounded by broken glass. A crowd of people were pushing through the broken glass panel on the door. "Close those doors! No one is boarding those trains!" a voice said across a bullhorn.

Nick knew this was his chance and pushed people out the way as he sprinted through the people making a break for the doors! Once outside everyone began scrambling in different directions to get to their train's platforms. People were running across empty tracks to get to platform G6 for Portland, so he did, too. As Nick climbed up onto the G6 platform, there was a train conductor at a door waving people to get in. As he climbed aboard, he was instantly hit with a wave of heat and the sound of kids crying. Nick made his way through the carriages to the middle where he found some empty chairs facing each other. He sat down after stowing his duffle bag in the spot above the seats. He slid his EDC bag under his seat wanting

167

to keep it close. Slumping into the chair he looked outside to see people still trickling out the station. What looked like soldiers were now trying to grab people which caught him by surprise. His attention was grabbed by some arguing coming his way. It was an older lady with faded red hair tied back, thick glasses, and a long beige cardigan with a brown skirt that went to her ankles. The lady was dressed like a librarian and was bickering with two children she had with her. A boy who must have been around five or six in a Minecraft t-shirt and a girl probably in her late teens in a Seahawks hoodie with holey jeans.

Quite the happy family, Nick thought feeling sorry for whoever was sat near this trio. Nick looked down to notice there was a purse under the seat directly opposite his. The boy in the Minecraft shirt jumped down into the chair next to Nick. Then the two others sat down in Nicks grouping of chairs both still bickering.

The boy leaned over Nick craning out the window. Nick got a whiff of sweaty child while getting close up of the boys buzz cut. Then the boy turned to Nick, "Anything cool?" The boy asked.

Before Nick could answer, a voice came over the intercom as the train started to move.

"Hello everyone and welcome to the early morning Amtrak service from Seattle to Portland, the doors are now locked and due to the present circumstances even though we are due for departure in 8 minutes, we will be departing immediately, unfortunately we may have to bypass some of the stops on our route due to the stations being closed but I will keep you up to date on this info as it happens, I do apologize for the lack of Wi-Fi on this service as it's currently unavailable," the voice clicked off.

As the train was moving there were still people running towards it! They were waving bags and tickets, but the train sped out of the station. The boy turned to Nick again, "We saw a guy get shot on our way to the station this morning, army guys were in the street and just lit him up," the boy said seeming pleased. The lady with the boy gave a dirty look "Michael! Keep quiet!" the lady snapped.

Looking at Nick, the lady said, "I'm sorry it's been a rough morning and he's a little excited," the lady told him, glaring at the little boy. The kid didn't seem to care, though, looking out the window on the other side of the aisle.

"No problem, there's a lot going on," Nick answered with a forced, close-lipped smile. Looking around the cabin there was still a bunch of empty seats so not all the passengers made it. Probably due to the melt down at the train station the driver must have thought it best to maybe just start up and go. Nick wasn't complaining things were only getting crazier and who knows what was going on with the Army arriving on the scene. Nick was glad he was on his way home, though, despite how crazy it was getting.

"You guys been on the train for a while?" he asked. He noted that the boy mentioned seeing someone shot but no mention of the shots that were just being fired outside the station itself.

The boy nodded then opened his mouth to talk but before he could answer the old lady cut him off.

"Yes, we were some of the first on the train, we've been outside the station all morning ever since we were woken up by the sirens and all the big Army trucks," the lady told him.

If a state of emergency was declared because of this outbreak then in a city the size of Seattle, the military involvement was a given. Nick was a prepper and had gone over scenarios in his head like this before. These people he was sitting with though, to them it was probably something they'd never imagined.

The lady reached under her seat and grabbed the purse he'd seen. Delving her hands into the purse, the lady brought out some knitting needles. Attached to the needles was a work in progress and a ball of yarn. "It keeps me calm," The lady said noticing he was watching.

The girl next to the lady sighed "Oh my God! You act so old!" the girl said, rolling her eyes and putting her head against the window looking out.

The girl jumped in her seat, letting out a squeal bumping into the lady who then swatted at the girl. "Heidi! For goodness' sakes what are you doing? Sit still, girl!!" the lady barked at the girl.

Heidi was sat sideways in her chair with her hand covering her mouth.

"What did you see?" the boy asked.

She turned to the boy "There was a guy just standing looking at the train covered in blood," The girl said scared

The old lady sighed then slammed the knitting needles down. "Heidi! Do not start acting up by trying to scare your brother! And this poor man probably just wants to enjoy his trip! Now enough!" The lady said sternly but the girl just sat back down with folded arms. The boy began rolling in the chair laughing. Nick knew better after the morning he had; he knew the girl probably had just seen someone like she described. It probably wouldn't be the last by the time this train journey had ended, he thought.

CHAPTER TWENTY-EIGHT
Alice

As Benny's yellow truck drove through the deserted neighborhoods, Alice only caught a glimpse of one person out in the street walking. She was sure everyone else was probably huddled indoors, fixated with the same repeated news broadcast of where to go and what to do. The virus seemed to have literally crippled the country in the last twenty-four hours. When Alice had finally gotten some sleep, it hadn't been for long. She had tossed and turned all night on Benny's couch unable to rest properly. Alice knew if she'd gone across to her own home, she would have been able to sleep even less. The lack of sleep may have been the cause of why she felt so groggy right now or it could have been the bump to the head. She'd gotten less sleep on some of the double shifts she'd pulled for VPD. So, Alice knew she could still function and still make good decisions. As they drove through neighborhoods, she was shocked by the amount of blood she saw. There was blood splattered on fences, houses, and even parked cars. It nagged inside her that she'd not seen a single body.

By the amount of blood she was seeing, some of the people should be lying dead in the street.

It was almost as if they'd gotten up and walked away, she thought to herself. Alice knew that thanks to this virus that's probably exactly what had happened.

"Oh, shit!" Benny mumbled slamming on the brakes as the truck turned a corner.

Alice leaned forward from the back seat to see a barricade across the street ahead of them.

The street ahead of them led to Mill Plain Boulevard. It was one of the major four lane roads that ran the length of Vancouver. Four men in army uniforms were manning the barricade armed with rifles. One of the soldiers started to walk towards the truck waving his hand for them to come forward.

"Shit, what should I do?" Benny asked.

"Pull forward slow," Alice said.

The truck slowly moved towards the soldier that was waiting in the middle of the road for them.

The soldier waved them to a halt then two more soldiers started to walk towards them. These two soldiers had their rifles raised and pointed right at them. The soldier in the middle of the road walked round to Benny's driver window. The soldier motioned Benny to roll down the window.

"Howdy, folks," the soldier began sounding eerily cheery. "Where you guys off to?" the soldier asked.

"We were headed to the Vancouver east precinct then the camp at Illahee Elementary" Benny said pointing towards the barricade. The soldier peered inside looking at Marcus then at her.

"I'm afraid that's a no-go, guys" The soldier said then waved at the two other soldiers to lower their guns.

Alice leaned forward "Why's that?" she asked.

The soldier glared at her. "Well the FEMA camp there isn't set up yet and probably won't be as most of the trailers are being redirected," the soldier said.

"Redirected to where? And we really need to get to the east precinct" she asked.

"I'm afraid I can't give you that information ma'am, so if you'd kindly turn the vehicle around and head home this situation should be resolved shortly and it'll all be back to business as usual once order is restored," the soldier finished.

"I'm an officer for Vancouver Police and haven't had any contact with my Precinct, is there anything else you *can* tell me?" she asked.

"Sorry, ma'am, your superiors should be in touch shortly, now please turn the vehicle around!" the soldier said changing his tone from happy go lucky to authoritative.

"No problem," Benny said raising his hands. The soldier nodded as the truck was shifted into reverse.

"What are we going to do now?" Marcus whispered as Benny reversed the truck to turn around.

"Try a different way, this happened to Jake and me yesterday. They only had busy roads blocked off, so we took the back-road home," Benny said.

"Head towards 136th and we can hit the precinct that way, they may have more info," she said.

Benny nodded as the truck turned off the blocked main street, they were on onto the narrower streets of a neighborhood.

As they neared the precinct the smell of smoke was heavy in the air. As they turned onto the street with the precinct, Alice felt her body freeze in horror. The whole precinct was rubble with tiny plumes of smoke coming from piles of smoldering debris.

"What the fuck…" Marcus said.

Benny stopped the truck and Alice got out trying to hold back her tears as she slowly walked towards what was left of the Precinct. It must have been burnt down, she thought, examining the scene. Looking around the scene, though, she noted that it looked more like there had been an explosion with debris scattered across the street. She felt Benny's hand on her shoulder, and she started sobbing turning into her friend's chest.

"What's going on?" she sobbed into Benny's chest.

She could feel his hands patting her back like she was a small child. Alice wasn't sure how long she'd been crying but Marcus got her attention.

"We gotta go, guys!" Marcus yelled from the truck.

Alice looked up from Benny's chest to see a group of people stumbling through the smoke of the precinct. There was a group of six of them, all covered in blood and charred black clothes with huge gaping wounds. All of a sudden, her sadness melted away and was replaced with anger and rage. Pushing off of Benny she walked towards the people stumbling through the smoke and pulled her Glock out from the back of her pants. Raising it up she squeezed off three shots that hit the first person that walked from the precinct debris onto the road. It was a man or had been a man with only one arm. Where the man's other arm had been it was missing from the elbow down. As the three shots slammed into the man's chest he fell to the ground.

Alice kept walking closer and aimed down at the man on the ground. The man looked up at her reaching with one arm and the other which was a cauterized stump. She fired three more shots into this thing with one going right into the forehead making the thing go limp.

"Let's go!" Benny said pulling her by the shoulder.

Once they were back in the truck Benny revved up the engine and peeled out, driving back the way they had come. Alice sat in the back seat trying to keep calm but could feel herself ready to explode inside. *The army guy had lied, the news had lied, who could they get truthful answers from?* she thought to herself.

"This is complete chaos," Marcus said from the front passenger seat.

Alice nodded to herself not saying a word as the situation only seemed to be getting worse and worse. "We can head to Jake's then the FEMA camp by his house, those guys might have been lying," Benny said.

"Yeah." she said softly, hoping that Jake and his family were okay.

CHAPTER TWENTY-NINE
Mason

People began pushing and running as shots and screams filled the air. Mason looked in the direction of the information boards where the shots originated. He could see soldiers standing on top of kiosks aiming down into the crowd that surrounded the boards. Other people were running in his direction towards the exit, but soldiers rushed past, forming a line. He wasn't sure what was happening, but he didn't want to get caught in the stampede of people about to clash with these soldiers.

"Follow me," he said to Alex who he could tell was terrified. He clutched his bags in one hand and lifted Sarah up with the other. He started walking fast in the direction the Exit arrows he'd seen were pointed. Looking at the entrance of the terminal he could see that it was blocked off by outside barricades and more soldiers. The arrows he'd noticed above pointed in a different direction from the entrance, however. He followed the arrows to some doors which looked like fire doors. Examining them he could see they weren't emergency doors as there was no bright markings or symbols.

The shouting and screaming was getting louder but there had been no more gunshots. The soldiers had formed a pretty solid line, keeping most of the rowdy travelers in the portion of the terminal the shots had come from. Looking at the door joints he couldn't see any kind of emergency exit alarm. Nothing that would trigger attention once he opened the door.

"Daddy, I'm scared" Sarah whimpered into his ear as he lifted her up higher in case he had to burst into a run. "It's okay, honey, we'll be okay," he told her, looking at Alex and nodding at the door.

Alex meekly nodded back as he counted to three in his head before knocking the middle bar of the door slightly to test it. It didn't make a noise, but he heard the latch click.

"C'mon" he whispered, pushing the bar and walking through. Once through he heard the door click closed behind them.

Alex was standing right behind him holding Abby in her car seat. They were in a long, dimly lit brick hallway with another set of double doors at the end. He could see these doors weren't as heavy as the ones they'd just come through. There was a square glass pane on each door with daylight coming through from the other side.

As they walked towards the double doors a single door opened to the side and a soldier burst out.

Alex jumped so he put his arm around her pulling her close.

"Ostanovites kuda vy idete!" The soldier shouted pointed an old, dirty looking AK-47 at them. Mason put his hands up dropping the bags but still holding Sarah whose head was buried in his neck.

"I'm sorry, I don't understand! Please!" He pleaded.

The solder stepped out of the doorway towards them saying again, "Ostanovites kuda vy idete!" He thrusted the rifle nozzle towards Mason.

Before he could speak again a man wearing the same polo shirt as the people manning the information kiosk came out the doorway the soldier had come from.

"Are you American?" the man asked.

Mason gulped and nodded not sure if this would be a good thing or a bad thing. The man stepped in front of the soldier putting a hand on the rifle urging the soldier to lower it.

"Oni poteryany turistami," the small man said to the soldier. The soldier looked at them and Mason could feel the soldier scrutinizing him.

"Ya zaberu ikh obratno," The man said, and the soldier nodded. The soldier then sighed and walked back through the door he'd come from, slamming it.

The man was looking at Alex and Abby smiling which made Mason feel a little uneasy.

"Thank you. I think" Mason said.

"No problem, I have a family, too, so understand" the man said in a sad tone.

"What's going on? Can you help us? We're trying to get home," he said.

The man shook his head, "To America? I'm afraid not," the man said waving for them to follow.

They walked down the hallway towards the two doors with the small glass panels.

"All flights national and international are grounded. All transportation has pretty much been halted," the man said.

Mason noticed the confusion on Alex's face, but he didn't want to ask for too many details with Sarah listening as his daughter clutched onto his shoulder tight.

"What's going on? Please you must know something," Alex asked from behind him.

The man turned and looked at Alex then at him. "How much do you Americans know? I'm guessing not much if you traveled here," the man said with a weirdly forced wry smile.

"Look! I appreciate what you did with the soldier back there but yeah, we don't know anything. Only thing we've seen is what was on the news out there…and looks like you guys are getting ready for a war," he said, waving his arm towards the direction they'd just come.

"Once we get out of here, I will tell you what I can but I only know what I've heard from soldiers and saw on the news myself and I've learned lately that they are two different things," the man said walking towards the double doors. As they got close to the double doors, Mason could see through and could make out green camo...lots of it.

"Can you get us to another airport?" he asked, grabbing the man's shoulders.

"First we need to get out of the city! I need you to do as I say! Please!" The man said.

This was the first time the man had said please, Mason noticed, and seemed a little on edge with all these soldiers outside. Mason still had an uneasy feeling about this guy. Right now, it seemed like the only way out of this shit storm was with this guy.

"Now, please be calm and do not do anything rash while I talk to some of these soldiers," The man said. Mason nodded putting his arm around Alex, pulling her close.

"Mason...that's my name," he said to the man.

"Dimitri," the man said opening the door.

Outside the double doors was what seemed like a staff parking lot fenced off. It was filled with army Jeeps, tents, and soldiers. Dimitri walked out, waving to a group of soldiers who were closest to the door. Mason couldn't hear what they were saying but Dimitri kept pointing over to them.

One of the soldiers walked over to them stopping a few feet away. The soldier looked Mason up and down then Alex. "Seek?" the soldier asked.

Mason knew what the man was trying to ask so shook his head. "No, we're not sick," he told the soldier. Dimitri walked up behind the soldier patting the guy on the back. The soldier turned and nodded before whistling to a group standing by a Jeep. Dimitri had a huge smile as one of the four walked over, throwing a set of keys to

Dimitri. Mason wasn't sure what was going on and didn't like it but would play along. "Let's go!" Dimitri said looking pleased with himself.

As Mason started to follow Dimitri the soldier in front of him put a hand up so Mason stopped. The soldier whipped out a flashlight and shined it in his eyes like a doctor would do. Mason was blinded for a second then when the flashlight turned off, he noticed the soldier was looking at his hands.

The soldier nodded patting him on the shoulder which Mason took as a signal that he was good to go. Mason put his arm tight around Alex he walked towards the Jeep that Dimitri had started up.

As a gate was opened for them to drive out of Mason knew he should be happy they were getting away from whatever was about to go down at this airport. He wasn't, though, as he was being eaten up inside with questions. As the Jeep's engine growled while they drove along deserted streets, he figured now was a good time to try to get some answers.

"Dimitri...what's going on? Why did those soldiers give you a Jeep and let us just leave?" He asked.

"Because I told them I'm taking you to the Embassy," Dimitri said continuing to drive along empty streets. "For several weeks there has been a disease affecting lots of countries and people. Most pointed fingers at America," Dimitri said looking at him with raised eyebrows.

Looking in the rearview mirror Mason could see Alex in the backseat snuggled with the girls. "What kind of disease?" Alex asked with an arm around Sarah's ears.

"A bad one" Dimitri began "It starts off as a fever with lesions, bleeding, dementia, schizophrenia, craziness, and even cannibalism!" Dimitri said.

"Why hasn't this been on the news?" Alex said.

Dimitri let out a deep laugh "It has been! You Americans don't care about us or the rest of the world, just yourselves. America has been getting the blame but now...now either America's big plan backfired, or you weren't to blame in the first place," Dimitri said.

Mason's head was spinning, and he could only imagine how confused Alex must be.

"What big plan? Backfired how?" Alex asked.

Mason didn't need to Dimitri to spell it out for him, he knew what Dimitri meant when he said that. Most of the world didn't like America or Americans in general due to their reputation.

When something happened globally, either America got involved even though it was none of their business and were seen to get something out of it or would just stand by while disaster struck.

"I'm sorry...I guess you've been traveling but America has been crippled more in the last twenty-four hours then the rest of the world has in the last four weeks" Dimitri said.

"So, this shutting down of transportation is basically a quarantine? Why now if this has been happening for weeks?" Mason asked.

Dimitri nodded, "Belarus, Russia, and most of eastern Europe has been doing pretty well isolating and keeping the infection from spreading, implementing methods that have worked successfully in other countries at slowing down the spread of the virus. Only in the last twenty-four hours since it erupted in America has the world gone into panic mode shutting down transportation and completely closing off borders," Dimitri finished.

"You said successfully? Are there countries that have been unsuccessful?" Alex asked.

Dimitri nodded somberly "There have been a lot but the virus itself is one thing, the things people are doing to each other and what's coming afterwards is much worse," Dimitri said as the Jeep slowed to a halt.

CHAPTER THIRTY
Nick

T hey train been traveling for what seemed like hours, but Nick knew by the scenery that they weren't too far outside of Seattle. The current state of events and failure to control what was going on wasn't confined to just Seattle. Nick had seen dozens of plumes of smoke and fires from the train window as it raced along the tracks. Sitting back in his chair closing his eyes closed, Nick thought over scenario after scenario in his head. Each scenario he ran though came with it dozens of questions.

Mainly, how he could find out what caused this? How contagious was it? How was the government handling it? And how long before it was under control? Everything had happened so fast in the last twenty-four hours. Had the lack of sleep and nerves about the meeting made Nick overreact in his decisions? Then he thought about the homeless man getting shot, the guy in the room next door, and the military's presence. No, the danger and severity of the situation was very much real.

Nick knew he had to remain as calm and as level headed as he could. He'd prepped for something like this. In fact, this is why most people like him prepped! To be prepared for when something happens to cause shit to hit the fan. From what Nick had witnessed and seen on the news it was definitely hitting the fan hard. He knew his main priority was his wife and daughter. He knew that in survival situations every decision was a big one. Lives could be changed, lost or saved in the blink of an eye. He'd remembered reading that somewhere as he slipped off to sleep.

When Nick woke up the train was at a full stop on the tracks. He wasn't sure how long he had been asleep but stretched out his arms, looking around. The youngish old lady was sitting knitting away while the boy was next to him was tapping away on some handheld video game. The blonde girl wasn't in her seat, though. The lady tilted her head down peering at him over the top of her glasses. "Enjoy your nap?" The lady said with a chuckle,

"Yeah, I didn't sleep that great last night," he said still stretching.

Nick was unsure why this lady seemed so normal and seemingly oblivious to the events unfolding. "How long was I asleep? We've stopped," he said looking out the window trying to pinpoint where they were. Looking at scenery outside all Nick could see was just trees and grass. The lady put her needles down and looked out the window. "Oh, I'm not too sure," she said with a puzzled look. "We've stopped and started up again a few times, not going very far," the lady said. "My name's Agnes," the lady said, reaching out her hand.

"That's Michael, my little brother and my sister Heidi is at the food car," Agnes said.

"Nick!" He said shaking her hand and was taken off guard by this lady telling him they were brothers and sisters. This lady dressed and the knitting had made Nick assume Agnes was the Mom or Aunty. As Nick went to shake her hand the girl jumped in front of them both and into her seat. The girl was laughing with a drink in her hand, "Yeah, she's our sister but dresses like our grandma and acts it, too," the girl said.

Nick wanted to smile as the girl was just saying what he was thinking. He didn't want to offend Agnes, though, who was clearly getting agitated glaring at the younger sister.

"Could I have a drink of your coffee?" Agnes asked.

The young girl smiled back, "Of course, but it's not coffee, they guy said they didn't have time to stock up at the station, so I got soda," Heidi said handing the older sister the cup.

"That to wash some xannies down, sis? Take the edge off having to deal with your rebellious siblings?" Heidi said laughing handing over the soda.

Sure enough, Agnes swallowed some pills before taking a drink and handing it back.

"Yes, as a matter of fact I do need medicine to help me cope with the stress you put on this family, sending you and your brother to that camp was supposed to bring you closer to our Lord and your family" Agnes said, glaring at Heidi. The younger sister just rolled her eyes, crossed her legs, and turned looking out the window.

"Do you have any kids, Nick?" Agnes asked him. He noticed Heidi glancing at him out of the corner of his eye. "Yeah I have a little girl, her name's Amber," he said, smiling. Before they could say any more about his baby girl, a member of the train staff came into the carriage. The man's badge said conductor.

"Attention, please!" The conductor said loudly, getting the car's attention.

"We apologize for the delay but for some reason we're having problems contacting the next station and without communication on the signals we have to remain here, sorry for any inconvenience we will keep you posted," the conductor said.

The conductor continued walking through to the next carriage ignoring questions passengers were trying to ask. Nick couldn't help noticing how badly the conductor was sweating. Not only that but why did he come through the cars instead of using the intercom. Nick got out of his seat; he knew he had to find out what was going on. Every second that they were stopped was more time away from his wife and daughter. More time that the situation was probably getting worse, judging by FEMA and the government's track record.

As he entered the next carriage, he could hear loud, harsh coughing. It was an elderly man sitting in the first row of seats having a coughing fit. There was an elderly woman beside the man trying to give him water. The crowd in this car were shouting questions at the conductor. They weren't taking it as nicely as car six that Nick was in. The conductor had his hands up as question after question was hurled at him. Nick walked down the aisle towards the conductor but just squeezed past heading to the area between cars where he waited.

Not wanting to join in with flurry of questions the guy was being bombarded with, Nick wanted to get him one on one. He knew he would get better answers directly and not in a carriage full of sweaty, pissed off passengers. As the conductor got to the doorway leading into the area where Nick, was a lady stopped the conductor. Nick heard the lady ask why her sister couldn't get on the train and why they had left. The conductor ignored the lady and continued into the area where Nick was waiting.

As the door slid shut with a hiss and the conductor walked towards him Nick moved to block the narrow walkway.

"Hey" Nick said as the conductor stopped in front of him. "I'm not an idiot! I would like some answers," he told the conductor.

"What?" the conductor asked, shrugging his shoulders.

"Why are we stopped? Why's it so hot in here and why didn't you use the intercom?" Nick hadn't noticed until now, but it was extremely hot. The conductor looked at the ground then at Nick with a confused look on his face. "We have no power, it keeps going out, we drive a bit then have to stop to let it recharge," the conductor said then looked up above them. "A/C uses a lot and the intercom works when it wants to," the conductor finished.

Nick nodded, satisfied with the answers even though they weren't the answers to the questions he was looking for. He started to move out the conductors way then stopped asking, "That lady said her sister didn't get on the train?"

The conductor turned and looked at the lady through the glass door. The lady was sitting with her face on her hand, looking out the window. Nick leaned in close to the conductor so he could talk quietly. "This train was cancelled, too, wasn't it? I heard the shots and saw the army arrive just as we were leaving," Nick whispered. Nick stepped passed the conductor and as he did, said, "You're going to want to start being honest and giving these people some answers before they start demanding answers," as Nick finished, the door opened to the carriage and the train shuddered and started to move again.

As Nick made his way back to his car, he could see the lady who was helping the man with the ghastly cough before. The lady looked worried and was standing at the end of the carriage outside the restroom door. As he got closer, Nick could hear her talking to the door. Nick looked down and the seats where the coughing man had been. The man's seat was empty, so he must be who was in the restroom Nick thought. As Nick got closer the lady started knocking on the door. "Alan? Alan! Are you okay? I still can't find your inhaler, dear!" the lady exclaimed.

Nick had to squeeze past the lady to get into the carriage his seat was in. As he walked towards his seat, Heidi got up and headed back the way Nick had just come. As he past her the girl flashed him a smile. Nick sat down then Agnes smiled at him, "On the move again," Agnes said. Nick smiled looking out the window, the Xanax had obviously kicked in, he thought.

Just as Nick sat down laying his head on the headrest there was a scream!

Nick looked down the aisle to see Heidi screaming! The old lady was in the doorway to the restroom wrestling with the old, coughing guy. Nick could see from his seat the man's eyes were all milky white and his face was red with dark veins throbbing. A man got up from his seat and pulled the old lady out of the restroom doorway away from the elderly man. The elderly man came out of the restroom swinging his arms at the old lady. The man who had saved the old lady threw a punch, sending the old man back. The old man then fell into Heidi who started screaming again. Somehow this set off the old man who turned, trying to grab and bite Heidi!

The old lady that was with the man initially stumbled up the aisle past Nick's seat. The lady was holding her face with blood coming through her fingers. The man who had punched the crazy guy grabbed the old man's jacket from the back. The guy swung the old man away from Heidi and back into the bathroom. "What the fuck, dude?!" The man yelled.

The elderly man didn't seem to hear, or care instead just pounced forwards. The man put his arm up to defend himself, but the old man sank his teeth into the guys arm!

The guy let out a grunt then slammed the arm with old guy still attached into the wall. The old man was still biting down trying to scratch and claw! The guy slammed the old man again and again into the wall but still the old guy wouldn't let up. Blood was running from the man's arm over the old guy's face and dripping onto the ground. Heidi was screaming and began hitting the old guy to try make him let go. Nothing was helping and people were out of their seats either screaming or watching in shock. Nick knew something had to be done fast! Getting out of his seat, he took one of Agnes' knitting needles from her hand. Nick stormed at a fast paced to the end of the car where he slammed the needle into the old man's head! The old guy let the man's arm go then turned towards Nick with jaws snapping! Nick quickly pulled the needle out then swept the old man's arms aside, thrusting the needle deep into the old man's eye socket.

The old man went limp then slumped down to the floor lifeless. The other guy was cradling his arm covering a huge gash. Nick just stood there not sure what had come over him then Heidi slammed herself against him, wrapping her arms around him, burying her head in his chest sobbing.

CHAPTER THIRTY-ONE
Jake

Jake stood in the kitchen in silence gazing out the window. It was still hot outside but there was no smoke in the sky anymore that he could see. He heard Emily walking up behind him,

"I love you," Emily said, resting her head on his back. "So, you want to leave?"

"Yeah, I think we should," he said nodding to himself. "Pete had the right idea, babe, I've seen what people are like out there, they're scared, and this virus is seriously dangerous," he said.

They'd talked about it in bed while trying to get to sleep amongst all the sirens and booms going off. Emily had eventually taken some sleeping pills to help her get to sleep. Then Jake had spent a lot of the night staring at the ceiling wishing this was a bad dream. The boys had been awake most of the night, too. He'd heard them chattering in the other room about what was going outside all around them.

Emily ducted under his arms to get between him and the kitchen window.

"Okay, honey, whatever you say, but are you okay? You seem kind of distant," Emily asked.

He wanted to cry, he wanted to just wake up from this. He wasn't sure why he felt this confused and conflicted. It was affecting him, and he knew it but couldn't figure out why. He did know if there was anyone, he could talk to it was his wife.

"When I was at work…" he began, "I killed someone, it was Mr. Parsons…" he blurted out.

Once he'd told her about Mr. Parsons the rest of the story came out no problem. The outbreak of the virus and everything that had happened in Hall 3, everyone turning into zombies, fighting with FEMA soldiers in the car park, Mr. Parsons trying to bite him as he was getting in the truck.

He didn't realize it at the time but there were tears rolling down his face. Emily kissed him on the lips and reassured him it was okay. That he did what he had to do to stay safe and get back to his family in one piece.

"That's why I think we should leave," he told her "I think we would be safer on our own with no one else," he said.

"Where would we go?" Emily asked and he could tell she was shocked with his idea.

"I heard Alaska's nice," he said with a lighthearted chuckle. "Seriously, though, it's sparsely populated, huge area and the cold should be a good defense against a virus," he said.

Emily just nodded and he could tell his wife wasn't into the idea of traveling across the country.

He couldn't blame her; all her family was here in Washington and who knows how bad it was out there.

"We'll think about it" Emily said.

There was a knock on the front door and both boys came running through the trailer to answer it. "Uncle Benny!" both boys screamed excitedly. As Jake walked into the living room to greet his friend, he saw Marcus and Alice were with Benny.

"Hey guys!" he greeted them then noticed the serious looks on Alice and Marcus's faces. Benny herded the boys back towards the hallway and their bedroom with the promise of playing some Minecraft.

Alice walked into the kitchen and began staring out the window much like he had been doing.

"All that haze from the smoke…" Alice muttered as he walked over to the window.

"Alice, are you okay?" Emily asked but Alice just stared out the window. Jake saw her eyes tearing up. Benny came into the kitchen and patted him on the back before taking a seat at the breakfast bar.

"Shots?" Benny asked. Jake nodded and knew this meant things were about to get more serious, especially with Alice here. Alice was a cop and was usually always cheery around Marcus and Benny. Right now, however, Alice was just staring out the window dressed in jeans, a loose shirt, and her police belt with holster.

Jake grabbed some vodka from the cupboard above the stove and some shot glasses. Marcus shook his head, but Jake poured them for Benny, Alice, and himself. They cheered and Jake looked at Benny as he took his shot.

"Alice wants to go back to Victory to talk with the FEMA docs," Benny said seriously picking up the vodka bottle and pouring everyone another round of shots. Jake couldn't believe what he was hearing.

He shook his head "We both know that's not going to happen, we barely made it out ourselves! That and they were blocking off all the entry and exits to Battleground" he told them.

"What the fuck is going on?" Marcus blurted out.

"I'm sorry...I...I…I just don't see how you are standing here taking shots while outside the world is going to shit!" Marcus buried his head in his hands. Benny patted Marcus's back while looking at Jake. Jake knew how Marcus was feeling, he'd felt this way too since yesterday.

"We have to find out what's going on," Alice said waving her hand at the window.

Jake turned on the TV to a red screen with "SAFETY INSTRUCTIONS" on the top of the screen. Below it was the A.D.D. acronym with the writing beside each big letter.

A - Avoid contact with anyone other than emergency services, Law enforcement, FEMA or the Military Aid in your area.

D- Denied entry to your place of residence or location from anyone other than the groups listed above.

D- Defend your location and place of residence from anyone trying to gain entry other than the groups listed above.

The screen switched to the list of updated FEMA camps with the one at the boys school near the top. "The boys school is five minutes down the road," he said.

"Soldiers told us on the way here that it had been redirected." Benny said.

"Yet, it's still listed as a safe place to go?" Jake said puzzled.

"Fuckers are lying! Just like everything else." Alice said angrily.

The news cut from the FEMA aid and shelter locations list to a news studio. Even though this was a local news station this wasn't the Portland studio like it was normally. This was the same affiliate but not the local state channel advertised. Two broadcasters sat at a desk looking at the camera.

"Again as has been reiterated earlier," one of them began, an elderly plump man with a bald, shiny head and thick grey moustache, "Please do not travel, avoid all major routes and highways if you must travel, then avoid high traffic areas," the man looked at the other anchor who looked at the papers on the desk. This guy was a lot thinner with long pointy nose and long black hair swept to the side.

"Reports and videos are coming in from various states of infected individuals failing to comply with law enforcement, also Portland and California protests turned into riots that are still trying to be brought under control," the man said as it switched to a clip showing police in riot gear defending themselves in a packed street. Rocks were bouncing off riot shields as were other objects. All of a sudden, a park bench filled the screen as it was thrown into a group of officers.

It switched back to the studio where the plump man was shaking his head.

"Clearly law enforcement are being overwhelmed on two fronts with the protesters and also responding to the overflow of 911 calls" as the man finished it switched again to an aerial view from a helicopter.

The other reporter began speaking "This is an aerial view from our traffic eye in the sky," the man began as the camera panned from a bumper to bumper freeway to a car lot.

"As you can see" the broadcaster narrated "This was an hour ago here in Houston and officers responded to reports of the car lot being vandalized," Officers could be seen like small bugs rushing between cars towards a few people who were on top of cars. Dozens of cars had smashed windows and some were even on fire.

"Officers quickly got the situation under control, but this area is again getting large reports of violence and destruction to public property," The newsman continued. Jake frowned as it wasn't clear how the situation had been brought under control. From what he was seeing the chaos seemed to still be going on. The news switched back to the studio where the plump man looked sternly into the camera. "Sadly, reports of situations like this are increasing all over the country, so please remain calm until authorities have this under control," The man advised.

"This is bullshit!" Alice piped up, "The authorities have lost control! The lack of information on this virus has people blinded!" Alice spat.

The screen switched back to the acronym while the skinnier broadcaster began reading the bullet points. The broadcaster also then mentioned if you are separated from family or loved ones then to check into a FEMA aid station.

Jake walked back into the kitchen. "Hey, Marcus would you mind staying here and looking after Emily and the boys?" he asked, knowing Marcus was on the fence about all of this and wasn't taking it too well. Jake understood as that's how he had been yesterday and just needed some time to digest it all. "I think we should go check out the boy's school anyway, see if there's anyone from FEMA there," he said. Benny was looking at Alice, who nodded.

"I'll go play with the boys for a bit while you get ready" Benny said heading towards the boys' room.

Alice filled Jake in on her night and what they found when they went to the Precinct before coming to his house. Emily came into the kitchen beside them. "Would anyone like some coffee?" Emily asked. Emily then looked at the bottle on the breakfast bar and smiled to herself.

"Never mind. Is…is it really that bad?" Emily asked. Jake could tell part of her still didn't realize just how bad it was or how much worse it could still get.

No…it's worse" Alice said pouring a drink.

"It's going to be okay, honey," he said putting his arm around his wife. "I promise," he reassured Emily, kissing her head.

"Do you have to go? We can just wait here till whatever this is passes," Emily said looking out the window.

"All that smoke," Alice said "It's from fires that weren't put out and burned all night. There is no one coming, there's no fire crews, no police, and clearly the news don't have a clue what's going on or don't want to tell people the truth," Alice said.

"What's the truth?" Emily asked.

"That we're fucked! All of us, anyone who has any sense is with their families and these infected are mindless crazy cannibals," Alice said.

Emily nodded at what Alice was saying and Jake saw the scared look his wife had on her face. "Honey, Alice is a cop, we'll be quick and in good hands," he reassured his wife.

As Alice and Emily talked, he slipped away into the back bedroom and into his lock box. He loaded his 9mm then tucked it in the back of his belt under his shirt. Benny appeared from the boys' room looking at him. "You ready?" Benny asked.

Jake nodded. "Let's get Alice and go do this," he said.

Emily's back was to them as they walked out into the kitchen, so he used this chance, walking over to Marcus. "Hey, can I talk to you outside for a second?" he asked, waving Marcus towards the front door.

"What's up?" Marcus asked.

Jake opened the door and stepped out then as Marcus stepped out, "Here," Jake said slyly handing Marcus the gun. Marcus was looking down at it and seemed hesitant to take it. Jake pushed it forwards. "I need you to protect them if anything happens, I'm not taking any chances," he told Marcus. Marcus gave a weak nod and took the gun with shaking hands.

"I hope you don't have to use it but just in case," he emphasized to Marcus who nodded back.

"Ready?" Alice asked walking out onto the porch with Benny.

"Love you!" Emily shouted from the door as they all got in the truck.

"Love   you   more!"   He   shouted   back.

CHAPTER THIRTY-TWO
Nick

Nick looked out the window wishing for some kind of sign to say where they were, a clue to let him know somewhere they were near. He didn't like being stuck in the middle of nowhere while things were going south. Right now, they could be only minutes from a station and didn't know it. Nick looked at the man who had helped, he was wrapping the bitten arm in a shirt another passenger had given him. Nick could see Agnes was helping the old lady calm down in some seats at the opposite end of the train car. Michael was sitting slack jawed with eyes wide open staring at him.

"Thanks, bro," the guy who'd been bit said to Nick.

Nick nodded then looked at the man's arm, blood had soaked through the shirt already.

"You're going to want to get that cleaned and bandaged," Nick said knowing there was something making these people act like this. He also knew it was probably contagious but for now decided to keep that to himself to avoid further panic. Heidi was still sobbing with her face buried in his shoulders. He wasn't sure just what to do, he brought his arms up awkwardly and patted her back. "Hey," he said softly, "let's get you back to you seat." He could feel her nod against his chest as he guided her back to their seats.

"Holy shit! You are such a badass!" Michael squealed as they sat down

"Michael!" Agnes shouted. The boy just smirked and continued to stare at him.

Nick helped Heidi sit down then looked around, people had left the carriage and the ones who hadn't were all just staring at Nick. He turned towards them all raising his arms.

"What?" he yelled.

"In case you people weren't aware, there's something making people act like this! They're not normal! They're dangerous!" he said pointing to the old lady who was sitting shaking.

Agnes had her arms wrapped around the old lady who looked terrified. The lady looked up at him. "He's…He's right, my Thomas wouldn't hurt a fly and his eyes… th-th-they were different like he wasn't there anymore. Like he was possessed," the lady said, sobbing while Agnes held her. The door at the end of the carriage opened as the conductor walked in.

"Someone hit the button to the driver! Is everything okay?" The conductor asked out of breath.

Nick watched the conductor's eyes widen when the guy holding a bloody shirt on his arm pointed to the old man slumped against the restroom door with a knitting needle sticking out of his head.

"I see. Okay, were you bitten?" The conductor asked the man. The guy nodded and Nick noticed the sweat pouring from down the man's forehead.

"We were told if anyone was infected, we were to isolate them," The conductor told the whole carriage who were all still silent with shock.

"Infected?" The man asked while wiping away sweat.

"Yes, it was on the news this morning there's some kind of super virus like rabies that's making people go crazy and it's highly contagious" the conductor said.

A woman who must have been with the man got out of her seat to stand beside the man.

"Highly contagious? How?" the woman asked. Nick was definitely interested in hearing the answer to this question.

"They didn't say for sure, but they think it's in the blood like HIV and saliva like rabies, I only saw the news before I left for work," the conductor said, shrugging his shoulders.

A man started shouting from a chair behind Nicks. "He needs to be kicked off the train!" the man said, sounding like the leader of a witch hunt. Nick looked over the chair glaring at the man. Nick knew throwing people off the train would not start or end well. It might start out like a good idea but would just be throwing fuel on the fire. The girl who was with the man didn't seem to like the old man's comments.

"If you're scared, gramps, then you get the fuck off!" the girl shouted. Nick was surprised by his role in what had just happened hadn't been brought up yet. Nick didn't want to attract any unwanted attention, so he wasn't sure of saying anything or if playing devil's advocate was a good idea right now. The man who had been bitten raised his good arm to calm everyone.

"Hey, I get it but I'm not getting off this train, how bout I just go into the restroom for the rest of the trip?" The man said gesturing towards the restroom. The conductor looked around the carriage as if looking for objection and Nick wasn't about to. The man had acted on instinct to help another human being. Nick thought he probably would have done the same.

"I think it's a good idea," Nick piped up looking at the old man again.

The old guy grunted but didn't say anything back. The girl sat in the seat next to the restroom door as the man went in waving. Nick could hear the man quietly reassuring the girl it would be okay, Nick felt his heart sink as he wasn't too confidant on what the man was promising. Nick also realized letting the man stay could be a bad idea but the time to be heartless with decisions hadn't come yet he told himself.

Once the man was inside, Nick watched as the conductor used a key to lock the master bolt on the outside of the restroom door. "There's two keys to this door. I have one the other is with the attendant in the cafe car," the conductor told them all. The locking of the restroom door from their side definitely made Nick feel a little easier about his decision. Now it was then time to address the obvious elephant in the room. As the conductor stood above the body on the floor with a knitting needle sticking out Nick got out his seat. "We should wrap up the body and move it to an isolated part of the train," he said to the conductor.

"I'll be right back," the conductor said, nodding in agreement then left the carriage.

A few minutes later, the conductor returned with a large blue tarp. The conductor placed the tarp flat as possible in the gangway. Nick nodded towards the old man's feet understanding what the conductor had planned. Nick cupped the head as the conductor grabbed both feet and they lifted the body into the tarp. After rolling the body up the conductor was looking at him.

"You think that's good?" the conductor said slapping the tarp.

Nick thought for a minute analyzing the tarp then turned and headed towards his seat. Opening his EDC bag, he pulled out a roll of black duct tape along with some paracord.

The conductor seemed awfully calm with the situation which made Nick feel a little uneasy like the guy knew a lot more than he was telling them. Then again Nick realized people were probably thinking the same about him after he dispatched the crazy old cannibal like that.

"You keep that kinda stuff in your bag?" the conductor asked.

"Yeah, you never know," Nick said as he tore off a long strip of tape.

Nick duct taped the seam of the tarp then used the paracord to tighten it at both ends. Picking up the human tarp burrito they shuffled out of the carriage into the area between cars then into the next. They carried the body slowly through carriage after carriage and Nick could feel the eyes of the other passengers on him. Finally, they reached the back of the train where the last carriage was empty.

"He'll be fine here till we reach Portland," the conductor said solemnly.

Nick nodded, agreeing in silence then the intercom crackled.

"Ladies and gentlemen, we apologize for the current situation, but we won't be going anywhere until we hear from the next station. As right now we're having some issues with communications."

There were eight cars in total, the conductor had told him as they'd carried the body through the last three. Nick was pretty sure the complaints and people shouting were coming from every one of the eight.

"What happens if we don't hear from the next station?" Nick asked.

He could tell the conductor was worried by the look on the man's face and this made him uneasy as the conductor hadn't even been worried too much when he'd seen the body.

"Then we go to Plan B," the conductor said.

"What's Plan B?" Nick asked curious that there was a Plan B.

"You don't want to know," the conductor said, turning to head back the way they had just came towards the front of the train.

CHAPTER THIRTY-THREE
Caleb

C aleb walked down the spiral staircase leading to the double car garage below that Nate used as his den. He wasn't sure what to expect when he headed down the stairs, but his son was sat slumped on the couch staring at a bong on the coffee table.

"Nate, you okay, son?" he asked.

Nate hadn't come upstairs all night and the girls had been worried all night as had he. Nate didn't answer so Caleb walked over to Nate who was still sat motionless, seemingly unaware of his presence.

"Nate!" Caleb said loudly as he shook his son.

"Ugh," Nate seemed to murmur, looking up at him.

He could tell his son had obviously been smoking pot all night. He couldn't blame him as at that moment as with the whole night before he'd wish he'd had some kind of outlet, too. Caleb wasn't sure what he needed to release but he felt angry and confused with a whole bunch of feelings wrapped in a knot in his stomach.

"Nate...Mark, we gotta get him to his mother, son," he said slowly and softly. He didn't baby his son ever, but he was making an exception as he'd never seen his son in this kind of mess. The world had never been turned upside down like it had been either though, so he knew this was unknown territory for both of them. Nate nodded without looking away from the table and the things cluttered on top from the struggle the night before. The only thing Caleb noticed had been picked up was the bong. "Nate, I know you're hurting and confused. We all are but we need to get Mark home," he said matter-of-factly.

"I...I know, Dad," Nate replied. This was the first time he'd heard his son talk lately without the attitude in his voice and it was sad.

After Mark's attack, they'd rolled him up in an old rug they had stored in the garage that Nate was supposed to throw out. After Nate had helped roll mark in the carpet, the two carried the body out to the Jeep then laid it in the back seat. Caleb wasn't a hundred percent sure on this virus and if these infected people were actual zombies, but he wasn't taking any chances. Mark's body was laid in the backseat with the carpet duct taped closed. He might have just been paranoid, but Caleb locked the doors setting the alarm just in case Mark came back to life again.

They approached the Jeep and peered in. Caleb could see red blood stains had bled through the rug. His stomach turned and he felt sick again, "Nate, jump in the front son," Caleb said, gesturing at the passenger seat while blocking the view of the body from his son through the window.

Once both in, he adjusted the mirror so he could see the body. Caleb wasn't taking any chances just until he was fully aware of the extent of what this virus did. Nate was unusually silent as they drove out from the driveway, any other time he would have been thankful for.

Looking up, he could see his wife on the balcony, he knew she was worried and didn't want him leaving the property. Caleb gave her a wave and mouthed, "I love you." He knew he didn't have to go right now; they could keep the body locked in the Jeep until more information became available on the news. Caleb didn't want to do that though; he'd learned more on their trip to the gas station than anything they'd heard on the radio or seen on the TV. Nobody knew as he'd done it earlier in the morning, but Caleb had put his shotgun in the car just in case.

As they drove up past Victor's place, there were more vehicles than the day before which probably meant more people, too. They stopped at the turning where the dusty road to the properties met the concrete main road. Two armed men were standing then slowly approached the Jeep once he'd stopped. Both men had visible AK-47's strapped across their bodies, which told him Victor and his cronies liked an open carry policy. Caleb waved as he rolled down his window, "Hi guys, everything alright?" Caleb asked.

One of the men stood at Caleb's window while the other walked around to Nate's.

"Yeah, just making sure no one tries to take advantage of the situation by trespassing on the properties," The man in front of Caleb's window said flatly.

"What's in the carpet?" The man in front of Nate's window said, nodding towards Mark's body in the back. Caleb didn't understand this situation or why these men were here, but he needed to think up something smooth fast. Before he could say there had been an accident Nate blurted out.

"My friends inside it, don't worry he's dead," Nate said without looking away from the dashboard.

Caleb could feel his stomach lurch up into his throat as the two men raised their rifles at them. Any type of damage control he wanted to attempt he knew he best tread carefully.

"Out! Hands where we can see them!" the man on Caleb's side barked.

Both of them got out with their hands up and the men both motioned with their guns to the hood of the Jeep. "Hands on the hood," the other man asked who seemed to be a lot calmer.

They did as they were instructed, and Caleb turned to see the man who'd been at his side of the Jeep was at the back of the Jeep.

The man opened the door and grabbed the rug and began sliding it out. "Careful!" Caleb blurted out.

He felt the muzzle of a rifle jab into his back, "Why?" the man beside him asked.

"We…we don't know much about what's going on, my son's friend freaked out, turning into one of those things," Caleb told them.

The guy slid the body that was partially out back in, then slammed the door. "Was he bit?" The man asked. Nate nodded.

"Were any of you?" the man behind them asked.

Nate shook his head.

"How did you kill him?" the man who'd had the rug asked.

Caleb looked at him but before he could answer was cut off, "Does this guy not talk?" the man behind him asked and he felt the muzzle of the gun leave his back. Turning, he could see it was now jammed into Nate's back.

"We fought him then killed him, don't worry we destroyed the brain," Nate said.

As if this had all been some kind of elaborate comedy skit both men lowered their rifles and burst out laughing.

Caleb could feel anger boiling inside him, "What the fuck is so funny?!" he blurted out.

Both men slowed their laughing, "You thought he was a zombie?" The man who'd been behind them asked. Caleb looked at Nate whose color had drained from his face.

"They're not?" he asked.

The man who'd been behind them looked into the Jeep then back at them. "No, he's a zombie," the man said and again the other man started to laugh.

"Why are you guys laughing?" Nate asked.

"Because you should have seen your faces," the guy laughing managed to say. Caleb could tell the other guy, the one who'd had the gun in their back knew it was time to stop the funny business.

"Look, I'm sorry you had to kill your friend but that wasn't your friend...not anymore. Not many people are willing to believe that this virus turns people into...well, zombies but as you've seen, it does." The man patted Nate on the shoulder.

"You guys can be on your way but if you're coming back, I advise you to be fast, do what you gotta do, then get back" the man said.

The other guy had come back over to the front of Jeep "The reason we're up here is to make sure no one infected tries to get onto the properties, be safe, and like Roman said, be quick, avoid contact as much as possible," the other man said.

"Thanks," Caleb said getting back into the Jeep. Just as he started the engine up, the guy who's name Caleb now knew was Roman walked up to the window. "If you do come into contact with anyone infected, don't get bit, if you do, don't come back" Roman said nodding walking away.

Driving along the road Caleb kept looking in the mirror at the body of Mark. He hadn't really thought this next part through and by how Nate was being he knew his son wouldn't be much help.

Turning onto the street Mark and his mom lived on, Caleb couldn't help but notice how quiet the street was. Knowing what was on the news that the people in this street were probably just following the instructions on the news. "This one" Nate said pointing at a run-down little two-story house near the end of the street. The street was small with only nine small houses, all had cars sitting outside in the driveways although the houses showed no signs of activity. The silence as Caleb turned the Jeep's engine off was eerie. As they got out, a dog ran over to them panting and drooling,

He looked at Nate who was smiling at the dog. Seeing his son smile eased everything and the tension lightened a bit.

"Dad, this dog's soaking wet," Nate said, patting it.

Caleb bent down beside Nate who was still patting the dog, "Nate, stop," he said quietly not to startle the dog. Nate looked up at him with a puzzled look on his face.

"Look at your hand" He told his son.

Nate let out a gasp as he looked at the palm of his hand which was red with blood. Caleb could see drops coming off the back of dogs coat onto the ground. Caleb watched as Nate backed away from the dog that just sat there wagging its tail.

"We better get on with this," Nate said.

Caleb nodded and they both headed towards the house. "Want me to do the talking?" Caleb asked. He knew his son wasn't in his right frame of mind so knew he should probably be the one to do it. His son just nodded as they walked up to the door.

Nate knocked on the door but there was no answer. Caleb took a turn at knocking but he knocked a lot louder than his son did. After a few minutes with no answer Nate shouted "Mrs. Buell! It's Nate, are you in there?" Nate asked loudly.

Caleb looked around the yard that was pretty messy, but it didn't look like it had just been done. Grass grew around some of the things lying around in the yard, letting him know they'd been there awhile. He turned when he heard the door open, but it was Nate who was opening it. Again, Nate shouted for Mark's mom.

"Mrs. Buell!" Nate said walking in. Caleb followed his son in.

"Nate, I don't think this is a good idea," he said looking back outside to see if there was any sign of people. The smell hit them like a fresh breeze only there was nothing fresh about it. The smell reminded Caleb of the buttery smell meat spoiling gave off. Nate walked down a hallway which Caleb could see was a kitchen. He headed into the living room which was right beside the door. As he looked at some pictures of Mark on a wall above an old unused fireplace, he heard a low groan. Looking around, he saw an elderly woman with closed eyes sitting in a chair in the corner.

"Nate! She's in here!" he said loudly but not shouting.

He could hear Nate's footsteps as he came from the kitchen, but it was too late. Mark's Mom's eyes shot open, revealing cloudy, milky, white vacant eyes. Then her mouth opened revealing old yellow stained teeth that gave off another low groan as what had been Mark's mom lurched out the chair towards him!

CHAPTER THIRTY-FOUR
Mason

Dimitri brought the Jeep to a halt and ahead of them in the street Mason could see what looked like an abandoned army blockade. It was made of long beams and what looked like large oversized plastic cones. "We have to clear the way," Dimitri said. Mason nodded, opening the door.

"There many of these on the way to the Embassy?" Mason asked.

"No, I don't think so, only at major intersections" Dimitri replied getting out the other side of the Jeep. Mason noticed his driver was glancing around nervously.

"So, what's going to happen when we get to the Embassy?" He asked as they both walked towards the hastily set up blockade of plastic beams and cones.

"We're not going to the Embassy; we're crossing the border and going to Tiraspol. It's the village where my family live." Dimitri said.

As Mason started to pick up the plastic barriers that were set up attached to tall looking traffic cones he decided to probe further. He could tell Dimitri had hesitated before answering.

"Seems like you kinda already knew what was going down?" he asked.

Dimitri nodded, removing some of the long plastic beams, throwing them to the ground.

"I had known for several days that at some point the airports might get shut down, I just didn't know when. The government wanted us to show as little fear as possible when it came to this virus, promising all of us would be safe, so we all carried on business as usual just as we were ordered," Dimitri said.

"Here's the thing, though" Mason said throwing a beam down hard to the side of the road.

"How come the army just let us go, handed you keys to a Jeep, and just let us on our way? Thinking you were going to take us to the Embassy. Surely if there was something going on, then two Americans they would want to take themselves?" He said looking Dimitri right in the eyes.

Dimitri chuckled a little. "Yes, in an everyday world that is correct my friend, but this isn't the everyday world anymore Mr. Mason. In fact, everyone is terrified, even the soldiers. They knew their safest course of action for self-preservation was to remain at the airport where they have access to aircraft, that and I gave them some money," Dimitri said with a smile.

Something wasn't adding up and Mason could feel it. "Why, though?" Mason asked.

"I told them you were an American scientist that had information on the virus and were trying to flee with your family," Dimitri said with a chuckle.

"What? Why?" Mason said getting frustrated now with Dimitri.

"Because I'm one of the directors board of tourism, I know the people at the embassy. I had no choice but to go to the airport today like the last few days to help oversee the shut down if it happened. It was the only thing I could think of to get myself and you out of there. I told them I would take you to the Embassy where the Army has set up a HQ" Dimitri said.

Mason knocked the last of the long barriers off with a kick, it clattered to the ground.

"I've been planning for days a way I could get back to my family if I needed to. I knew how scared the soldiers were and how they were ordered to not abandon their posts but figured if I could give them something important enough for them to give me a Jeep, they would, and they did." Dimitri smiled.

Mason nodded back, partly satisfied with Dimitri's story but knew for now he had to go along with Dimitri regardless, as he didn't have a choice.

Dimitri put a hand on Mason's shoulder, "Please my friend try to be quiet, anyone infected are very agitated and can become extremely violent with noise," Dimitri said nodding down at the beam Mason had just kicked.

"Sorry," Mason apologized.

Looking around it didn't seem like there was anyone around to hear it. The streets were mainly stores locked up and the windows above were all dark. The other streets they'd driven down had all pretty much been the same since leaving the airport. "Where is everyone anyw-" Mason was cut off by the roar of five jets that soared over head.

"This is not good," Dimitri muttered.

They both hurried back to the Jeep and once inside, Mason looked in the back at Alex. She had been quiet since the airport.

Dimitri must have sensed his concern and spoke "Shock, probably from the gunshots and the commotion at the airport. We need to keep them warm and hydrated," Dimitri said, revving the Jeep.

"I thought you said we had to be quiet?" Mason said

"To late for that now, moy drug," Dimitri replied starting in English then finishing in Russian.

Before Mason could ask what that meant or too late for what, there was a thud on the back of the Jeep, then another and another. Mason looked round the seat to see Alex sitting up and covering Sarah's eyes. There were six sets of hands on the rear window that

210

disappeared as the Jeep accelerated forward. "It's okay, baby" Alex said softly to Sarah brushing the small girl's hair.

Mason looked out past his wife and daughter out the rear window to see three people walking slowly, following their Jeep. Within minutes, the three people had disappeared into the distance, satisfied whatever danger they were in had passed he leaned back to kiss Sarah on the forehead. "Don't worry, honey, mommy and daddy are here," he told her.

"And baby Abby! Don't forget baby Abby, Dad," his daughter said.

"I won't, honey" he said beaming with pride at how innocent his daughter was in all of this and still her only thought was of her baby sister.

"Were those people infected?" Mason asked quietly as he could in the cramped Jeep.

Dimitri nodded.

"How could you tell?" Mason asked.

Dimitri pointed up at the sky which was dark.

"It's night and curfew began over two hours ago. Anyone on the streets are either infected or using the curfew to exploit others. Either one, we want to avoid." Dimitri said.

Mason understood that, he'd seen plenty of videos online of people in bad situations like during disasters. People looted and used the chance at the breakdown in society to take advantage of people. "Have you seen these infected people?" Mason asked.

Dimitri nodded again while looking in the rear-view mirror, Mason saw Dimitri was looking at what was behind them and then at the girls.

" I've seen some videos on the news but that didn't prepare me for seeing a Strogi up close..." Dimitri's eyes were getting cloudy and teary.

"Strogi?" Mason asked.

"Yes, it's what we call them…umm…I guess the English is Zombie perhaps, it's what they turn into once they die" Dimitri said.

"Zombies? Are you fuckin' serious? And what do you mean turn into? You said they were infected, not zombies" Mason said, finding this hard to believe. Then again if he'd been told before leaving the US for Scotland that he'd be caught up in the middle of an international pandemic and quarantine he wouldn't have believed that, either.

"Oh, I understand now, when I told you virus and disease you took it literally as you Americans do. However, the disease is just how it starts once you've been infected it's a slow and what looks like agonizing process leading to a slow death then…well, then you come back as a Strogi…sorry, zombie" Dimitri's tone was sounding sadder as his voice choked.

"You okay?" Mason asked, sensing the emotion in the man's voice.

"Two days ago I watched Pietr, my colleague, who'd been bitten by a crazy homeless man a few days before turning into one of them…I watched as soldiers at the hospital in the city center filled him with bullets but he just kept walking towards them…gurgling and making an awful, awful sound…then a bullet hit him in the head causing half of his skull to explode and the thing he'd turned into fell to the ground. Then he was picked up and taken away like garbage by the soldiers," Dimitri said sadly.

Mason felt a wave of sadness come over him as he saw the tears rolling down Dimitri's face, he could tell the man was being sincere this time.

They drove for almost an hour in silence mainly because Mason didn't know what to say and he wanted to give Dimitri some time to himself. The roads now were all rural with the odd house here and there but seemed deserted.

The Jeep slowed and Mason could see someone in the headlights. There was a man in the road. As he slowly turned into the light facing the Jeep, Mason could tell the man was old with a bald head and grey beard. The man started to walk slowly towards the Jeep in tattered stained clothes.

"A Strogi," Dimitri said as the Jeep accelerated. Passing the man, Mason could see the man was covered in blood. Part of the skin on the man's face was missing with just a red gaping hole where the man's right cheek would have been. Mason watched as the man feebly reached out trying to grab the Jeep as it swerved around him.

"We can't stop, he was infected" Dimitri said.

"Yeah…I…I see that" Mason said in both shock and disgust at what he'd just seen.

Dimitri must have been able to tell that he was a little creeped out as he felt Dimitri slap his leg.

"It's okay we're safe, comrade," Dimitri said, laughing.

"Dimitri…" he said quietly looking back to make sure his girls were asleep, and they were. "What can you tell me about what's happening? Not just here but everywhere? And please tell me the truth," Mason asked hoping the man would continue to be honest about what he knew.

CHAPTER THIRTY-FIVE
Jake

As they drove through the park there wasn't much activity, but the air was thick and stuffy with smoke. Nearing the park exit they saw a Hispanic family loading up their car, Jake couldn't help but think to himself that might not be a bad idea. Jake thought about the day before when his neighbor Peter had tried to warn him. He didn't understand at the time what was happening so Peter must have seen something pretty serious. As they pulled out onto the main road, Jake looked behind them in the direction of downtown past the apartment blocks. All he could see was the sun making the haze of smoke that filled the sky glow.

The drive to the school would be a short one, it was a straight road from the park to the school passing only the rock quarry and a Wal-Mart. As they passed the rock quarry, this was the first time Jake had seen it empty with all the machines ground to a halt. That was an eerie sight he thought to himself.

They pulled up to a four way stop. If they drove straight, the school was on the other side. Looking across they could see it was deserted with only two trailers parked on the school grounds. They looked like the ones Jake and Benny had saw the day before at the Battleground High School.

"I don't see a single person," Benny said leaning forward. Jake could see his friend scrunching his eyes trying to see if anyone was over at the school.

"Looks like the Army guys could have been telling the truth," Alice said.

214

Benny started to turn the truck into the right lane to turn into the Wal-Mart parking lot.

The parking lot was packed! Jake hadn't seen it this busy since a black Friday! Benny found them a space towards the back of the lot.

As they walked towards the store, they were met with people rushing out of the store with arms full of merchandise. "Looks like the looting's started." Alice said dully.

Jake could sense the lack of optimism in Alice's voice but still hoped they could get in and out of here quickly despite how busy the store seemed. As they walked through the double doors, a man ran past clutching a TV. Jake couldn't believe that some people's priorities were with material things instead of their families and other people.

Entering the store, they agreed to split up so they could get what they needed and be out faster. The store was packed with hardly any elbow room at all. Benny was going to head to the pharmacy section for first aid supplies, Alice was going to get what food and water she could then meet Jake in the outdoor and sporting goods department. He figured he could get a lot of stuff to help if the power went out and long-term things to help if this situation lasted a while.

Jake pushed through some people as he headed to the back of the store where sporting goods was. He noticed there were no employees, but there were pallets of merchandise strewn in the aisles like they were halfway through unloading when this mob of people hit. Jake got to sporting goods but just like the rest of the store, it was crammed with people. Apparently, a lot of people had the same idea. The shelves were starting to be picked clean as were the pallets and merchandise was lying all over the floor. He saw a crowd of people around the ammo case with an employee behind the counter selling the ammo. This was the only employee he'd seen; the poor kid was being heckled and bombarded with handfuls of cash. Jake bypassed the crowd heading into the camping and survival aisle.

Jake had lay in bed most of the night thinking about stuff they'd need. Propane or other items for fire starting, things that could be used for purifying water as, even though the park had well water, right now he didn't trust that. The aisle, like the rest, was packed with people. A big huge tank of a man who Jake recognized stood in the middle of the aisle looking at a shelf of thermos flasks. The man saw Jake then nodded in acknowledgement. Jake was always reminded of a giant Viking when he saw this guy around the trailer park. He was over seven feet tall with a bald head and huge long grey and black wizard biker type beard.

Jake returned the nod as he headed for the propane which the man also had arm full of, he noticed. He wasn't able to get a basket and the store was too hectic for him to have grabbed a cart. Jake grabbed a few in one hand then got the last couple of Lifestraws off a peg.

Jake had read about them with some great reviews and looking at what was left those, and some purification tablets were his only option.

There was a scream that grabbed his attention away from the camping water supplies. He looked at the end of the aisle where there was a flashlight display. It was a young Hispanic boy maybe around his boy's age struggling with a large rich looking white guy in slacks. The guy had grey curly hair with a flushed red face. The guy obviously didn't work here, and the boy was looking around. The boy seemed to be looking for help as the man tugged at the flashlight they were both holding. Jake rushed towards them, "Hey, let go!" he said.

The flushed faced man just grunted pulling the flashlight out the boys hand with a fierce tug sending the boy tumbling to the ground.

"You back the fuck up, mister!" the man snarled, pointing a finger at Jake. Jake looked at the man's arm. There was bandaged showing under his shirt sleeve with blood spots seeping through.

Jake helped the boy up and heard someone walking up behind him. Glancing over his shoulder it was the big guy from his park. The big guy stepped past Jake,

"The fuck's your problem dude!" the big guy said to the man, "He's a kid," The big guy continued looking down at the man who was still pointing at Jake.

"I saw it first! He snatched it before I could get it," the man whined.

Looking at the display Jake could see there were no more flashlights. "Where's your parents?" he asked the boy who was visibly shaking and seemed scared.

The boy looked over towards the other side of the store, "My dad went to get water and told me I could get a toy, but I didn't want a toy, I wanted a flashlight," The boy said meekly. Jake nodded putting his hand on the kids shoulder as they backed away from the man.

"Hey, kid!" the big guy shouted as they both began walking away, "here you go, better than anything here" The big guy threw the kid a small black flashlight, "it's five thousand lumens, glass breaking rim and strobe, spot and wide beam settings," The man told the boy seeming proud of the functions.

The boy took it then looked up at the man, "Thank you, but don't you need it?" the boy asked.

The giant let out a deep laugh, "Nah, I got tons of them," the man said.

"Got some your kids can have too, always see them zipping around the park on their bikes. You guys might need them when the power goes out," The giant said matter-of-factly.

Jake smiled then before he could say they were interrupted by gunshots that rang out from the end of the aisle. Looking back, he saw the guy who the boy was struggling with was laying on the

217

ground. There was a man standing pointing a gun at the body on the ground.

"He was infected!" The man said popping off three more shots.

The shots started off a chain reaction as the whole store went crazy. People began scrambling towards the front of the store. Jake saw people tripping over each other and displays as more shots rang out, echoing through the store. Jake grabbed the back of the boy's shirt as they started running for the exit. The big guy ran in front of them pushing a path through the sea of people.

As they got to the front of the store the boy cried out, "Dad!" Breaking free from his grip the boy ran into the arms of a tall Hispanic man. Jake watched the man bend down to kiss the boy's head. "Are you okay?" the man asked the boy.

The boy nodded, "A guy took my light from me," the boy told the man who was glaring at Jake but the boy continued, "He pushed me down then these guys helped me and gave me a flashlight…it's a tactical one," he said, proud of his new toy. The man smiled, nodding at Jake in thanks.

The boy waved as the two walked towards the exit of the store with a basket full of food.

There was still a lot of screaming and shouting as Jake could still see people grabbing things from shelves but no more shots.

Jake saw Alice smiling, pushing a cart towards them as they stood near the exit. Benny was with her. "Guess everyone panicked. Found ourselves a cart," Alice said with squinting eyes. Jake realized she was staring at the big guy beside him.

"Hi, I'm Charlie" the giant said, putting out a huge hand which Alice shook.

"Alice," Alice replied.

Jake could see Charlie eyeballing Alice's belt.

"Your boyfriend a cop?" Charlie asked.

"No, I am! Is yours?" Alice replied back nodding towards Charlie's waist. Jake looked but didn't see anything then noticed the bulge near Charlie's crotch.

"Laundry day, these pants are too small… it's a python" Charlie replied.

"Course it is!" Benny chuckled chiming in.

Shots rang out from somewhere in the back of the store, "Let's get the fuck out of here!" Alice said getting no objection from anyone.

As they walked out of the store there were guys with guns circled around the exit. They were wearing camo and tac vests.

"Billy!" Charlie shouted waving at one of the guys in camo. A guy with a bucket hat and shades stepped forward smiling.

"Local militia…Bunch of yahoos," Charlie whispered as Billy waved a hand signaling the other men to lower their weapons.

Billy nodded behind them at the store. " The fucks going on in there? You boys code four? Heard some shots," Billy barked with a mouthful of chew.

Charlie nodded "Yeah, guy went off the deep end, think he was infected," Charlie said.

"Really?" Billy asked, taking the shades off then spitting the chew out.

Billy whistled then pointed into the store, four more guys in camo came forward. Billy patted Charlie on the shoulder, "Shit's hit the fan big guy…Not for everyone, so stay frosty!" Billy said then headed into the store with the other four men.

The group walked unimpeded past the rest of the men with guns. "Jesus Christ," Alice muttered.

"You don't feel safe with the likes of Bad Ass Billy protecting us, Mrs. Officer?" Charlie joked.

"Oh man, I love this guy!" Benny said laughing.

Jake couldn't help but smile at the attitudes of his friends and neighbor.

He saw Charlie looking at him, "Things are going to get a lot worse, you better get ready, that family of yours, too! Cause shits about to get real and Billy over there and his piss patrol will do more harm than good," Charlie said stopping at a huge Ram truck throwing his items in the trailer bed.

"Yeah, we've seen some scary shit and know there's no government help coming" Jake said, looking over at Benny.

Charlie nodded, "Good you know that, the governments a joke, this FEMA and this Red Cross bullshit is a joke, Billy and his crew have the right idea to stick together, it might be awhile before the government gets round to sorting shit out so until that happens people are definitely better sticking together," Charlie said climbing into the truck.

Jake nodded then gave the gentle giant a wave as the truck started   up.

CHAPTER THIRTY-SIX
Rob

The dull pain throbbed in Rob's back reminding him it hadn't been a dream as he sat with his back against the wire fence of the sectioned-off area he was in. They'd been looked over when they arrived here the night before, both Brandi and he were given a sleeping bag, a bag of food, and told they were safe here until the situation was brought under control. That was the last time any military personnel had spoken to them. Brandi had gone off to talk to other people in the quarantine area to try to get more information on what was happening. Rob had tried to get some rest as they'd been kept up all night by gunfire and screams coming from outside the "safe zone" as they'd heard it being referred to by the soldiers on the way in.

In reality, it was more like a fenced off compound about the size of two football fields. The area they were in was about half of the compound. It comprised of people who'd been rounded up and brought here. From what he'd heard, it was the same for most people. They were put into the back of a vehicle; told they were being taken to a joint FEMA/Military safe zone until the virus had been brought under control. As they entered, they were all given a brief exam then given a bag with toothpaste, toothbrush, cereal, milk and a protein bar. Rob had seen some people separated on the way in. Those people were taken to the quarantine tents which he summarized were for people who were infected.

The compound was right beside the I-205 bridge from Vancouver to Portland. It was surrounded by an eight-foot fence.

The bridge itself had barricades and a roadblock on both sides, he'd seen the bridge being blocked off when they arrived here. He rubbed his back as best he could, blaming the ground he'd chosen to sleep on. There were tents inside the area they were in, but he felt uneasy being enclosed in a tent after what he'd seen. He was starting to nod off when a boot dug into his side. Looking up it was a soldier.

"You okay?" the soldier asked.

Rob nodded, "Didn't get much sleep," he told the soldier.

"Well get up and head over to the gate, they're giving out lunch sacks," The soldier told him then wandered over to another guy who was snoozing away.

He got up to make his way over to the large gate where the lines were forming to get some lunch.

"Rob!" Brandi shouted. Brandi was with two hillbilly looking guys who were giving him a weird vibe. "You make some friends?" He asked sarcastically.

Brandi smiled, "This is Tommy, he went to my school," Brandi said gesturing at one of the men with her. The guy was of small frame with square shaped forehead and curly red hair.

"Nice to meet you," Rob said politely.

"Likewise," Tommy said, "This is my cousin Gus, we were brought here this morning. Apparently for our safety until order's restored and back to normal," Tommy said.

"Yeah, us, too" Rob replied.

"Thing is, we don't think it's going to be brought under control. It's gotten crazy overnight and we were safer where we were at than in here." Tommy said.

Rob knew where this was going, he'd seen plenty of guys like Tommy. Instigators, troublemakers not content with the pace things were going.

"Gus and me…we're thinking of trying to get out. Tonight, or maybe tomorrow." Tommy said.

Rob knew instantly this was a bad idea, he'd seen the soldiers mow people down last night. They may have been infected or zombies he understood that. The distance they had been from some of those people, especially on the drive here, there is no way the soldiers could have known for sure.

"You're telling me why?" Rob asked. He wanted to make it completely clear he wanted nothing to do with it.

"We could use some more muscle. You're a big guy," Gus said stepping in front of Tommy.

Rob let out a snigger then looked at them both in the eyes. "There is no way in hell I'm going to do something stupid that could get me shot," he told them smiling.

Rob could tell this wasn't going over too well as Tommy had clenched fists. Part of Rob's job was to access people and how they were feeling to best deal with a situation. Right now, he could tell Tommy didn't like his position on an escape attempt.

"No worries dude, just figured a guy like you didn't want to be cooped up in here while family and friends are being taken advantage of," Gus said, walking away.

Tommy stood for a few moments still staring at him, "If you change your mind, let us know. Brandi knows what tent we're in," Tommy said dryly before following Gus.

Brandi was looking at him, "You want to stay here? Really?" Brandi asked.

"You think it's any better out there right now?" He replied back. He knew these people were scared. He understood why but he also knew that for the US Army to be setting up FEMA shelters and shooting up hospitals then the situation outside of these camp walls must have been spiraling out of control. "It's not, not if there's places like this being set up on American soil," he told her.

Brandi nodded then forced a smile "I'm glad you're here with me," Brandi said.

"Me too, now let's go get some food," he told her, putting his arm around her in reassurance.

The line moved pretty fast for them to get some food which they took and sat down by the fence. Rob looked inside his brown paper bag at the squished, sweaty sandwich that was shrink wrapped and the badly bruised banana. Brandi made noise in disgust at the contents of her bag that made him laugh. "What!" Brandi asked.

Rob shrugged his shoulders, "I figured you were high maintenance but didn't figure you were this bad," he told her unwrapping his sandwich slowly like it was a delicacy.

He laughed again as Brandi squinted her eyes at how he was savoring the unwrapping of the sandwich. The moment was cut short by a woman screaming from the other side of the fence.

"Please No! Nooo!" a woman yelled.

Both of them were sitting with their backs against the fence and turned to see what was going on.

The other side of the fence was the compound where the soldiers and FEMA wandered freely between tents. The lady who had been screaming was standing in front of two soldiers. Behind the soldiers Rob could see some FEMA people or doctors in white coats dragging a young girl away. The lady tried to run past the soldiers but one of them tackled the lady throwing her to the ground. Rob wasn't the only one who noticed what was going on as people on his side of the fence lined it to watch what was unfolding. The other soldier must have noticed as he raised his rifle at the fence. "Like they're going to topple this fence," Brandi said quietly.

The lady scrambled again to try and get past the soldiers to the child being dragged away but more soldiers appeared.

There was another scream but not from the lady. This time it was a man that screamed then the child who had been dragged away came running around a tent corner back into view. The child had blood around her mouth and was growling, snapping her jaws. The

224

soldiers seemed frozen in place as the lady pushed past them to the small child. As the lady got close to little girl Rob could hear her talking softly to the child. This was cut short when after a loud boom, the child's head erupted in an explosion of blood and brain matter. The lady seemed frozen in place with outstretched arms covered in blood. The little girl's body slumped to the ground as cries went up from the people watching on their side of the fence. More soldiers were appearing with guns drawn walking towards the fence.

"BACK AWAY FROM THE FENCE!" a voice boomed across a bull horn.

The two soldiers who had been involved in the altercation with the lady were ordered to drop their weapons. Rob stepped back away from the fence keeping Brandi close but also kept his eye on what was going on. The two soldiers along with two doctors who had been dragging the little girl were marched away towards a large white tent. The large white tent was where he'd noticed a lot of people being taken since they arrived. There was a sign outside marked "quarantine."

The lady was surrounded by soldiers as was the child's body and Rob couldn't see what was going on. He felt sick to his stomach at what he'd just seen, and he could hear Brandi sniffing back tears.

"C'mon let's go take a walk," he told her, guiding her away from the fence and the horror that had just unfolded. As they began walking away the other people on his side of the fence didn't seem to share his want to get away from the situation. The fence was clanging as people banged things against the steel, shouting and screaming in anger at the soldier on the other side.

The tension was rising fast, so he hurried Brandi past some tents away from what was going on at the fence. The angry mob got a little quieter the further into the city of tents FEMA had erected on their side of the fence.

Rob took Brandi into a tent, thinking they could find a quiet spot to gather their thoughts. That idea was short lived when gunfire started to fill the air. Brandi squeezed him tight as what sounded like rain on a roof magnified by a lot was a hail of gunfire.

He didn't want to think about what was going on at that fence line but knew he would have no choice once it crossed into their side of the fence.

Over the echo of gunfire Rob heard scuffling coming from outside the tent. "Stay here!" he told Brandi sitting her down in a camp chair. Brandi shook her head terrified as tears streamed down her face. "You'll be safe in here! I need to see what's going on," he told her quietly with hands out for her to stay seated. "I'll be right back, I promise," he told her.

Brandi nodded wiping tears away.

Rob peered out the tent door to see a soldier lying on the ground between tents being kicked and stomped by a group of men. There were three of them and Rob didn't need to think twice, he ran out and pushed them away from the soldier. The soldier rolled over and Rob could see it was the one who told him to get food earlier.

"Fuck is wrong with you!" he shouted to the three men.

Three men stood there staring at him as the soldier began to get to his feet.

"Where's my rifle?" the soldier asked the men.

The men didn't say anything, but Rob could see the weapon lying on the ground behind the three men. The shooting at the fence had stopped, "You hear that?" Rob asked.

"That's the sound of his buddies about to come through that gate and round up idiots like you," Rob said dryly.

"We're trying to help you people!" The soldier said as the three men turned walking away.

"Save it, kid" Rob told the young man as he walked over to pick up the soldier's rifle.

One of the men stopped then turned around, "Help us? Are you kidding me? You're fuckin Nazis and this is just an internment camp," the man spat.

Rob glared at the man to walk away but inside knew there were similarities in the two. Something like that would never happen in this day and age. Let alone on American soil could it? This was something that would linger with Rob for a long time.

CHAPTER THIRTY-SEVEN
Caleb

The yellow puzzle piece teeth that Mark's mom had snapped with ferocity as the lady shambled across the room. Caleb backed away from the old lady as Nate ran into the room.

"Dad!" Nate shouted running in then pushing Mark's mom away. As Nate pushed, the lady tried frailly to grab onto his son. "Mrs. Buell can you hear us?" Caleb asked.

He knew it was probably futile by the twisted animalistic expression on her face, but it was worth a try. As what had been Mark's mom started to get up again, Caleb stepped forward kicking the lady in the chest sending her back into the recliner they'd found her in. As she landed in the chair again Caleb saw Nate rush over to an old fireplace in the corner. Grabbing a poker Nate threw it to him. Caleb caught it then gritted his teeth as he swung the poker as hard as he could at Mrs. Buell. There was a loud wet crack as the poker smashed into Mrs. Buell's temple as she was again lurching out the chair towards him. This time instead of teeth snapping at Caleb, Mrs. Buell's whole body fell to the floor in front of his feet. He looked down and wanted to cry, he could feel his eyes welling up, but he needed to snap out of it. "Dad!" Nate shouted.

Caleb looked over at his son, "Thank You," he said, mumbling.

"Dad, it's okay, we should go," Nate said but he was having a hard time concentrating, he wanted to throw up. Letting go of the poker he hadn't realized how hard of a grip he had on it as his hand was throbbing. It seemed like a dream, he wanted it to be a dream, but he could smell the rot and decay in the room. Looking down he could see thick chunks of blood on the poker he'd dropped. This wasn't a dream; this was a nightmare and it was one he didn't want to be a part of or his family. "You know where there are tools?" Caleb asked.

Nate nodded and Caleb could see the confusion on his son's face. "We gotta bury them, son," he said.

"Is that a good idea? What if we get sick? Shouldn't we burn them?" Nate asked.

Caleb knew burning them would be the best but if things went back to normal, he needed proof they'd done what they did as self-defense.

It took them a little over an hour to bury mother and son in the small back garden of the house Mark and his Mom had lived in. He hammered a wooden cross in the ground to mark the grave in case they needed to come back here with authorities. He'd sent Nate into the kitchen to gather supplies for the farm. As they were loading them into the Jeep, the dog returned and began barking again. "Go! Shoo!" Caleb shouted, waving his hand.

The dog kept barking, but this time wasn't sitting wanting petted, it seemed to be agitated, pacing.

"Dad! You hear that?" Nate asked.

Caleb looked at Nate shrugging his shoulders. "All I can hear is that blasted barking," He told Nate.

"No," Nate said looking into the air listening, "It's a baby crying!" Nate said looking toward two houses on the other side of the street. Caleb froze listening intently then he heard it faintly, it was a baby crying. As they both started to walk towards the houses on the other side of the street, he realized they weren't the only ones who'd heard the crying. Three people were slowly hobbling from the rear of one of the houses. Looking at them, Caleb could tell they were definitely infected so opened the rear door of the Jeep and pulled out the shotgun he'd stashed on the floor.

Something turned on inside of Caleb and all sense of self-preservation went out the window as he cross the road shotgun in hand. He knew he had to check on that baby!

The three infected were heading to the front door of one of the houses which seemed to be the one the crying was coming from. Pushing a rickety, wooden, waist high gate open he leveled his shotgun with the shoulders of the closest infected to him. All three of them seemed oblivious of Caleb and his son until he squeezed the trigger. He must have been ten feet from the infected when the slugs slammed into the one he'd been aiming at. The infected tumbled forward into the two in front like a bowling ball. The two that had been in front began getting up fully aware of Nate and him behind them now.

The one Caleb had shot lay on the ground with its upper shoulder, neck, and head wide open on the path leading to the front door. Nate rushed past him swinging a baseball bat at one of the other two cracking it on the head. It fell to the ground, but Nate didn't stop swinging. Caleb watched as his son reigned down a barrage of blows to the infected man's head. The last was a young woman whose shirt on her shoulder was torn open showing white, bloody muscles and tendons.

This last one had milky glassy eyes fixed on Nate. Nate was too close for him to shoot so he flipped his shotgun round making sure he had a tight grip on the barrel. Stepping forward he swung the shotgun with as much force as he had the poker. The lady's neck snapped as the butt of the gun connected with her jaw with a loud crack. As the head turned at an unnatural angle, the infected still seemed obsessed with getting his son. The shotgun stock obviously hadn't been as effective as the poker he thought as he swung a second time. This time he swung higher catching the front of the infected's face just before it reached Nate. This time it after he made contact with his make do baseball bat it fell and didn't get up. Nate was standing above the one that's head he'd turned to pulp. "Uhh, feel so much better now!" Nate said.

Caleb wasn't sure what his son meant by this, but he felt sick, he'd let out something he knew needed let out but felt sick as the sight and smell of what was in front of him.

Both were quickly reminded why they were there as the baby's cries grew louder. Without thinking, Caleb kicked open the front door then quickly surveyed the inside of the house. All the rooms seemed clean with no bad smells like Mrs. Buell's house had. He found the baby upstairs lying in a crib furiously crying. Caleb was dumbfounded at the fact someone had left this baby here alone. "Nate! Check the rooms!" He said but his son came walking in shaking his head at no sign of anyone else.

"Dad there's a lot of blood out back" Nate said standing by the window in the baby's room.

Caleb swaddled the baby in its soft baby blue blanket, it had been years since he'd done this. Holding the baby in his arms he began swaying and humming. The little guy seemed to like it as the crying stopped but he continued humming to soothe the child.

"The baby whisperer," Nate said with a snigger.

Caleb smiled knowing he still had it, he hadn't swaddled or calmed a baby since his girls. He could feel his cheeks stretch as his smiled widened. This was a sign he thought, a sign that things would definitely get better. That they would survive this, if this helpless little baby could survive then he knew everyone else could, too. Looking over, he could tell Nate thought the same thing as his son was smiling just as big as he was. Then Caleb froze as his heart sank at what he saw on the wall next to the baby's crib. There was a picture on the wall of the baby and its mother. It was the lady who was infected outside that he'd killed with his shotgun.

"I am so, so sorry little guy," he whispered to the baby boy he cradled   in   his   arms.

CHAPTER THIRTY-EIGHT
Nick

Nick looked out the window trying to gauge by the tree line and smoke plumes just where they were on the train route from Seattle to Portland. The train hadn't moved in over an hour. The train car was getting hot and the people inside not just the carriage, but others were getting agitated, he could hear them. The conductor hadn't been back to give them any more information on the situation or what was going to happen next. The little boy, Michael, hadn't stopped looking at the body in the tarp between the carriages.

"It's okay, he's not getting back up," Nick said to reassure the boy.

Michael just nodded still not looking away from the tarp wrapped body.

Heidi, like her brother, hadn't moved from beside him since the conductor left, either. Only unlike her little brother Heidi's attention was fixed on the bathroom door.

Agnes had taken the old lady to the cafe car to get away from the scene of what had happened. It had been the old lady's husband for who knows how many years. Nick couldn't imagine how hard it was or what the poor lady was going through. A few people who had been in their carriage had left into other cars, too. Nick had heard the whispering, saw the funny looks he was getting.

Nick knew enough of what was going on to understand that the man was infected. Infected with whatever virus this was and needed to be put down. The fact that the conductor was calm about it made Nick a little wary. The conductor obviously knew more about the

232

situation than he was telling them. Nick got up, reassuring Heidi he'd be right back, then walked over to the bathroom.

The man's girlfriend was still sitting back against the bathroom door. The lady hadn't looked in Nick's direction the whole time while sat there. Nick could tell the girl was scared but didn't know if it was because of what could happen to the boyfriend or of him. If the boyfriend was infected, then turning into one of those things was the next step. He knew he'd probably have to be the one to deal with the guy in the bathroom like he did the old man. This was probably another reason why the girl hadn't looked in his direction.

Nick calmly walked over beside her with the intent to try start a conversation, but the girl spoke first. "He hasn't talked for a bit... please..." the girl began but couldn't finish as tears flowed.

"It's okay, I'm just going to check on him, that's it," Nick said with his hands out.

The girl nodded as he leaned over to knock on the door. There was no reply from inside, so he put his ear against the door.

He didn't hear anything at first then there was a loud thump against the door that made him jump. The girl let out a scream at the thump from the other side of the door. Then a low dull groaning came from the other side, "ugghhh I...I'm...okay," the man said, sounding strained.

The girlfriend smiled, wiping away some of the tears. Nick knew from the guy's labored heavy breathing and strained voice that it wasn't a good sign. The guy definitely shouldn't be hurting this bad just from a bite. Nick gave the girl a forced smile then headed back to his seat trying not to think about what would happen next. As he turned, he saw Heidi peering down the aisle at him. Michael was looking over the headrest at him as if hiding to see what was happening.

"He's fine," he told them as he sat back down to set their minds at ease. Michael let out a sigh of relief then looked out the window.

"He's fine?" Heidi asked not as easily convinced.

Nick nodded trying not to give away his concern while trying to think of something else to say.

Just then the intercom crackled, "Attention please, we would ask that you all safely and slowly gather your belongings and exit the train using your nearest available exit, a crew member will meet you on the tracks outside," a voice said.

Everyone was looking at each other as they all started to get up. Michael was staring at him,

"Isn't it a bad idea to get off the train? Isn't it dangerous?" the boy asked.

Nick knew the boy was right, but they also had to do as instructed. Then Nick realized it may be safer to get everyone off the train. If anyone was infected then ended up like the old guy, being in an enclosed space wasn't too smart. It was only a matter of time before the guy in the bathroom turned and Nick wasn't sure the timeline of the virus.

As everyone headed to the door, Nick walked back over to the girl sitting outside the bathroom "Hey, do you want to come with us?" he asked her.

The girl shook her head and he nodded in understanding. The conductor hadn't been back through with the key. Nick bent down beside her, "I'll find the conductor or if I can't, I'll get a key so we can get him out," he told her.

"Thank you," the girl said looking up at him with eyes swollen from crying.

Nick knew he shouldn't be so concerned for some strangers, but he also felt he owed these two. If it hadn't been for this guy being a hero who knows what would have happened. How many people in the train car would have been attacked or infected with whatever this was? Now he had these two kids looking at him like they were his responsibility now. He knew Agnes was busy in the cafe car so hopefully he could hand them back to her care outside.

"Let's go," he told them as he grabbed his bags from the overhead. They began gathering up their stuff that was strewn over the table. Nick looked at both ends of the carriage, there was a line at one end to get out. The other was the end with the body between carriages and had no line.

He started heading towards that door but stopped as Michael grabbed his shirt. Looking down, he could tell Michael didn't want to go that way.

Nick smiled nodding then turned to walk towards the other end with the line of people.

"You're such a pussy," Heidi said teasing. Michael didn't seem to care, and Nick couldn't blame the boy. *There was a dead guy laying on the ground at the other door, how many kids Michael's age had seen a dead guy*, Nick thought.

As they got off, he couldn't believe how much better it felt outside of the train. The stale musty air inside and muggy heat was getting to be unbearable. He could see the train staff all standing on the other side of the tracks talking amongst themselves. Nick looked both directions seeing no sign of civilization except a plume of smoke in the distance rising above the trees to the north. Before the train had stopped, he remembered there was a road crossing a little way back. So, he knew they weren't too far out from people.

"Stay close" he said helping the two kids down from the train doors. Without a platform the doors were a few feet above the ground. Nick looked around for Agnes then heard a woman scream. This wasn't a scared scream but a scream of someone in pain. Looking a few carriages up he could see people gathered around a door. The crowd parted as two men were helping Agnes stand up. Agnes's arms were wrapped around both men's shoulders as they walked slowly down the tracks.

"Are you okay?" Michael shouted, running towards Agnes.

Agnes nodded but Nick could see Agnes was clearly wincing in pain. He looked down at her ankle, it was already starting to swell.

"Here take a seat," Nick told Agnes putting his bag down. He motioned for Agnes to rest on it while he looked around for some water.

A guy who had been in their car handed him a bottle which Nick gave to her. Kneeling down beside her, he rolled Agnes' pant leg up. "Think she landed wrong and twisted it," one of the men who'd helped carry Agnes said, Nick nodded when he saw a big ball starting to form on the side of her foot.

"You need to elevate it and rest," he told Agnes, who nodded. Nick looked at the two men who helped her, "We need ice," he said. One of the men nodded then headed in the direction of the food car. Heidi and Michael both had looks of concern so Nick backed away a little so they could get closer. He looked over at the train staff talking in the huddle apart from everyone. A lot of train commuters were looking over at them, too. Once the guy came back with the ice, Nick told Michael to keep it on Agnes ankle. Nick hoped that would keep the boy busy as he didn't want Michael worrying too much. Nick knew anything the train staff was going to say wasn't going to be good if they'd made them all vacate the train.

One of the train staff stepped forward waving people closer then started shouting trying to get everyone's attention.

"I'll be right back" Nick said to Michael patting the boy on the shoulder as he walked, Nick could hear Heidi following right behind him.

"Please! Please!" The conductor began.

"If you could keep your questions for a few minutes we want to tell you what we know first," another train worker said, stepping forward. Nick looked at the man's Amtrak name badge. It read Stephen with title of driver underneath it.

"We were told not to leave Seattle station, but we did, we panicked when we heard gunfire over the radio and since then we have had no communication with Seattle," Stephen said.

"The last message we got from Portland was to not go there and not go back to Seattle either as people are getting infected with this virus. It's running rampant and the military has been called in to try get it under control. FEMA has been setting up shelters for displaced people which is where we've been told to head. We sent out calls asking for FEMA or the army to send help with our location," The driver said.

Nick knew this was bad as he could feel the tension growing in the crowd. The train staff then came under fire from a barrage of questions from the passengers. Suddenly something caught Nick's eye from the tracks behind the train. Nick began walking towards the rear of the train not wanting to cause any alarm or panic.

There was lady crawling along the tracks behind the train towards them. The lady was wearing a tattered blood splattered white dress with chunks of flesh missing revealing red stained bones. Jaws snapped as the lady slowly crawled towards the train dragging two mangled legs behind. Nick was about to check if Heidi had noticed the lady when screams erupted from the crowd of train passengers. Nick looked around for something to use as a weapon but there was nothing in sight. He didn't want to waste too much time so started towards the crawling corpse unclipping his knife. He kept it clipped reverse in his pocket, so it wasn't noticeable but also easy to access. Nick really didn't want to get infected or contaminated blood on his knife that he used every day. He used this knife for lots of things on a daily basis but right now he had no other option. Nick stood over the mangled body lying on the tracks, gasping and clawing at the air. He knew there was no time for over thinking decisions in situations like this. There was only spontaneous action for preservation in survival situations he reminded himself.

Nick flicked the blade out while looking into the soulless white eyes of this poor girl. He felt pity for who this lady had been and whatever horrific accident had left her like this.

Thick slimy drool ran down the ladies twisted torn open face as Nick slammed the knife into an eye socket. The jaws stopped snapping instantly as the ladies whole body went limp like the legs that had been dragging. Staring down at the body, Nick slipped back to his habit of making up back stories for people. This lady seemed really young, was in a nice dress, she may have been on her way to something important. Then was attacked by infected people or just simply in a bad accident then set upon by infected people. Nick was brought back to reality when his attention was brought back to the train passengers screaming. Passengers began to scatter as shapes of more people were rounding the corner of the tracks behind the train.

CHAPTER THIRTY-NINE
Mason

The girls were fast asleep in the back of the Jeep which was good as Dimitri had been explaining some of the videos, he'd seen in news broadcasts. Mason had no idea this had been going on for so long. "At first there was a curfew, which right now we're past! Then there was martial law in the cities. No one was allowed on the streets unless with armed designated escorts. Then today…today was when there was collapse. This has taken time to hit us but had been happening in other countries much sooner. A few days ago, when the army presence increased, I sent my family home to our village just across the border. I'd hear the soldiers talking about places like Korea and China that had tried to curb the spread by isolating town centers. Removing nails and teeth. Most of this wasn't on the news. I think for the same reason as I was ordered to stay, to not show weakness to the people. I think eventually this virus will destroy the countries from within. Now armies are bombing and attacking their own cities. That's what I was watching on the news right before you got caught in that access hallway," Dimitri said.

"So, any advice on what to do next?" Mason asked.

"We're almost at the border, once there, my village is just down the road, you can drop me off and I can give you directions to where you want to go from there," Dimitri said.

There was some stirring in the back seats, so Mason looked back to make sure everything was okay with the girls. Alex was sitting up awake looking out the window while still holding on to the children. "Where are we going?" Alex asked.

"Dimitri's hometown across the border in Poland," Mason told his wife.

Alex nodded then snuggled up tight with the girls keeping them warm. Mason could feel it was starting to get cold. The weather here was definitely unlike the heat wave they had just left back in the US. The road started to get a little rough as the Jeep was rocking with every bounce on the beat-up road. Both girls woke up with Abby screaming at the top of her lungs. In a small confined space like the Jeep the crying was almost unbearable. Sarah immediately started to comfort her baby sister. "It's okay, baby Abby, Mommy's here and Daddy, see!" Sarah said to Abby while patting the baby's back.

This melted Mason's heart, seeing his daughter being brave taking care of her baby sister. "Scenic route?" he asked Dimitri rhetorically. The road evened out again as Mason reached in the back to pick up the baby out of her car seat.

"C'mon, come to daddy, little lady," Mason said in his best baby voice. Glancing at Alex he was surprised to see his wife asleep again. Feeling a little uneasy he felt his wife's forehead which was clammy with sweat. "Dimitri, I have to change her diaper, you might want to hold your nose" He said to the driver smiling.

"No problem here, and we've arrived" Dimitri said motioning at a border crossing blockade that was dead ahead.

Mason nodded as the Jeep slowed in the middle of the road to a stop.

"Sarah, can you pass me the diaper bag, honey?" Mason asked his older daughter.

Sarah pulled the diaper satchel off the Jeep's floor then passed it forward to him. Abby started to cry as Mason laid the baby in his lap then pulled the dirty diaper off. As he wiped then put a clean diaper back under the little girl, he heard Dimitri muttering something.

"What's going on?" Mason asked attaching the Velcro on both sides of the diaper.

"There was something in the trees, probably attracted by the sound of the girl. A baby's cry can mimic several different animals cries for help or mating or to anyone infected it's just an attraction," Dimitri explained.

Mason began patting Abby's back as he lifted her up into the crevice of his neck to comfort the baby. He could see in the rear-view mirror Sarah was snuggled up with her mom.

"Dimitri this virus…what are the symptoms? How do you get it? And why did you say infected are attracted to noise?" He asked.

Dimitri reached back putting a hand on Alex's temple. "Don't worry your wife's not infected if that's what you're worried about," Dimitri reassured him.

Mason didn't want to say it out loud but since the airport his wife had barely spoken a word, was starting to develop a fever and seemed to have little or no energy. He'd assumed it was jet lag or shock from what had happened at the airport.

"The virus itself, many have speculated where it came from. The most popular theory as you know is that it's an American designed super virus. The news said it's contracted like an STD or via any kind of bodily fluids. The army was instructed not to touch or come into close contact with anyone infected. So, I'm not sure if that means it's airborne or not but if your wife or any of your children were infected, they would be burning up with fever right now. Other symptoms reported are violent outbursts, skin breaking, and bleeding easily." Dimitri said while constantly looking nervously outside of the Jeep.

Mason looked out surveying the border crossing which was locked down and seemed deserted. The four-lane roadway to let traffic through was closed with heavy barriers in place across each of the lanes. The toll booth looking things on each side also had shutters down.

" How do we get through? Place looks empty" Mason said still rocking baby Abby against his chest.

"We have to get into one of those booths and open a gate manually, as far as I knew the border crossings were still to be manned. They must have had to close the borders if things got too bad," Dimitri said.

"Yeah, too bad on which side of the border is what I'm worried about" Mason answered back.

"We should leave them in here and us both go out, make it fast" Dimitri said enthusiastically.

Mason nodded laying his daughter who was now asleep in the back seat beside Alex and Sarah. "Daddy, where are you going?" Sarah asked.

"Honey I need you to look after your sister and wake your mommy up if anything happens," he told the bright-eyed girl.

"Happens? Like what, Daddy?" Sarah asked catching him out.

"Like if your sister wakes up, honey," he hesitantly replied.

Sarah just nodded then buried her head into Alex again while putting an arm around Abby.

"You feel comfortable using this" Dimitri asked handing him a rifle.

Looking at it Dimitri must have sensed his concern. "If you have to," Dimitri continued.

Mason took the AK sliding back the bolt then nodded. He understood what Dimitri was referring to. They were about to illegally cross a border and not just any border. This was a Russian military-controlled border crossing that had been locked down. Anyone else that was here probably wasn't supposed to be since the military had bugged out.

"You know how to get one of those barriers open?" He asked Dimitri who nodded.

The four-lane border checkpoint was gated with each lane having individual barriers as well as steel gates on each lane. "We will head to the gatehouse at that end, check it's clear then I'll open one of the middle gates and barrier. You come back and drive through then wait on the other side for me. I will close the gate then come out the other side," Dimitri said.

"Sounds good" Mason acknowledged.

Mason looked back at his family in the back seat all huddled together. He didn't know how he would get them out of this or even home. All he knew was that he had to keep them safe and get them somewhere safe as quickly as he could. Mason opened his door feeling the chilly wind hit him as stepped out into the cold night. It had been hard to see through the Jeep's grimy windows but on either side of the border checkpoint was a huge chain link fence. The fence was topped with razor wire that ran with the fence in both directions away from the gates. As he began to walk towards the checkpoint, he heard Dimitri close the Jeep door. On one side of the check point was a small gatehouse then a little further down the road there was a two-story building. The building had a sign outside that Mason couldn't read. He assumed it was some kind of security or immigration building.

"The switch to open the gates in there, right?" Mason asked

"Yes, in the gatehouse for the steel gate, then in the booth for the barrier," Dimitri replied.

As Mason cautiously walked towards the gatehouse, he suddenly froze in his tracks fixated by what he saw on the ground.

"Dimitri, I think I know which side of the border stuff went bad on," he said looking at blood splattered all over the ground. He turned to see Dimitri kneeling down picking something up.

"Shell casings. Lots of them," Dimitri said.

Before they could elaborate on what could have taken place the Jeep's horn began to blast causing both of them to jump. Looking over, Mason could see Sarah leaning over into the front of the Jeep pounding the horn with her fist. Then he saw them, dozens of them coming out from the trees. It was too dark to make out details, but they weren't moving very fast, two of them had already passed the Jeep which is what Sarah must have seen. As the horn kept going off the people that had come from the tree line in his direction had turned towards the Jeep.

"The horn! She's attracting them to her!" Dimitri blurted out.

Masons heart froze for an instant then he realized he didn't want it to break as he saw the look of fear on his little girl's face. Leveling the rifle with the two things shuffling towards him he squeezed the trigger sending blood splattering into the cold night as bullets ripped through both of the bodies. Mason bit his lip and pulled the trigger again when he saw they didn't fall.

"Dimitri, open that fucking gate!" He screamed, running towards the two people that had just sponged up the bullets.

"The head!" he heard Dimitri yell as he charged forward closing ground fast towards the Jeep. As he got close to the first shape, he swung the AK high like a bat catching the man on the chin. Mason heard a sickening crack as the man fell to the floor with a wet thump. The second man who was in a suit riddled with bullet holes lunged for him. Mason moved to the side avoiding contact with the man who let out a growl. Mason was focused on one thing and that was getting to the Jeep.

A few of these things were already at the Jeep so he aimed the rifle at the feet then let out barrage of bullets sweeping the rifle from left to right and back again. The group all crumpled to the ground then turned towards him. They began clawing their way towards him dragging themselves across the road. Mason had never seen anything like this before at all. He felt sick at the sight of the twisted, shattered, and burst open lower limbs. Raising the rifle to the closest crawler to him he pulled the trigger. A bullet pierced the forehead of the closest crawler sending it limp face down to the ground. They weren't moving very fast on the ground, so he ran around to the driver side of the Jeep. Once inside Sarah wrapped her arms around him bawling with Alex in the back, holding the baby close. Looking past the girls out the back window, he could see even more of them coming out from the trees. Mason put his foot down as he drove the Jeep towards the gate. One of the middle gates was open but the barrier was still down.

"Daddy, go! Go! Please!" Sarah begged.

Looking out he couldn't see any sign of Dimitri. He didn't want to leave him, but those things were getting closer. "Alex put Abby down and come up front!" He said to his wife.

"Wh-why?" Alex asked anxiously.

"Look, pass Abby to Sarah and hop up front, I need to go open the barrier. Soon as I do that, floor it through, okay? I'll meet you over there," he told them.

"Daddy, no! Don't go! Please stay!" Sarah said, crying hysterically.

Mason pulled her in close kissing her on the head and taking a big smell of his daughter's hair.

"Daddy will be right back, honey, trust me I'm going nowhere, I promise," he said before opening the door then jumping out. As he did Alex hopped up front while he watched as Sarah held Abby close while not taking her swollen eyes filled with tears off him. He'd never felt so powerless yet so responsible before.

He ran into the toll booth with the barrier of the lane the Jeep was sitting in. The door was already open with blood all over the ground. As he looked in at the desk where someone must usually sit, he could see some buttons. "Fuck," Mason muttered to himself as all the button descriptions were in another language. He was about to start pushing every button when he heard something behind him right at his back. Mason whirled round with rifle up pointing directly at Dimitri who was standing with hands in the air. One of the hands had some keys dangling.

"They're for the barrier," Dimitri said as Mason moved out the way.

Mason moved back outside the booth and fired more shots at the oncoming group of people who seemed more like mindless zombies than people. It worked and the group turned from heading towards the Jeep to heading towards Dimitri and him. A buzzer went off as the barrier raised then the Jeep flew through the gate and across a bridge on the other side of the checkpoint gates. Mason hadn't seen the bridge while the gate was closed.

"We gotta go!" Dimitri shouted as the buzzer went off again. The barrier came back down with a thud. The steel gate slammed shut stopping any of the infected people from following the Jeep. They instead turned their attention towards him then Dimitri pulled his arm towards the door leading out the other side of the checkpoint gateway onto the bridge.

CHAPTER FORTY
Jake

As they drove towards the trailer park, Jake could see down the road to the apartments. The road was completely clear of cars, which was unusual. Jake could see the people at the apartments were pretty busy.

They were pushing cars out onto the road creating a makeshift barrier. The barrier blocked off the small two-lane road that connected the apartments, trailer park, and the big wide main road.

Pretty smart, Jake thought looking past the jerry-rigged blockade to the four-lane road leading to the freeway and downtown.

As they turned the corner into the trailer park, Jake could see the assistant manager was outside a trailer on a ladder. Ken had been the assistant manager since Jake had moved in here. Ken did more than the actual managers did which Jake respected. Both Ken's trailer and the manager's trailers sat at the entrance as you drove into the park. The only time Jake or Emily had seen the managers was when they were out around the park handing out notices. Ken was in his early sixties but a picture of health with short white hair and well-trimmed beard. Ken definitely didn't look in the sixties, but Ken's wife Marcy did. Marcy rarely left the house, spending a lot of time on the porch reading.

Pulling into the driveway both boys were working on their bikes. Emily was on the steps with Marcus standing beside her. This made Jake feel a little more normal than the trip to Wally World had made him feel. "How was it?" Emily asked walking towards them.

"It was fine, but we won't be going back to Wal-Mart anytime soon so have to make what we have last" he said. Emily looked a little shocked, so he kept going "We met one of our neighbors, the big biker Viking guy who lives around the corner, his name's Charlie" he told Emily with a smile.

They said goodbye to Benny, Marcus, and Alice who said they would try to check in every couple of days. "Stay safe!" Jake said and Benny nodded.

"Honey, I think when they come to check in if things aren't better then we should leave," Jake said as they took the supplies into the house.

Emily didn't say anything so Jake knew he would have to explain to his wife his reasoning if it came down to it. He'd thought it over while coming back from Wal-Mart.

Jake thought about how many people were in this trailer park.

If someone here got infected then turned into one of those zombies, then the whole park could get infected in no time. This confirmed his idea he'd had to leave, to travel as far away as possible. He remembered in history class that they did a project on the black plague.

When it hit small towns, most successful people who survived had isolated themselves. They traveled out in the wilderness away from people. The hard part he remembered learning was they would kill anyone who came close. They couldn't risk the chance of infection from outsiders. Jake knew that wasn't something he could do. He also didn't know much about this virus or how it was spread.

While they were putting the food away there was a knock on the door. Jake opened the door to see their neighbor, Kristy.

"Hi Jake, just thought I would let you and Emily know that most of the park are gathering at the manager's office," Kirsty said pointing towards the front of the park.

"Really? Let's go see what's happening," Emily said walking out the door putting an arm around him. While walking towards the Manager's office the two boys came flying around the corner on their bikes then skidded to a stop in front of them.

"The assistant manager wants to see everyone at his place," Paul said, short of breath.

"Yeah we were headed to the park to play then people started gathering and shouting, then Ken came out and said he wanted to wait until everyone was there," Greg blurted out, not taking a breath.

Jake was taken aback when he saw the crowd that was circling the porch of the assistant manager. Ken was stood on the porch above the crowd with arms outstretched like he was trying to calm an angry mob. Jake noticed Marge was at the front of the crowd shouting so of course this was an angry mob if Marge was the instigator he thought. Jake saw Marge's cousins, the Jones brothers standing by their beat-up green ford truck. The truck was parked in the bark dust of the play park that was meant for the kids. CJ, the middle of the three brothers was stood with a beer in hand. Jesse the other brother was leaning over the trucks hood looking at the crowd of people. Jake saw as they got closer Jesse's gaze switched from the crowd in front of Ken's trailer to his wife. Emily must have noticed this too as he felt Emily take his hand squeezing it tight. Joining the back of the crowd, he could hear Ken being asked about park security.

Ken explained that the managers had left for a vacation and not returned. That's when Marge seemed to take her cue.

"What about rent Ken? If the managers aren't here, I'm not paying rent! Any scumbag could steal it from their mailbox!" Marge said in a rough gravelly voice that Jake always assumed was from the constant smoking.

"Y'know I can't say I blame you guys with what's on the news for your concern so until I hear otherwise from the management company who owns the park rent will be frozen!" Ken said which led to a big smile spreading across Marge's face. The Jones brothers cheered along with some other residents.

After what Jake had seen he couldn't help but feel sick inside at what he was hearing. Even after what was on the news these people were more concerned with saving a few bucks. They had no care about what was going on outside of their small little selfish worlds. Seeing this gave another reason why he knew he had to get his family away from here as fast as possible.

The Jones' truck door opened then Hank, the oldest brother of the three, got out. Hank stood by the side of his truck.

"Hey!" Hank bellowed, swaying a little then stepping towards the crowd.

"So, what are we going to do about these damn infected? The news says we can defend ourselves," Hank said looking away from Ken.

Hank was one of the people who bent the rules as much as possible. Marge was his neighbor as well as cousin. From the gossip Emily was always hearing from the neighbors, Ken and Hank had gotten into it many times over park rules. Jake could feel the tension in the crowd as it got quiet. He heard the deep breath Ken took in before looking around the crowd that were looking up for an answer.

"This park has been my home for over twenty-eight years, and I am not going anywhere! I will not let some hooligans or some crazy people high on drugs come in and damage this property in any way shape or form," Ken stated boldly. The crowd cheered but Jake looked at Emily shaking his head. These people had no idea what they were in for if they thought they could just scare these infected people off. Jake was about to pluck up the courage to say something himself when Charlie spoke up.

"Listen!" Charlie shouted, getting everyone's attention, even the Jones brothers fell silent. "We can stand here in a scared huddle all we want, worry about rent, worry about defending our homes if they try to get in but what we should be more concerned about…is making the park more secure, more defendable!" Charlie began to slowly walk to the front of the crowd.

As the crowd parted at the front, Charlie walked up Ken's steps then turned to the crowd. "Listen, these infected who've gone bat shit crazy aren't the only issue! Help ain't coming! Not anytime soon! When downtown gets overrun with infected or they run out of food or whatever because there just simply isn't enough for them all then they will travel outward from the city and come this way!" Charlie said authoritatively. As the giant of a man was talking Jake could see people in the crowd nodding agreement. Charlie continued, "You can bet when they make their way this far up from the freeway, and they will, they'll want what we have! Our food! Our well water! What would you do to feed your family? So, we have to start preparing! We have to board up our homes! Secure our fences! "Charlie said, stepping beside Ken pointing at the park entrance.

"Do those work?" Charlie asked.

"Yes, I think so… they haven't been closed in over ten years, Charlie," Ken said looking bewildered.

To his relief Jake could tell Charlie had just taken over control of this crowd from Marge.

"That's where we start!" Charlie shouted.

"We close the gate! Set up some watch posts and keep it safe for the people who live here and only the people that live here should be let in!

"These are our homes and we have to defend them!" Charlie said as more cheers went up from the people gathered. CJ smashed a beer bottle on the truck as the brothers cheered. Then Jake's relief got shaky as he realized that this could turn ugly very fast. If people came to the gates to asking for help, they shouldn't be turned away.

Charlie seemed like a nice guy, but the Jones brothers were too pumped for this.

Charlie stood silently for a few minutes then continued, "It's not just thugs, thieves, and desperate people looking to steal some food we need to defend our homes from! It's these infected too and they're not just druggies on bath salts!" Charlie said looking wide eyed.

Jake knew this is where Charlie would either get the crowds 100% backing or they would think the guy was crazy. Most of them probably hadn't seen what he had or what this virus does to people.

"They're zombies! The people infected are dead folks come back to life infected by some disease that causes them to feel no pain! Just a hunger for human flesh! Only shooting them in the head will do the trick so ya gotta get all your firearms ready." As Charlie finished, Jake could see people in the crowd turn talking amongst themselves. To these people Charlie was starting to sound like a guy gone off the deep end. Jake had seen the infected for himself, so he knew what Charlie was saying was right. Jake watched Charlie walk over to the entrance then grab the handle of the gate. The gate had been slid to the side in the open position ever since he'd moved here. Charlie's brother Nathan walked over grabbing onto the gate, too. Both of them tugged at the gate to try move it closed. The gate creaked but didn't budge as it was rusted in position. Emily squeezed Jake's hand then he felt her lean in close to his ear.

"You're right, we have to leave," Emily whispered.

Jake nodded then as they turned to head back to the trailer, he could hear Charlie grunting. Charlie was trying to force the gate closed but it wouldn't budge. The Jones brothers had started laughing as they still stood by the truck.

"We don't need the gate! We'll shoot any fucker stupid enough to come near our place but we ain't jumping on your zombie crazy train!" CJ said chuckling. Hank started the brother's truck up spewing black diesel fumes then drove off. Charlie seemed unfazed by the antics as the big man still kept trying to close the gate. Nathan's feet were digging into the dirt as both struggled with the gate.

Jake let go of Emily's hand so he could go over to help them. He walked over knowing the park and the families in it could use all the help in defending it that they could get. People like the Jones brothers couldn't grasp the severity of the situation. Jake hoped at some point they would as how they wanted to handle things wouldn't end well. Charlie nodded as he joined in the struggle to close the gate. After a few seconds of pushing, the gate finally squeaked as it moved a little. A couple of people came to help push then slowly it started to move. As they all pushed the gate started to pick up momentum. "Keep going, it's moving!!" Charlie roared.

Cheers went up from the crowd gathered as the gate rolled across the width of the entrance then slammed closed. Jake was out of breath and looked over to see Emily squinting at him.

"Thanks, partner!" Charlie said slapping him on the shoulder.

"Yeah, thanks, man," Nathan chimed in then thanked the other two guys who'd helped.

Jake knew one of them, his name was Dom. Dom was a small guy who lived a few trailers down from him with two girls. Dom's wife Kristy was who'd told them about the meeting.

Jake looked around at the other families gathered knowing if those infected got in here it would be far worse than the old folks home.

CHAPTER FORTY-ONE
Nick

T he train staff were trying to calm people, but Nick knew what was about to happen would spiral out of control. He darted over to Heidi grabbing her by the arm. "Here take your brother and run that way! Follow the tracks!" Nick said pointing in the direction the train had been headed.

Nick had noticed when he got off the train there was nothing but trees on either side of the tracks for a good few miles ahead of them. Behind them, however, they had just passed a road crossing where these infected must have come from. Attracted by the sound of the train he assumed as they seemed to be drawn to sound.

Nick began to help Agnes up "C'mon, little lady, you're with me," he said, hoisting Agnes up and wrapping her arm around his shoulder.

"PLEASE! GET BACK ONTO THE TRAIN AND WAIT UNTIL EMERGENCY SERVICES ARRIVE!" Steve the train driver shouted out. No one seemed to be listening to Steve as they were all scrambling in different directions into the trees. Some people did jump back on board the train Nick noticed but that was just a death trap. As he hobbled with Agnes along the tracks, he could hear screaming coming from whatever was unfolding behind him. Nick saw Michael starting to turn around.

"Don't look around and keep going!" He shouted.

Heidi started to pick up the pace with her little brother in tow, but Nick and Agnes weren't going very fast. He was glad these infected seemed slow and docile otherwise carrying Agnes wouldn't be a smart move. Smart moves were how you stay safe in survival situations, you can't think with your heart just your head.

Agnes groaned as he kept trying to keep up the pace with Heidi and Michael. He had to though as he didn't want the kids to get too far ahead. A noise of feet crunching on gravel came from behind them. It got louder as the person running got closer. Nick paused for a second to glance over his shoulder at whoever was running to catch up with them. What he saw wasn't at all what he expected. Nick thought it would be someone from the train who'd noticed they'd made a break for it. It was the conductor of the train who had clearly been infected. The eyes weren't cloudy white but extremely bloodshot. There was a gaping gash on the conductor's shoulder that was pouring blood. Agnes groaned as he removed her arm from around his neck then lowered her to the ground. "What-" Agnes began to say.

"Don't worry, I'll be right back! Heidi!" He told Agnes then shouted for Heidi's attention to help her sister.

Turning to deal with the conductor it was too late the conductor lunged at him. They both fell to the ground with the conductor on top. Agnes was screaming, kicking the conductor with the good foot. Nick put his forearm across the conductor's chest to keep a barrier between him and this monster's snapping jaws. Blood mixed with drool dripped onto Nick face, but he turned to the side so as to not get any in his mouth or up his nose. The conductor's body felt like dead weight bearing down on him. The conductor's arms weren't grabbing at nick but flailing around to the side like a bird trying to fly. Nick used this to his advantage wrapping his free arm over one of the conductors's then used it as leverage to pull the monster to the side rolling him over. Now Nick was on top he kept his forearm across the conductors collar bone pinning him to the ground then elbowed the man in the face, but the conductor wasn't fazed as jaws kept snapping. Nick was about to try for another elbow when two hands around a rock came past his face. The rock smashed down into the conductors face sending blood spouting into the air. Nick looked up to see Heidi standing above him. Growls came from the conductor who was now in even more of a frenzy. The rock cradled in Heidi's hands came down again and again onto the infected conductors face. Nick felt the man's body go limp under him as the snapping jaws now full of broken teeth stopped. Nick fell back with a sigh looking at the clouds in the clear sky. He was out of breath struggling to get his heart rate back down as it felt like it was going to explode out his chest.

Quickly he rolled over then got up then started to walk away from the group. He began checking around his nose, eyes, and mouth for blood from the conductor.

"Stay back!" He shouted putting a hand back to make sure none of them came near him.

"You're not one of them" Heidi said walking towards him.

"You don't know that yet, I could have gotten it in my eyes or in my mouth without realizing it," he told her.

Heidi stood staring at him waiting, he wasn't sure what she was waiting for. In fact, he wasn't sure what he was waiting for, he didn't know how long this thing took to kick in. So even if he was infected, he still had time to try to get these people to safety wherever that was.

"Okay, let's get going," he told her.

Heidi nodded as they both walked towards Michael who was sitting by Agnes.

"If I start acting weird or funny, you need to leave me and go. You hear me?" Nick stressed to her quietly before they reached Michael. Nick noticed a sad look in the girl's eyes when she nodded. Nick nodded back, silently acknowledging their agreement.

Helping Agnes back up, getting her settled around his neck to hobble on, he looked back in the direction of the train. He couldn't make out what was going on, but he could see movement in the distance. It was time to put some more distance between them and whatever these infected were.

CHAPTER FORTY-TWO
Caleb

The road was empty on the way out from Marcus's Mom's. house towards Amboy which felt a little unusual for Caleb. Nate was sat in the back cradling the baby that they'd found. They were going to stay to try to find more family, but it was just too dangerous so they both agreed to keep the boy safe until this blew. Once everything was back to normal then they could reunite him with some family. As they approached a freeway exit there was a car wrapped around a signpost with another car beside it that had mounted the sidewalk. The car on the sidewalk was surrounded by three people who were pounding on the windshield. Caleb could see two small girls maybe around five or six in the back seats screaming. Caleb brought the vehicle to a screeching halt.

"Dad, what's up?" Nate said from the back seat.

"Those folks are in trouble, keep the baby quiet, Nate I'll go see what I can do," Caleb said while reaching for his shotgun. Caleb pumped the shotgun as he stepped out, but the three men seemed to not hear it. The sound of a shotgun being racked was one of the most recognizable and most distinguishable sounds in the world. The fact none of these three men were bothered by it sent a wave of terror over Caleb.

"HEY! HEY!" Caleb shouted to get the men's' attention.

Only one of the men turned around and immediately Caleb raised the shotgun towards the man who was clearly infected. The cream shirt the man had been wearing was soaked on one side with blood from a huge chunk of missing meat from the man's shoulder. An eye was also missing from the man with blood streaked from the socket down the man's cheek. A blast rang out as Caleb pulled the trigger sending fragments of bone and flesh hurtling out from the infected man's knees. The infected dropped to the ground with a groan then the other two turned towards him, their attention grabbed by the shotgun blast. Caleb walked towards them then one of them began to move quickly towards him. This other man didn't look as infected as the one still writhing on the ground. This one had bloodshot eyes instead of the cloudy white he'd seen. There was uncontrollable drooling as this one came right at him. Caleb pulled the trigger again only this time he aimed for this one's chest. The infected flew back like it was yanked by an invisible cord attached to its back.

The third was slowly shambling with a large lengthwise slice on one thigh and blood trickling from a gash on its neck. Caleb leveled the barrel of the shotgun with this one's white glassy eyes then fired again. This time the skull of this infected erupted as the shotgun's shell spread tore through the infected's head. This infected fell to the ground silently then lay motionless as the other two infected groaned.

"Thank you! Thank you so much!" The driver of the car said getting out. It was a small Asian man who froze when the first infected Caleb had shot flopped around on the ground.

"It's okay," Caleb said raising a hand.

Walking towards the small Asian man, Caleb looked at the infected he'd shot in the knees. It rolled around on the ground just snapping its jaws with no indication of it feeling any pain. All it seemed to be focused on was eating or biting. Caleb put the barrel to its head then fired again sending blood spray up in the air. There was a growl coming from the infected he'd shot in the chest. This time as the infected began to rush towards him he knew he had to put it down for good. Again, putting the shotgun barrel in line with the infected's head as it came towards him in a crazy frenzy. The shot tore through the left side of this infected's head sending it tumbling forward. "Are you okay?" Caleb asked the man as nothing had just happened.

"Yes. I mean no," the man said hesitantly.

"Can we help?" Caleb asked confused with the man's answer.

The man looked at the two girls in the back of the car who were holding each other and obviously terrified. Caleb had two daughters and didn't like the idea of being left with the feeling of selfishness at not helping someone in need.

"We were at the Ilani casino when everyone went crazy. We left and headed north home but the army has blocked off the freeway. They offered to take us to a relocation center where we could get relocated home as soon as it was safe. When they checked us to see if we had this disease, they said my wife was infected then shot her. My girls didn't see it happen but heard the noise as they shot her and some other people. Other people started to go crazy, so I took my girls and headed back south this way. Please my girls are very scared is there anywhere near where I can take them?" the man asked. Caleb looked back at his son sitting in the back of his vehicle holding a baby they just rescued. He wasn't sure why he was about to suggest what he was about too. All he knew was that it was the right thing to do.

"I have two girls myself, a lot older but my children, nonetheless. I have a farm just a little bit down the road but out of the way away from the freeway and main roads. You and your children are more than welcome to come and stay, at least till all this blows over. There's a lot more of these," Caleb said pointing back at one of the infected.

"Thank you, thank you!" the man said gratefully.

"Follow me close till we stop at a checkpoint then let me do the talking," Caleb told the man.

Getting back in the car he could feel Nate staring at him from the back.

"You told them he could come home with us, huh?" Nate said.

"Yeah, yeah, I did, with everything going to shit we need to help each other. Poor bastard was at the Ilani and said he saw his wife get shot by soldiers...What the fuck is happening, Nate?" Caleb said sadly.

The drive back towards the farm was quiet without a single other vehicle or person in sight. They slowed as they got to the turning lane leading down to past Victor's house to the farm then stopped right in front of the two men who were standing guard at the makeshift check point on the corner. Caleb got out expecting the men to have guns raised at their arrival, but they just sat on the hood the Tahoe parked on the grass by the side of the road.

"Hey fellas, we uh... we got some company. Old friend of mine I saw that needs a place to stay till this blows over," Caleb explained.

One of the men hopped down from the hood then looked at the car behind them.

"How many people?" The man asked.

"Just three, my friend and his two daughters," Caleb explained.

The other man still on the hood was looking at the girls in the back seat of the man's car.

"Any of them infected? Acting crazy?" The other guy asked.

"Nah, they're fine" Caleb replied shrugging.

"No cuts or bites?" the man standing with Caleb asked but Caleb just shook his head.

The man next to Caleb smiled then gestured for them to head on their way.

"Thanks guys, appreciate you boys keeping watch and keeping us safer" Caleb said as he got back in the vehicle.

The two Russians gave a wave as Caleb began driving down the road leading to the farm. He gave them a smile then realized he

261

hadn't even considered if the two girls or even the dad might be infected. "Nate when we get to the house, I need you to keep an eye on our new friends for a bit, make sure they're not infected with whatever's going around," He said looking in the rearview mirror at his son.

"Sure, what you want me to do if they are?" Nate asked

"Tell me" Caleb replied.

"What will we do then?" Nate asked.

" If they are then…then they gotta leave, your sisters and your mom comes first. I don't want to risk anything happening to you guys," he said.

Nate nodded acknowledgement but Caleb knew even if they were infected, he wasn't sure if he could just cast out this man and two young girls. If they were infected what's to say he wasn't infected? After all, he did get blood spray all over his clothes and was in close contact with infected.

As they pulled up to the house, he saw his wife tending to plants outside. Caleb saw the expression of relief on her face then confusion at the other car parking behind him. After getting out he walked over and gave Janice a long hug then stepped aside as Nate brought the baby over.

"We rescued this little guy; we'll look after him till we can contact and find family. Caleb told as Nate passed Janice the baby. "And this is…" Caleb began then realized he didn't know the man's name.

"Sung," the man said, walking over to them with a handout.

"Caleb," he said taking Sung's hand and shaking it. The girls came running out the house then stopped when they saw Sung. "Girls, this is Mr. Sung and his daughters, he'll be here for a bit. Can you guys play with his daughters?" he asked.

Both nodded then went towards the car to introduce themselves to the two young girls.

"Hey, let me get you settled in," Nate said to Sung.

Caleb looked round at his girls by the car bonding with Sung's daughters. Janice was fixated with the baby in a way he hadn't seen in a long time

That's when he knew what he had to do and headed over to his truck.

"I'll be right back! Want to stick some food on," Caleb said to Janice while getting in.

" Uh, you have some explaining to do!" Janice said looking down at the baby then over at Sung's girls.

"I will, later, I promise, hun," Caleb told her as he started the truck up.

Caleb pulled out onto the main road waving at the two men at the corner as he headed back out. After just under half a mile he pulled over to a big sign then got out shaking a spray paint can.

Walking over to the big sign giving directions to the freeway he spray painted over the directions.

Once he was done Caleb took a few steps back to examine his writing then nodded knowing he'd made the right choice to try and help.

It read: "Sanctuary! Safe place! Caleb's Farm, follow arrows." and with that Caleb began the drive home determined to get out every so often to put arrows on the road leading people to his farm and safety. Until this was over, until life was back to normal, he would do what he could to keep people safe.

CHAPTER FORTY-THREE
Mason

Dimitri pulled Mason out of the rear door onto the walkway leading to the bridge without saying anything. Dimitri didn't need to; Mason already knew the infected were attracted by noise. He just hoped there wasn't a bunch of infected waiting for them on the other side of the bridge.

They both ran towards the Jeep that was stopped on their side of the bridge. Sarah opened the door for them with a grunt. Jeep doors were pretty solid, especially to a five-year-old, Mason thought as he jumped in smiling as his daughter. Dimitri ran in front of the Jeep towards the other side of the bridge. Mason could see another set of steel gate with barriers like the last set in each of the four lanes. "Drive forward then stop right before the gate to let me out," Mason told his wife.

"Daddy, no! You just got back! Please don't go!" Sarah begged sadly.

"Honey, daddy has to go help his friend again then we'll all be safe, okay?" he said more than asked.

He looked at Sarah's eyes that were cloudy with tears. "I'll be right back to keep you safe, I promise," he reassured her.

Mason jumped out once the vehicle pulled up to the gate. Dimitri was tugging at the door, but it wouldn't budge. As Mason got closer, Dimitri began shoulder ramming it to try to open it.

"Step back" Mason said.

Once Dimitri stepped out of the way Mason stepped in, kicking the door like a fireman would but again it didn't budge.

Dimitri was looking at the door as if trying to analyze a way in, but Mason knew they didn't have the time to stand around wondering alternatives. Mason brought the AK up a little then squeezed the trigger turning the handle and lock into swiss cheese. There was smoke coming from the door handle as he brought his foot up for another fireman's door kick. This time the door swung open then Dimitri patted him on the back before running in. Again, the buzzer sounded as the gate shutters opened then the barrier lifted. Mason watched as his girls drove through then he followed Dimitri into the control booth then out the other side of the checkpoint.

As they exited on the other side of the checkpoint flood lights came on forcing Mason to bring his arm up to shade his eyes. A PA system crackled as a man's voice came over it.

"Lower your weapons and raise your hands above your head," the man's voice said calmly.

Mason did as he was instructed placing the assault rifle on the ground and saw that Dimitri was doing the same. The light shut off as some double doors that were the entrance to a large building beside the checkpoint opened. A group of armed men walked out with guns trained on them.

"Keep your hands up, American," the man who was leading the small group said.

"How do you know I'm American?" Mason asked keeping his hands up.

The man stopped two feet from Mason then looked him up and down while the other man stood back. "Cause you look like one," the man said softly as the rest of the men chuckled.

Two of the men in the group began walking towards the Jeep with rifles raised.

"Wait! That's my family! We're just trying to get home," Mason told the man in front of him.

The man's face squinted in confusion Mason noticed.

"Family? In an army vehicle?" the man asked with raised eyebrows.

Before Mason could reply, Dimitri stepped beside him. "We escaped the airport, it's much worse on the other side of the border my friend...Pozhaluysta pomogi," Dimitri said finishing in Russian.

Mason could almost hear the ticking in this man's head as he thought about what Dimitri had just said. "Infected any of you?" The man asked.

"No," Mason said as Dimitri's head shook. The man seemed satisfied and nodded then waved for them to lower their arms. The man then turned towards the Jeep and the two men pointing rifles at it. "OSTAVIT' BYT'" The man shouted. The men nodded lowering the rifles then gestured for Alex and the girls to come out.

"Name's Sergei and I'm afraid things are a lot worse on this side of the border my friends, please come inside. My men will take your weapons," Sergei said.

"Name's Mason" Mason told Sergei.

"Dimitri...if we're friends, we can't get our guns back?" Dimitri asked.

Sergei smiled putting his arms out wide. "The fact we're all alive right now makes us friends but I don't trust you and you shouldn't trust me. There's too many people exploiting other people right now. Once I'm satisfied you're on the right side, you can have them back, but first come eat," Sergei told them.

"Right side?" Mason asked hesitantly.

"I'll explain inside," Sergei said nodding then turned and headed back towards the large building. The building looked like the one on the other side of the border. Two story brick with lots of windows along the second floor but not many on the first. Mason walked over to the girls who were out of the Jeep and heading over to the building. Sarah was running over to him then when she got to him, Mason scooped her up in his arms and held her close.

"Told you daddy would be okay," Mason said kissing Sarah on the head.

Alex put an arm around him, so he did the same pulling her Alex and baby Abby close to him.

After walking through the heavy looking double doors, two of Sergei's men closed it then put a barricade back in place. Mason eyeballed it then looked around the rest of the entrance way which was fortified to stop intruders. There were riot shield type standing barricades lined up inside the entrance way, razor wire, and wood covering the windows.

"You guys expecting company?" Mason asked.

Sergei kept walking not answering before stopping at the bottom of the steps leading up to the next floor. "We were here when the border was shut down yesterday and all the soldiers left. We were waiting to cross for safety, but they just locked it up and left us out there standing. No explanation then the Infected came so we moved our families in here until we feel it's safe to move. There's children in the room down there playing." Sergei said nodding down a hallway to a large meeting room that had glass wall. Inside the room, Mason could see about six children around Sarah's age all playing. Sarah must have heard the kids laughing and playing as he watched as his daughter looked then took a few steps towards room. Sarah turned to look at him, and he just smiled, "Go on, you can go play," he told Sarah.

Alex was looking at him, so he smiled to reassure her he thought they were in a safe place, then nodded for her to follow their daughter. Abby must have heard the kids, too, as even the baby started to make excited noises.

"There are a couple of mothers in there with the kids, your wife will be fine. We have a couple of guys downstairs working in the kitchen to make dinner if you're all hungry." Sergei said.

Both Dimitri and Mason nodded, Mason hadn't eaten since this morning and the thought of some warm food made him smile. Sergei led them into what must have been a meeting room then gestured for them to sit down.

"So, I'm not sure what your plans are but you are more than welcome to take some food and anything else you need that you can find in this building with you," Sergei told them.

"My village is not far from here, I'm headed there, and Mason here is trying to get his family back to America so he's hoping to get to an embassy," Dimitri explained.

Sergei's eyes widened then the big man shook his head. "I'm sorry, my friend, most of the major cities have been over run. It happened in a matter of hours. The army was stretched too thin and cities here in Poland were over run. There are still some sites I believe that offer protection and even transportation to other areas less affected. Perhaps you could use these as a way to get closer to home." Sergei said.

"That sounds like a good idea, thank you," Mason said trying not to sound too disappointed. By the sounds of it, Lithuania was worse off than the other side of the border in Belarus.

"The closest city is Vilnius, the soldiers left more than a few Jeeps outback. You are more than free to take one as you probably don't want to be seen in the one you're in" Sergei said.

"Why not?" Mason asked.

"Well, that other side I mentioned. A few people who were here and there are bound to be others feel like the army let them down as did the government. That they weren't given enough protection from this attack or whatever it is" Sergei said

"When the dead rise, they will fill the streets, turning neighbor against neighbor until the world goes dark," an old man said who was sitting in the corner.

Mason hadn't noticed the man as he was hunched over a chair, wrapped in a sleeping bag. Laughs went up around the room from most of the men. Mason couldn't help but feel uneasy about what the old man said. "Don't listen to Amon's ramblings, he had too much to drink today, didn't you old man!" Sergei said with a smile.

"Thank you for being kind, comrade, we need to get on our way as soon as possible" Dimitri said.

"Of course! As time passes it gets worse and worse out there and you have a village to get to yes? Which one?" Sergei asked.

"Sums kas" Dimitri replied.

"Ah, I understand, then let us get you all some food and get you on your way. I hope your village is well. I know a lot of smaller villages have been untouched by this plague, so I hope yours is one of them" Sergei said.

Dimitri nodded in agreement as Sergei got up motioning them to follow. Sergei walked them to the room with all the children in it. "You can wait in there with the children or anywhere else on this floor. I'll have someone bring you all some food. We will get two Jeeps ready for you. I just ask that you stay away from the windows. There was a couple of infected lurking outside earlier and I would rather not have them test our defenses here" Sergei explained.

"We totally understand and thank you! Seriously, I don't know what to say," Mason said.

"It's okay, we're all human, helping each other is in our nature and if it's not, well then you're on the other side and more like one of them," Sergei said, pointing out the window at a man outside. Mason squinted noticing the man was tied to the tree with a rope around his neck like some kind of dog.

"He's infected, isn't he?" Dimitri asked.

"Yes, he alerts us when there's someone close by infected or otherwise. He was my friend before he got bit yesterday helping my little girl." Sergei said with sadness in his voice.

CHAPTER FORTY-FOUR
Jake

Jake kissed Emily taking her hand as they started to walk back towards their house, leaving the crowd that had started to dissipate. Once they got home, Jake headed into the living room and slumped himself on the couch. "You want some coffee?" Emily asked.

"Sure, thanks, babe," Jake said as he looked out the window over at Pete's place.

Emily came and sat down beside him handing him his coffee.

"So, are you going to tell me what you're thinking?" Emily asked, widening her eyes in interest. "Because I know there's something going on in that head of yours so tell me what it is."

"We should stay," Jake said firmly as he snapped out of his daze. Emily was giving him a strange look.

"But you just said less than ten minutes ago we should leave… is that what the helping close the gate was about? You feel like you owe them something for him being there at Wal-Mart?" Emily asked. Jake shook his head thinking about how he could word all the stuff going around in his head. "This is our home, it would be pretty hard to just pack up the boys' stuff and get out of here not knowing what state the place would be in when we came back, if we ever came back," he said.

"We could go to my Aunt Janice's place in Amboy, that's out of the way and come back when this blows over," Emily said.

"Honey, like I said we may not have anything to come back to if we're not here to protect it and I've seen those things, our neighbors don't deserve for us to run out on them." he explained.

Jake could tell his wife was thinking about it hard, so he had to let her know he was serious.

"Honey, I love you more than anything in the world and honestly the best choice is for us to stay here with safety in numbers, I was selfish to think we could run away if something were to happen to us, the boys would be on their own but at least here they know people," Jake said.

Emily leaned in hugging him tight and in that instant, he felt happy, content, and safe.

"I love you! We are so lucky to have you," Emily said.

Jake looked into her big brown eyes, the same eyes he first looked into years ago. He knew then he would marry then grow old with Emily. As he looked at her smiling, Emily leaned into kiss him. As his lips touched Emily's, the front door burst open as the boys came crashing into the house. "Mom! Mom!" Jeff yelled excitedly "Dad's here!!!"

Behind Jeff standing on the porch was Jeff's dad, Simon.

Simon raised his hand, "Uh, hi," Simon said meekly to Emily. Simon was a big guy usually pretty loud. Right now, Jake noticed Simon wasn't being very loud and obnoxious. The journey from downtown Vancouver to here couldn't have been easy one Jake thought.

"Well, this just got weird," Paul said, walking past Simon into the house.

Jeff grabbed Simon's hand "C'mon, Dad, come in," Jeff said, leading Simon into the living room. Jake walked into the kitchen gulping down his coffee. Jake grabbed the coffee pot for more while Simon was laughing in the living room.

"I love you, son! Daddy had to come get you! My God, downtown is a nightmare! Those people! Those things are everywhere!" Simon told them. Jake had never gotten along with

Simon. In fact, he despised this man but had to admire the fact that he made his way here from downtown.

"How is it downtown?" Jake asked.

"It's a lot like it was on the news about Portland, people looting, rioting…chaos! That and they're getting infected fast then turning on each other," Simon explained.

Jake could imagine how a densely populated area could become a cesspool for a virus in no time.

"I'm so glad you're okay and here, Dad! "Jeff said hugging Simon.

"We're going to keep bad guys away! So, you'll be safe here with us," Jeff said proud.

There was a knock at the door, so Jake opened it to see Charlie and Nathan standing there. Jake invited them both inside. Dan invited them in then led them into the kitchen where they could talk. "What can I do for you guys?" Jake asked

"We came to ask for your help," Charlie began "We're going to go see Ken and want to propose a few things," Charlie said.

Jake was a little confused as Charlie had made great points in front of Ken's place, so he wasn't sure why they needed him.

"Such as?" he asked them.

"You seem like a smart guy, you're a doctor and Ken likes you, so we need him to agree to let us put up watch posts in some gardens and use empty trailers for storage for supplies" Nathan said speaking up.

Jake smiled, as he was about to correct them about him not being a doctor. Emily spoke up from the living room. "Course he'll help! We need to make this place as safe as we can," Emily said smiling at him.

"Oh, he's not a doctor, he looks after old people" Simon said, chuckling.

"And who the fuck are you?" Charlie said, glaring at Simon.

Charlie looked at Jeff then at Emily "Oh, sorry for the language," Charlie said like a kid in trouble. Emily smiled, waving her hand that it was fine.

"C'mon, let's go see Ken," Jake said as he walked towards the door.

As the three made their way towards Ken's place, Charlie looked at Jake, "So who the fuck is that guy and what was with the tension?" Charlie asked.

"That's Jeff's dad, guy's a dick" he told them.

"Seems like one, smug prick," Nathan said, smiling.

"Emily and me got together when Jeff was three, but that clown kept trying to break us up and was possessive and abusive of her their whole relationship," Jake told them.

"Yeah, that's why I don't fuck with relationships," Nathan said. Jake could tell the guy was trying to lift the mood.

"You don't fuck with relationships because you can't get one which is why I think you bat for the other team" Charlie added. Nathan just replied with the middle finger.

Once they got to Ken's place, Charlie stopped at the steps, looking at Jake.

"Age before beauty, lil' fella," Charlie said. Jake walked up the steps then stopped turning back to Charlie.

"You guys know what you want to do?" he asked before knocking on the door. Charlie nodded yes then before Jake could knock on the door it opened. Ken was standing looking like a parent who had waited up for their kid to come home.

"I was hoping someone would come see me," Ken said inviting them in.

"You were expecting us?" Jake asked.

Ken nodded gesturing into the living room. "I know it's going to get rough," Ken said.

Ken rubbed his white, short, well trimmed beard. "I know if we want this place to be safe, we need some young bucks to help get it going and I'm just glad it wasn't those blasted Jones boys who came knocking right now," Ken said with a smile.

Jake looked at Ken but wasn't sure what to say, so he turned to Charlie. Charlie took his cue stepping up and detailing his plan.

"See this," Charlie said pointing to a map of the park on Ken's wall by the door. "When we helped out at Katrina we had a cross we would paint on every house that let us know who or what was inside, we go door to door and mark it all down here on your map and we also mark empty and vacant lots that we can store supplies in, which we'll need to gather but we'll need to do a perimeter walk to check for gaps, holes in people's fences. Also set up a couple of watch points on people's roofs or sheds that overlook the fence in all four directions," Charlie grabbed a pen. Ken handed Charlie some paper as Charlie looked at the map then started scribbling notes.

Ken looked at Nathan, "What about the front gate? You guys closed it but what if people want in?" Ken asked.

"We'll also need round the clock watch on that gate, too, and also take a tally of guns and ammo to put away," Charlie said handing the pad of paper back to Ken.

"These supplies I think we can gather from around the park and also the management supply shed but the guns..." Ken paused while reading the list.

"What if people don't want to give them up, I mean the news said they should defend their homes," Ken continued.

"If people think we're going to keep their means of protecting their family then they might lie about having them and we can't start off like that, we need full disclosure and everyone in this park on the same page, we don't want to have to worry about people inside the park as well as people outside the park," Jake said.

"Well, we keep a tally and itinerary then of weapons," Charlie suggested.

They all agreed then planned to go in twos, house to house, around the outside of the park first since it was basically one big huge circle. Charlie went over what was marked on the notepad about where to put up the watchtowers. The first was at the entrance on top of the mailroom shelter. The second was in Pete's yard on the tall shed in the back, they could set up on the roof. The third was over by the Jones' place overlooking the rock quarry. Looking down into the quarry meant it didn't need to be too elevated.

They agreed while checking homes they would let people know of a signup sheet they would post on the mail shelter bulletin board for watch shifts.

As they headed out, Jake paused as he noticed a shotgun by Ken's front door.

"As I said I knew someone would come knocking I just wasn't sure if it would be a friendly face or not," Ken said.

Ken had given them all paper to keep track of numbers. Ken went with Charlie taking the east side of the park. Nathan and he took the west side, which meant he could stop in to see Emily. He wanted to fill his wife in on the plan of action of what they were doing.

As they started out, Jake felt good about his choice to stay. He thought he'd use this opportunity as a chance to get to know Nathan. This whole time he'd lived here, he hadn't really tried to get to know anyone. Nathan apparently had the same idea as just after putting the sign-up sheet to the bulletin board, Nathan asked about Emily and the boys.

"So, it just your wife, you, and your two boys?" Nathan asked,

"Yeah, Paul's my son from another marriage but his mother's not in the picture and Jeff's Dad, well that's the prick you met earlier" Jake said with a smile.

"So, wait with all this going on..." Nathan paused. "Is he going to be crashing with you?" Nathan asked with raised eyebrows. Jake hadn't really considered it, but he couldn't just toss the guy out despite how much he disliked the man. He wouldn't want to see anyone leave who was safe in here as he knew this was the safest place to be right now. Strength in numbers was important just like Charlie had said earlier.

"Maybe we can get him a tent, or he can stay in a vacant trailer," Jake suggested.

"I got a couple of tents in my shed he can use, they'll be nice and ripe smelling too from the last time Charlie and I took a trip on Larch Mountain," Nathan offered.

Jake couldn't tell if Nathan was joking or serious, but Larch Mountain was pretty isolated. A good idea he thought to bring up later if they ever had to leave here or stash some stuff.

It was Jakes turn to ask a question now as they stopped outside the first trailer.

"So, you guys in the military?" he asked.

"Charlie was, he was in the Marines for eight years then had enough, said he was tired of seeing the American people getting treated like shit in bad situations. He helped out in New Orleans when Hurricane Katrina hit and that was it for him," Nathan told him.

"I see, well hopefully, we won't need the government's help to get through this" Jake said trying to stay positive.

FEMA and the Red Cross where nowhere in sight and Jake's only interaction with them since this started wasn't a very good one.

CHAPTER FORTY-FIVE
Rob

The camp was busy with helicopters, trucks and hummers coming and going for the last couple of hours. Rob had been watching what was going on in the inside of the camp from the fence. The army had been expanding the size of the housing area they were in. Clearly, they were expecting more people. There had been trucks going on the dirt track on the other side of the freeway, too. This made Rob think they were possibly building another camp like this one on that side of the road, too.

Heavy machine gun fire ran out getting his attention. It was coming from the bridge above the camp. The 205 bridge connected the I-205 from the Washington side to the Oregon side over the Columbia River. The army had set up barricaded secure checkpoints on both sides of the bridge.

The gunfire was coming from the Oregon side across the water. Rob couldn't see what was being shot at, but the gunfire was echoing across the river.

"Sickos trying to cross the bridge," a voice said from the other side of the fence.

It was the soldier Rob had helped earlier. "Hey kid, how you feeling?" Rob asked.

"I'm okay, not supposed to be over by the housing section after earlier but saw you standing here and just wanted to come say thanks," the soldier said with a smile.

"Housing section? That what they're calling this fenced off part of the camp?" Rob asked.

"Well, this is general housing, secured and safe from the barracks, medical units, and quarantine" the soldier said waving at the rest of the camp. The large fenced off area Rob was in was definitely secure but it was more to keep them in rather than safe, he thought.

"Anyways, thanks again" the soldier said.

"Wait, hey what's going on up there? On the other side of the freeway?" Rob asked before the soldier could walk away.

"We're expanding, there's more and more people needing evacuated and the housing area you are in is getting pretty full. Tensions are already getting high so we're building another part of the camp on the other side of the road," the soldier said.

"Evacuated?" Rob repeated, puzzled.

"Yeah, most of Portland's going dark except the people in PGE park stadium and The Moda Center so we're trying to get as many survivors out as quick as possible with some place to go," the soldier said.

"Going dark? I thought this thing was being brought under control? We'd be getting to go home soon?" Rob said confused.

"Not anytime soon, I'm afraid. This is going to be one of the main safe zones in the area. They're calling it Camp Hope," the soldier said before walking away.

Rob looked up at the 205 bridge covered in razor wire, mounted machine gun emplacements, and flood lights. This place was definitely well protected but the fenced off area he was in was already getting pretty crowded. If there were more people going to get packed in, then he knew it was only a matter of time before guys like Brandi's friends tried to break out.

Rob walked back to the tent he'd slept in to find Brandi laying on a cot. There had been cots in each tent but now there were more people than cots.

"You asleep?" He asked.

Brandi didn't say anything, so he didn't want to disturb her as she'd been pretty upset and crying a lot. Rob knew the girl needed rest, so he left her. The other cots in the tent had other people laying on them, too. Some were whimpering, some were sobbing, but the feeling of despair was thick in the air. Rob's heart got heavy as he looked at the people laying on the cots upset. This was something he never thought he'd see in his country. The government was meant to take care of its people, keep them safe. What Rob was seeing he knew deep down inside this wasn't the government taking care of its people. This was damage control and made Rob think maybe Brandi's friends were right.

The government was cutting its losses if they were just going to abandon Portland. The soldier may have been convinced by the line of bullshit given but he wasn't. Even with another area the size of the area he was in there is no way they could house people from Portland. Rob saw those infected up close, so he knew how vicious they were. If one of them was to get loose in an enclosed area like the one he was being held in, it would be a massacre.

He looked at the armed guards standing inside the camp. Even inside a secure camp with civilians locked up in this pen the guards were still armed. The higher ups clearly didn't have enough confidence in their perimeter security or men. Rob knew he needed to make a plan, just in case things went south and he needed to get out   of   Camp   Hope.

CHAPTER FORTY-SIX
Jake

After checking out the side of the park they'd been given, Jake looked over what they'd tallied up. Eight out of the thirty-six trailers they'd checked had no one home. Jake knew this either meant they weren't answering or were out there somewhere. Satisfied, they headed back to Ken's place to put their list together with Charlie and Ken's. This way they had a total of how many people were in the park, the number of weapons, and how much free space they had. As they approached Ken's, Charlie was standing out front talking to whoever was at the gate. Charlie looked at them and started waving at them to hurry up. Jake wasn't sure what could be going on but hoped it wasn't infected at the gate. As they got closer to the front of the park Jake saw Benny, Alice, and Marcus inside the gate talking to Charlie. Jake was a little surprised as they'd just left a little bit ago with their supplies from Wal-Mart.

"You guys okay?" Jake said, still surprised to see them.

"Yeah, the army has roadblocks and diversions up everywhere." Alice said, sounding frustrated.

"Every time we got stopped heading back to our side of town, they told us to either go back or follow them downtown to the military facility being set up to help relocate displaced people" Benny said.

"Displaced? By what?" Nathan asked.

"Probably by all the roadblocks, shut down sections of road and quarantine parts of town," Benny said.

Jake thought about all the empty trailers they had; if people were stuck out there when this all kicked off that would explain why so many are empty. The families could be trying to find a way around roadblocks or at a FEMA or Red Cross facility. Waiting until it was safe, or they got the go ahead to return home.

"Quarantine? It's getting that bad already?" Charlie asked.

"Yeah, we saw parts of town fenced off with a lot of soldiers. The freeway's jam packed too! They have hummers going up and down the shoulder and carpool lanes, they advised us to take an alternate route to get downtown to the I-205 bridge to this safety and relocation zone they're setting up" Benny said.

Jake wasn't surprised as from what he'd seen at the old folks home this virus spreads fast. Keeping the park secure was definitely a priority now if areas on this side of town were being quarantined.

"Did they say anything about the virus?" Jake asked.

"No, we were about to ask when some people, I'm assuming who were infected, ran at the soldiers," Alice said

"Yeah, we took that as our cue to book it but thought since we couldn't get answers from a camp here maybe head to the one downtown. Take some back roads like we did yesterday from work," Benny suggested.

This idea made Jake a little nervous as they really didn't know how bad things were towards downtown. The last thing he wanted was to be stuck somewhere and not be able to get back to his family.

"That sounds like a great idea! We sneak our way towards the 205 bridge and ask Uncle Sam for the what's what on this zombie crackhead cannibal conundrum. Come back and set everyone's mind at ease with the news straight from the top," Charlie said matter-of-factly.

"Simon just came from downtown, we could ask him for details of what it was like," Jake said

"Yeah, if that clown made it here from downtown sure we can make it halfway there to the bridge," Benny said, smiling.

Jake felt a little more comfortable now with the idea now. Benny was right in that the bridge was halfway between here and downtown. Simon seemed to have made it no problem so if things hadn't gotten much worse, they should be fine.

"One problem we might have to deal with first," Alice said.

Everyone's attention turned to Alice as both Benny and Marcus both nodded.

"Your neighbors in the apartments over there, they've blocked off the road with cars and a school bus. They barely let us through," Alice told them.

"We should go talk to them," Nathan said.

This was a good idea as Jake knew if they're neighbors were coming home, or any family was trying to get here they would need past that blockade. The only problem they might have was that there was a lot of people living in those apartments and if they didn't want to open that road there was really no way to make them.

"I say a few of us go over and try talk to them, not too many as they're probably just as freaked out as we are," Jake said.

"I'll go with you...y'know since it was your idea and you gotta go," Charlie said smiling.

"Yeah, I'll come, too" Alice said while unbuckling a police belt and holster. That was the only identifiable piece of clothing Alice had that said Police. Jake thought this was a good idea as the police probably weren't that well liked over at the apartments.

"Okay give me a few minutes to go tell Emily. Benny, you and Marcus good to stay here with the kids?" Jake asked.

Marcus nodded but Benny shook his head.

"Fuck, no. I'm coming with you guys, I ain't missing out on anything" Benny said cheerily.

"Meet you back here in fifteen," Jake told Charlie. Charlie just replied with a nod then headed off with Nathan towards their trailer.

When Jake arrived back at the gate he was greeted with Charlie and Nathan both armed with two more rifles extra in hand. "You gotta be kidding me," Benny said excitedly.

Charlie was beaming from ear to ear. "Got a stash, so figured we could use these," Charlie said.

"No," Jake said shaking his head. Everyone looked at him with a look someone would get if they'd suggested something utterly ridiculous.

"We're trying to negotiate and make friends, not start something," Jake said.

"Jake's right, there's a lot of felons over there, a lot of bad people who will use any excuse to exploit others but there is also a lot of families. We don't want to seem like a threat. They're blocking off that road for a reason," Alice said, making sense.

Charlie and Nathan nodded in agreement then handed the guns off to the two men who Ken had asked to watch the gate. "You mind if we use two of them?" Dom asked.

Dom was one of the people Ken had asked to watch the gate. Ken had been working on shift rotations and had a volunteer sign-up sheet pinned on the board at the mail shelter.

"Course, just take care of them. You know how to shoot them, little guy?" Charlie asked poking fun at Dom's height.

Dom rolled the AR over examining it then flipped the single shot to semi burst then back again. "Yeah, I got it," Dom said smiling.

"Okay, let's do this! Who's doing the talking?" Charlie asked.

"Jake!" both Benny and Alice said at the same time.

The gate closed behind them and Dom shouted good luck as the group crossed the road. Once on the other side, it was only a small walk to the apartments which were about three blocks away. Jake couldn't help but look over at the other park next to the one he lived in. It was an adult only park with no kids allowed mainly for the elderly. The whole park was in complete darkness, which made him feel uneasy. There was only a small field and high fence between his park and the old folk's one. As they got close to the apartments, Jake could see the bottom floors of the apartments were all boarded. The stairwells at each apartment building were blocked off too as was the road just like Alice had said. The school bus blocked half the road while some cars and a truck blocked the other side. Armed men were on top of the bus as well as some of the apartment balconies. They were definitely more prepared for something bad than the park was which made Jake wonder if these people knew something they didn't.

A group of men came walking from the barricaded road towards them with guns drawn.

"Knew we shoulda brought them guns," Charlie whispered.

Jake put his hand up to silence everyone as the men walked over.

" Fuck you people want?" the man in front said.

Before Jake could reply another voice came from a balcony above them.

" Eduardo! Wait I know these guys! They're cool, stand down, homie," A man on the balcony said before disappearing. Jake didn't get a good look at him but was relieved all the same.

"You heard the man, lower the fuckin' gun" Charlie said.

Jake was already feeling uneasy about the tension and Eduardo wasn't lowering his gun.

The man who had shouted from the balcony walked down some steps and Jake immediately recognized him from Walmart.

"Holy shit! You guys are my neighbors?" The man asked smiling.

"Yeah, the Great Western across the street." Jake nodded.

One of the men said something in a language Jake didn't understand to Eduardo. Eduardo seemed to be in charge of the armed group that was manning the blockade.

"We were coming to ask you guys about the blockade, we were going to send some people out and just wanted to make sure you were okay with it. Seems like you got the roadway pretty secure." Jake said.

"Yeah, yeah, we do. A lot of shit happening and we gotta keep ours safe. These things are vicious. We lost eight people last night. Had to put three down then the five they bit we had to put down too when they turned. So, yeah, we blocked off the road. We don't know more of them fuckin' infected coming this way. You guys want to leave you are more than welcome, we'll even let you guys back in but you gotta secure the road coming from the quarry and wally world, you feel me?" The man said.

"Sorry to hear that about your people, we've not got anyone infected at our park but the place I work got hit pretty bad, so I know where you're coming from," Jake said.

Jake knew all too well what the infected were like and understood why they'd secured the apartments like they did. Eduardo spoke to one of the other men with guns then looked at him.

"Oh, you'll know soon enough when those fuckers get through those fences you got, bro," Eduardo said nodding over towards the old people's park. Jake was confused and the look on his face must have gave that away as the man whose name he still didn't know explained.

"Some ambulances and a fire truck went in there last night and never came out, we sent two guys over to check it out and the people in the homes are all infected. Hopefully they stay there but if they get out, they'll probably head straight for you guys," the man said.

The men with guns all started to chuckle which Charlie didn't seem to like.

"Fuck, you think this is funny?" Charlie shouted. People came out onto balconies while more men started walking towards them from the blockade.

"Something you want to say?" Alice asked.

Eduardo shrugged his shoulders, "Do you guys? Bringing someone that big is trying to make a statement and Lamar says you're a cop," Eduardo said looking at Charlie then nodding at Alice.

"Eduardo enough! They helped Diego! They're good people," the man said.

"If you say so, Remmy," Eduardo said to the man.

Jake could feel the anxiety of his people and sense the tension from Remmy's, but this had to work. "Look we can stand here, and we can bicker, or we can work together! We're neighbors and we might not like each other, we might not get along normally, but right now we don't really have a choice. If infected or people wanting to take stuff come from that direction, we have to rely on you guys, if people or infected come from the other direction you guys have to rely on us. So, let's just put our differences aside and work together. " Jake said putting it all on the table.

Everyone was nodding in agreement. Then Eduardo lowered his gun and signaled for the others to lower theirs as well. "Thank you" Jake said.

"No problem, we don't really need to get into a whose dick's bigger contest right now." Eduardo said nodding. Remmy walked over smiling then put his arms around Jake and Eduardo.

"We can help each other, and we might have to come together if they get out," Remmy said nodding over towards the old folk's home.

"I agree, hey we're sending a group to an army camp set up to try get some more info on this virus. So, we'll need through the blockade later" Jake told them.

"You got guns? Those things are tough and the army ain't really fuckin' around either," Eduardo said.

"Guns? Does a bear shit in the woods, Eddie?" Charlie said smiling.

"It's Eduardo! Gringo," Eduardo said back to Charlie with a smile.

They all were smiling now which felt good to Jake and gave him a sense of ease that things would work out. He was glad he'd decided to stay as he felt they had more of a chance now all together than he would have if he'd taken his family and left.

CHAPTER FORTY-SEVEN
Nick

T he group emerged from the trees into an empty derelict street. Nick had to stop for a rest as he'd been carrying Agnes through the woods from the train tracks for what seemed like hours. Nick didn't want to leave the tracks as they were a steady route to where they were headed. The problem was that it wasn't a straight route. When he mentioned to Heidi and Michael about cutting through the woods, they were both scared. Agnes had helped talk them into it, but it had been a slow walk with lots of stops for Agnes to catch her breath. Looking round the street they had spilled out onto; it was eerily silent. "Should we keep heading this way?" Heidi asked.

Nick nodded looking down at some flyers that littered the ground. It read A.D.D. then had some bullets points but he didn't bother to pick one up. It was the same stuff he'd seen on the news and none of that information had prepared him for what he'd had to deal with. These infected didn't have just some nasty virus, they were completely changed.

As they walked along the empty streets the sun was right above them beating down furiously. "Where is everyone?" Michael said.

"Not sure but we should keep moving, at least until we find somewhere, we can settle down safely," Nick said.

"Or someone who can help us," Heidi mentioned.

Nick didn't care too much about finding help. He knew they should avoid people in general at all costs. There was no way for him to tell right now who was infected and who wasn't. He didn't even the state of the government or emergency services. One thing he did know was that Agnes needed medical attention and to rest.

The houses in this small neighborhood were small with a lot of trees, plants, and very well decorated. As they crossed a road, Nick didn't notice them at first but heard Michael gasp.

Turning looking down the cross street, he saw probably a dozen infected littering in the middle of the road. "We gotta keep moving quick!" Nick said struggling to move quickly with Agnes.

"Where they sick?" Agnes asked sounding labored.

"Yeah," Nick said.

They didn't have to be close for Nick to know they were infected as they were all covered in blood and gaping wounds. The weird slow swaying shamble they did gave them away too. The conductor still stuck in Nick's head though as did the old man. They both moved fast and seemed almost amped up in their movements. Still this was something Nick knew he could think about another time. Right now, he had to focus on the task at hand.

They reached the end of the road they were on as it turned a corner, but the corner was taped off with yellow caution tape. Nick set Agnes down on a small wall of the house that sat on the corner.

The house seemed empty, but he knew if anyone in there was smart, they would stay hidden. The yellow tape read quarantine then he looked further around the corner and saw bodies littering the ground beside a shot up army truck. Heidi came up beside him.

"Don't look! Make sure your brother doesn't come over here," he told Heidi. The young girl was speechless but nodded before walking back to Michael who was sat with Agnes.

Examining the scene, it looked like the truck was meant for people, but all the tires were shot to shit and bullet casings all over the ground sparkled in the sun. The bodies on the ground weren't moving which was a good sign, but Nick knew going down that road wasn't an option. He couldn't risk more than one of those things attacking if he was carrying Agnes. Turning around looking at the sky taking in the sun, he noticed a small dirt road leading down a hill. Nick walked over to the hill and looking down the tracks path, he saw a house. It was huge and probably cost more than Nick would ever earn. It sat at the bottom of the hill surrounded by open fields. The real payoff was the for-sale sign that Nick could see.

"C'mon, let's go! I think I have us a place to take a little break!" Nick told them.

Walking up to the huge, heavy, double doors, Nick noticed there was a key coded padlock on the door. Setting Agnes down, he opened his wallet pulling out his lock pick kit. "What's that?" Michael asked.

"Part of my EDC," Nick answered.

"Are you going to break in?" Michael asked, sounding surprised.

"Kind of, it's for sale so isn't anyone's and no one lives here so it's as safe a place as any," Nick told the boy. Everything about this house seemed like a good choice to Nick except that there were windows everywhere! The architect of this house must have loved the things as they were everywhere on the side of the house.

Once the padlock clicked the key popped out. "Tada! Bob's your uncle!" Nick said with a smile, pleased with himself.

"Who's Bob?" Heidi asked.

"It's an expression, dear, one I've not heard in a while," Agnes said, clearly in pain.

"C'mon, let's get you inside, hopefully it's fully furnished," Nick said jokingly, with a smile, trying to lighten the mood.

Once inside the house look as expensive inside as it did from the outside. Nick closed the heavy doors behind them as they walked into a huge open living room area. There were two long L-shaped couches and two small loveseats. Nick set Agnes down on a couch while Michael hopped up beside her. "Can we sleep in here?" Michael asked.

290

Nick nodded as it was in the middle of the house with only windows facing out towards the fields behind the house.

Nick heard the sound of the ice machine grinding up ice chunks then falling into a glass. "Oh my God! There is so much nice food in here!" Heidi shouted from the kitchen that was adjacent to the living room. Nick was surprised but maybe the realtor kept a stocked pantry and fridge to show possible buyers the storage capacity. Then he realized he was doing it again, making up background stories in his head again. Nick elevated Agnes' foot onto the arm of the couch then smiled at Michael. "You want some food, buddy?" Nick asked.

"Yes please! I'm starving!" Michael said with a huge grin.

"Thank you," Agnes mouthed to him, he smiled back.

"No problem," he told Agnes.

Walking into the kitchen, Heidi was sat up on a counter drinking water. "You okay?" he asked.

Heidi shrugged her shoulders. "Seems like everything's going to shit, I feel like I should be sad but I'm not," Heidi said.

"How come?" Nick asked confused.

"My world was already going to shit, that's why I ran away to Seattle. Now you're stuck with us and get to be miserable, too, as the world goes to shit," Heidi said staring into the empty glass.

"Listen, you're young! Way too young to be worried about your life being shit. We'll get you home and things will eventually get back to normal. Then, well, then the rest will be up to you but running away isn't the answer. I don't know you or what you're going through but I know as a parent your folks must be worried sick, especially right now," Nick said.

Heidi's legs swung out from the counter as Heidi leaned back laughing. "Do you really believe that? Things will go back to normal? People are turning into fuckin zombies!! ZOMBIES!!! I'm actually happy I think for the first time and my parents…Fuck my parents," Heidi said starting to get teary eyed.

"Oh, I can assure you they're prob-" before Nick could finish Heidi cut him off.

"We should stay here!" Heidi blurted out.

"Well, we might have to, at least until your sister's foot gets a little better or I can find a decent car around here," Nick said.

"No, I meant *stay*. There's more than plenty of food and it's nice and big in here!" Heidi said.

"Sorry, that's not an option, I have a wife and daughter I need to get home to. If you guys decided to stay that's up to you guys, but I gotta get going and sooner rather than later," Nick said. Inside part of him hoped they would want to stay here. It would be much easier for him traveling along with no one to watch out for.

"Really? You would do that? Just leave us? We're fuckin kids! What would your wife and daughter think of that? Of you abandoning some other kids," Heidi said with a tilted head obnoxiously.

Nick forced a closed, wry smile then walked away. He knew what his wife would say, and he knew what his daughter would say. That's why he knew he couldn't leave them outside the train or leave them now. Nick stopped then turned around looking at Heidi, "Okay you win...for now. What should we make everyone for dinner?" He asked   Heidi.

CHAPTER FORTY-EIGHT
Mason

The guy tied to the tree swayed back and forth, head perking up every time a sound went in that direction. Mason stood holding baby Abby to his chest in the freezing wind unable to stop staring at the poor soul tied to the tree. *Did he have a soup?* Mason wondered, he didn't know what these people were or if they were even people at all. A door behind him opened with a creak, it was Alex with Sarah holding hands. Mason smiled at his wife who smiled back then Dimitri came out with Sergei. "The Jeeps are full of gas and ready to go my friends, I had my men put in blankets as well as some food and MRE's to help you both incase anything happens" Sergei said.

"I really don't need any, my village is just down the road, the people here need them more than me" Dimitri said but Sergei held up his hand in objection.

"Then maybe if travelers arrive in your village in need of aid you can pass the vehicle and provisions along to them," Sergei suggested.

Sergei was a good man, Mason realized now, at first, he was hesitant to trust this man, but all the guy was trying to do was look after his people. Mason understood that as he was trying to do the same. Sergei had given them everything they needed and even made sure they had their own rooms in the building to sleep in. They all agreed it would be better to get some rest before leaving today. Sergei walked them over to the Jeeps then shook their hands. "Good luck my friend to you and your family," Sergei said, shaking Masons hand.

"Udachi brat," Sergei said, shaking Dimitris hand.

Sergei waved farewell then disappeared back into the building leaving them all outside with the wind howling by. Dimitri came and hugged him. "Thank you, my friend, I hope you and your family get someplace safe. If not, I've marked directions from here to my village where your all more than welcome," Dimitri said.

They all said their farewells and Alex loaded the girls into the Jeep while Mason took one last look at the infected tied to the tree. Mason waved as Dimitri started up the Jeep then drove off down the road in the opposite way they would be headed.

"C'mon, Daddy! Let's go!" Sarah shouted from inside the Jeep. Mason turned to see Sergei watching from a window upstairs in the building. He gave one last farewell wave before climbing in the Jeep and drove off.

Sergei had gone over with Mason the safest route to and into the city. Soon they would be coming up on a big hill that divided the countryside. The city was on the other side of that hill so they would have to go through a tunnel. Mason could see the tunnel and the orange lighting inside, which was a relief as he didn't fancy driving through a pitch-black tunnel. The tunnel itself was free from traffic and relatively unobstructed except a few tents he noticed on the other side of the road. As they exited the tunnel, they were shocked to see the smoldering ruins of what must have been a beautiful city. Mason saw his wife's jaw drop as tears filled Alex's eyes. Buildings were charred and still smoking. The ground itself lay cracked with gaping holes in the road like giant wounds. The streets were filled with clouds of smoke but there was no sound, no movement of any kind.

"Oh my god" Alex said.

Mason knew as soon as he saw the blackened brick and burnt-out vehicles littering the road from all those planes they'd seen the day before, this is where they'd come, here to this city to burn it. Dimitri had said governments were trying to get rid of this virus by horrible means. Mason stopped the Jeep on the road then got out. Alex got out with the girls behind him as he heard their doors opening too. Masons eyes welled up with tears as he saw burned, charred bodies all over the road. He felt like he was going to throw up as the world spun around him.

"This way, girls" he heard Alex say. Mason was in shock and hadn't had time to tell them not to get out of the Jeep. He watched Alex take the girls into a small park away from the site ahead of them. Mason couldn't believe it, all these bodies all these people just wiped out by whoever had made the decision. "Look, Mommy a bike! My size!" Sarah squealed.

"Can I ride it, Mommy? Daddy?" Sarah asked.

"Of course," Alex said.

Mason felt a tear roll down his face as he looked at a small body lying on the road. It was obviously a small child about Sarah's size. He wiped the tear away realizing he was crying. Then he looked around to see Sarah smiling on the little partially burnt tricycle. Time slowed down as he heard Sarah ring the bell on the bike. As the bell rang and rang the sound of groaning came from behind him. Mason saw the look of horror on his wife's face at whatever was behind him. Mason began whispering "No...no...no" to himself. "Alex! Get to the Jeep now!" He shouted to his family.

Mason turned to see two blackened corpses walking towards him with hands outstretched. He'd left the rifle in the Jeep so reached for a knife Sergei had given him that he'd fastened to his belt.

As the first walking corpse got to him, Mason thrust the knife out into the man's chest, and it sank deep as the man's chest cavity seemed to collapse under the pressure. The man fell forward onto Mason, sending him falling backwards to the ground with the man on top still groaning. Mason pushed him off as the man didn't have much weight to him. The second corpse lunged down at him, but he rolled then slashed with the knife but all he cut was air. The Jeep horn honked and honked which Mason took as a signal they were ready to go.

Running towards the Jeep, Mason saw more infected walking corpses coming towards the Jeep from another street. He almost froze in place then snapped out of it as the roar of gunfire filled his ears. Alex was standing half out the Jeep with an Ak-47 with smoke coming from the barrel. Mason didn't need much more prompting as he jumped into the Jeep and peeled out. Turning the Jeep around the mob of the dead converged on them. Mason put his foot down as the Jeep thundered into the tunnel with the engine echoing.

Mason had studied the map the night before and the routes Dimitri had marked to get to his village. Instead of going back the way they'd come, there was another route marked going straight from the tunnel exit to the village. Mason decided that would be the one to take to get to Dimitri. It had next to no towns on the way and avoiding people living or dead seemed like a good idea right now. Mason wasn't sure what Dimitri could do but anything was better than going through the city of the dead they'd just saw. Maybe there were other routes Dimitri could show him around major populated areas. He would have to ask the man himself when he got there, he thought. He felt Alex take his hand. His wife squeezed it.

"I love you," Alex said.

"I love you, too, honey. Thanks for that" He replied.

"No problem, we're a team" Alex said back smiling.

"I love both you guys!!" Sarah chimed in from the back

CHAPTER FORTY-NINE

Jake

"**A**re you fucking kidding me?!" Emily screamed glaring at him. Jake had tried to put it as best he could. Emily was not happy about his suggestion of taking a group to the army base at all.

"Babe, we need to know exactly what's going on and the only way to get answers is from them," Jake said trying to reason with his wife.

The two of them were standing in the kitchen while everyone else was in the living room adjacent. "Boys, go to your room or outside," Emily barked.

"Do you want us to go outside too?" Benny asked.

"Oh, no, you can stay right there, Benny and you too…what was your name?" Emily growled.

"Charlie, ma'am, but please it wasn't all your husband's idea" Charlie said trying to be helpful, which Jake appreciated. "Oh, I bet it wasn't, but he just follows along to try and keep everyone happy," Emily said. "And no, you are all going to wait right there! Because I want to say this to all of you!" Emily said turning to the group gathered in the living room.

"I understand we don't know what's going, I understand everyone's scared, I'm fucking terrified and want to know what's going on, too. If anything, and I mean *anything* happens to my husband those infected fucks will be the least of all your problems, if you come back here without him! Do you understand?" Emily demanded.

The whole living room was silent as they all stared into the kitchen at Emily and him. Jake put his hand around his wife's shoulders.

"Babe, I love you! Nothing will happen I promise! We'll be straight there and back real quick," he reassured his wife.

"Emily if anything seems not right, we'll turn around and come straight back," Benny chimed in.

"I know and I know you would do anything for my husband that the only reason I'm allowing it," Emily said, walking past the group towards the back of the trailer.

" I woulda went anyway" Jake said quietly.

"That's what you think!" Emily shouted from the back of the trailer.

The group laughed which lightened the mood. "Give me a few minutes and I'll see you guys at the gate," he told the group. Once they were all gone, he headed into the back of the trailer where Emily was sitting on the bed crying. "Honey, it's going to be okay, we're going to be okay," he said.

"I know, I just keep thinking about my family, the people I work with just everyone and how fucked this situation is," Emily sobbed.

Jake sat beside her, pulling his wife in close to he could hold her tight. When his wife was in his arms, the whole world seemed to stop and melt away. Jake had no worries and felt content; this was a feeling he knew he'd come back to. "I love you" he said wiping the tears from her eyes.

"I love you more" Emily said.

"I'm going to have Alice and Marcus stay here if you are okay with it till I get back?" Jake asked.

Emily didn't say anything but nodded. "There's a few empty trailers in the back so Simon can crash in one of those Ken said," he told her.

Jake gave her one last hug, "I'll be back in a bit" he said kissing her on the forehead.

At the gate Benny and Charlie were both in their trucks. Nathan was in Charlie's passenger seat with Dom in the back. Jake jumped into Benny's then Ken came over. "You boys be safe and be quick, we don't have many folks here if anything happens and the Jones brothers have already been talking about going out hunting for infected so they can see what the virus is like up close," Ken said, sounding worried.

"No problem, Ken, we'll be fast and find out what we can then come straight back, Alice is here if they give you any problems, go see her at my place," Jake told Ken.

Ken nodded then slapped the side of the trucks farewell.

After turning out onto the main road, the trucks slowed down at the blockaded road in front of the apartments. Remmy and Eduardo walked over to the trucks. "You guys be safe" Remmy said.

"Here, if you guys get into any beef between here and the freeway, we can send a car to help," Eduardo said handing Charlie a flare gun.

"Thanks, Eddie," Charlie joked, taking the flare gun.

Remmy waved for some of the men manning the blockade to open it up. As the trucks drove out, Jake turned and saw Diego, Remmy's son from Wal-Mart, standing on a balcony waving. He gave the boy a wave back. Jake then sat back in the seat to try and relax and ready for whatever they'd find at the army base, or Camp Hope   as   it   was   called.

CHAPTER FIFTY
Dr. Ferguson

The results on the computer screen in front of him were not what he wanted to see. He threw his coffee cup in frustration. These results baffled him as had the results before that. None of the markers he'd found in the initial set of infected samples he got matched any of the newer samples. It didn't make sense as it was the same virus. There was a knock at the door.

"Come in" He said.

A soldier walked in looking flustered.

"Dr. Ferguson, sir, I've been ordered to let you know to back up your intel and prepare for evac." the soldier said.

"Evac? Where? Why?" he asked, confused as to why they'd have to evacuate after just setting up here.

"The safety zone perimeter was breached over an hour ago sir, I was just instructed to tell you to back up the drives and pack up any intel you had or needed," the soldier said.

"Do you know where we'll be going?" he asked.

"Camp Hope, sir, it's a site that's been set up on the other side of the Columbian river by I-205, I believe" The soldier said before leaving.

He slumped into his chair gazing into the screen in front of him. The infected markers still baffled him as did the mutation he was seeing. The only way he could unravel this virus further was with more research. Since the OHSU hospital had been breached this new Camp Hope would have to be where he continued his research.

THANK YOU

There are so many people in my life that helped make this possible! From encouraging me or just giving me ideas, this story would not be possible without a lot of people. Thank you to my wife Kimberly: without you I wouldn't have been able to put my story into words. You let me sneak away and lock myself away to finish chapter after chapter. You supported my crazy idea 120% from the beginning. Thank you to my family for putting up with me missing out on things to get this done. Thank you to the late George Romero, the pioneer of the Zombie Genre, for *Night of the Living Dead*! He made the undead legacy what it is today.

Thank you, Chris Weatherman for the *Home* series which awakened my love of books and writing. Both Shawn Chesser and Joe Zuko who are fellow scribblers for the motivational words, great advice and some phenomenal books!

Terra and Samantha from ACE Publishing for making it easy for me to just get my head down and write without having to worry about anything else.

My amazing editor Sabrina Bourque who was able to decipher my mess!

Lastly, Thank You for taking the time to read what I put down on paper. I hope you enjoy it!

ABOUT THE AUTHOR

D.K. Fraser is an emerging author of spy memoirs.

Douglas Fraser was born in Fife, Scotland where he grew up in a small village called inverkeithing. Douglas moved to America to coach Kickboxing at a martial arts acadamy and now lives in Vancouver, Washington with his wife and four children.

He spends most of his time reading, writing and is very active in the Survival and Prepping communities. This plays a big part in the current book line he is writing "When the Dead Rise" book series.

When the Dead Rise is a mixture of Apocalyptic survival and horror.

In his spare time he enjoys creating costumes for comic cons and cosplay contests as he is very active on the convention scene.

Printed in Great Britain
by Amazon

19242753R00181